BY A THREAD

Never stop fighting. ♡

R.L. GRIFFIN

18 17 16 15 14 13   10 9 8 7 6 5 4 3 2 1
By a Thread
ISBN: 978-1482761801
ISBN-10: 1482761807
Copyright © 2013 by R.L. Griffin

CONTENTS

To the two guys who mean the most to me, Trey and Griffin. Without your love and support, I would have nothing.

PROLOGUE

An explosion burst through her ears just as she turned to look at the door of the makeshift FBI field office. She didn't even have time to shield her eyes. The force of the explosion knocked her out of her rolling chair and onto her back, where she lay stunned. After a few minutes, she glanced around the room, attempting to see what was going on in the office where just a short time ago, she'd sat down at her computer for only the second time ever. The entire front of the office was gone. Searching frantically around the office, she couldn't see the four agents who had been seated at their computers minutes ago. Three of the missing agents were from ATF. The other was a seasoned FBI agent assigned to clean up the mess created by the ATF in Montana.

Three masked figures in dark clothes moved through the opening created by the blast. She rolled to her stomach and through the haze attempted to take inventory of her body parts. She put her hands under her shoulders, pushing herself up, and tried to stand. Everything seemed to be moving in slow motion. Suddenly, strong hands grasped her biceps, lifting her with ease.

"Whoa there, honey!" the broadest figure of the three yelled at her. The man lifted her to her feet and was holding her firmly, her back pressed against his soft belly. She started to separate herself from him, to move toward the back door of the office. "Hey, Jack, you ever seen a cop this *hot* before?" The man jabbed his gun into her back. "Where you going, sweet thing?"

Stella froze; she hadn't heard the man, but she felt his gun. The man gripped her arm tightly and easily swung her around to face him. She was still taking stock of her body parts; obviously she couldn't hear.

He slid his gloved palm down her face, his chest heaving up and down from exertion.

"Ooooooweeee, you sure are a pretty thing," he said, ripping the buttons off her button-down shirt and exposing her bra. "Hey, Jack, come look at this."

Stella shifted away from the man's hands. The other two masked figures paid no attention to the man pawing at Stella, but she couldn't really make out what the other men were doing. She was trying to put together what was happening and why anyone would bother bombing their makeshift field office. There was no money, and nothing to steal other than paperwork.

"Cat got your tongue, baby?" The man grabbed her chin hard, forcing Stella to look at him. She grimaced.

"She probably can't hear, you idiot," the man rummaging through the piles of blown-apart desks barked. "We don't have time for you to play with her. Come on."

The big man pushed Stella hard enough that she fell flat on her back, knocking the wind out of her. "It won't take long, will it honey?" He got down on one knee and started unbuttoning Stella's pants. Although still in shock, Stella fought back, kicking him in the face with the heel of her boot. Rolling on her stomach, she started crawling, only to be pulled roughly back him. He flipped her over like she weighed no more than twenty pounds and ripped the button off her pants.

A figure loomed behind him, the third man. "Dude, you're kidding, right?"

"Just give me a few minutes." The man was breathing heavily from fighting with Stella.

"No." The third man pulled out his gun and shot her in the chest.

Her eyes locked on the third man, her mind reeling. She'd know those eyes anywhere. Her thoughts didn't fully form as her world went white. Pain shot through her chest and then her head. Then everything went black.

CHAPTER ONE

The Future's So Bright

Jamie kissed her this morning while she still slept in their bed, whispering his goodbye. Hours later, she rolled over and nuzzled his pillow taking in his scent. She missed him immediately. She never thought she would be one of those girls who did everything with their boyfriend and missed them when they were gone. She'd been wrong. Jamie had changed everything. The two had just moved all their things into the house they were renting along with two of Jamie's friends in Alexandria. Last night was their first official night together in the new house. Jamie recently had been hired as an ATF agent and was flying to Savannah today to drive his truck back to Virginia. Patrick, one of their new roommates, was a friend of Jamie's from Savannah. He was a few years older than them and already worked for the ATF. Patrick had driven Jamie to the airport before dawn. Stella grabbed her phone from under pillow and checked her phone. Jamie was already in the air, but had texted her before take-off.

I miss you already

I love you

She texted him back so that something from her would be waiting for him when he landed.

I'm so excited to start our new life together

hurry home

we have many rooms to christen

She smiled as she hit send and then threw her phone on the bed. Her black hair splayed over her pillow and she contemplated getting up to start unpacking. The sheer volume of boxes lining the windowless walls in their basement room made her feel claustrophobic. When her cell phone screen went black, she found herself in complete darkness.

Their other roommate was a friend of Patrick's that Jamie had met during the summer. All she knew about Billy was that he worked for the Department of Justice. Stella was going to meet him tomorrow. It was weird living with people she didn't know, but she figured if she was with Jamie it would be fine.

Stella had always wanted to be a lawyer and was starting law school in a few weeks. Her uncle was a criminal lawyer and ten years younger than her mom; Stella loved hearing his stories. He was always regaling her family with his adventures from courts all around Georgia. He was so funny around her, but she knew he must be very good at his job. A few years ago, he represented the man who wrestled a female deputy's gun out of her holster and killed a Superior Court Judge. Before she took the LSAT, the test required to gain entrance into law school, she'd gone to her uncle's office to grill him about being a lawyer. Uncle Rick had made it sound so easy. She started to question his sanity when just the law school application process was wearisome and tedious.

Rubbing the sleep out of her eyes, she smiled. She was here, about to start classes at a great law school, and she and Jamie were starting this brand-new life together. Life couldn't be any better. She couldn't wait to get started. Sitting up in the bed she scanned the perimeter of their basement room, boxes were piled everywhere. The only boxes labeled were hers. Jamie didn't bother labeling boxes or organizing their contents, for that matter. He'd basically pulled out his drawers and dumped them in boxes. It was difficult for Stella to watch something so unorganized, but she certainly wasn't going to pack for him.

Digging through her box labeled "workout," she pulled out shorts and a tank top, grabbed her iPod and the leash. She changed quickly because her dog, Cooper, was already bouncing up and down at just the sight of the leash. Jamie had given Cooper to Stella for her birthday two years ago. He was six months old when Jamie adopted him from a no-kill shelter and she'd fallen in love with him instantly, just as she had with Jamie. Cooper was a blond labrador-golden retriever mix with light caramel-colored eyes and the sweetest face she'd ever seen on a dog. While she loved Cooper more than any person in the world, training him had been a nightmare. He was supposed to weigh forty to sixty pounds; by ten months old, he'd tipped the scales at eighty pounds. Cooper had finally stopped growing at 105 pounds. Stella had almost given him away when he was a year old. She came home from class one afternoon and found Cooper in the middle of her bedroom, surrounded by white down and torn leather. Cooper had destroyed her down comforter and the bat bag her Dad had given her when she was thirteen. She cried, spanked him as hard as she could with a leather belt, and called Jamie to come get the dog. That lasted four days.

She'd already mapped out a good six-mile walk to the Potomac and back to their house. According to the website, there was a huge dog park down by the river that she wanted to scope out for her daily run with Jamie and Cooper.

Turning left on King Street, she walked down a road lined with shops, bars, and restaurants on both sides of the street. This part of Alexandria was called Old Town and was very cool. She loved it; they could walk to eat, drink, and shop. She loved it. Stella smiled to herself, knowing the next few years were going to be fantastic.

After a while she reached the Potomac and walked along the water until she saw the dog park. The river was lined with slips bearing very pretentious boats. Once he saw the dog park, Cooper immediately began pulling her. "Okay, okay." Stella bent down and took him off leash, letting him into the fenced-in park. She smiled as Cooper ran around the entire park before deciding to play with a brindle boxer. The two dogs instantly started wrestling and playing.

"Your dog seems to like Brutus." Stella looked over to find a guy with a Nationals baseball cap pulled down over his eyes, smiling at her.

"Oh, hi. Is that okay?" Stella said, looking back to where the two dogs were playing chase.

"Sure. What's his name?" She took a closer look at the boxer's owner. He had chiseled features, but the hat kept her from making out details. She could tell he was in good shape through his T-shirt and athletic shorts.

"Cooper," she said, smiling and putting her left hand to her mouth while still watching the two dogs.

"I'm George," he replied, extending his hand to Stella.

"Stella," she said with the same big smile that had been on her face all morning.

"Congratulations," George motioned toward her ring.

"Oh, thanks." Stella twisted her engagement ring around her finger. "Nice to meet you," she commented, not losing her manners, as she admired the river. "This is awesome."

He pushed his cap back to rub his head and eyes. His eyes were a gray-green color and his hair was very dark, black or dark brown. A touch of sadness showed around his eyes. "Not from here, are you?" George asked.

"Nope, you?"

"Actually, yes. I'll probably be the only person you'll meet that was actually born and raised here."

"I love it here." Stella's gaze toward the Potomac was full of innocence and promise.

"I do, too. How long you been here?"

"This is my first real day."

"A novice, huh?" George pushed himself off the fence and whistled. Brutus ran over to his owner without delay.

"I guess," she shrugged, still smiling, but at Brutus now. The boxer ran towards her and jumped on her, his paws on her chest. Stella steeled herself against the boxer's weight.

"Brutus!" George yelled and Brutus hopped down and tucked his little nub of a tail down, along with his head. "You know better than that." Brutus ran away, looking ashamed.

"Shit, I'm sorry about that." George walked over to where Stella stood and inspected Brutus' paw marks, which just happened to be on Stella's chest.

Stella blushed at his inspection. "It's fine."

He smiled at her. "Well, good luck, Stella. I hope DC is all you want it to be." George walked out of the park with Brutus trailing behind him.

Cooper ran up to Stella and nuzzled her legs with his head, wanting attention. "Yep, this is going to be amazing," Stella said to herself.

CHAPTER TWO

Six-Pack

S tella clutched her throat; she couldn't breathe. She felt a ripping sensation in her chest. As she collapsed to the floor, a guttural sob escaped her throat. Not sure how long she stayed that way, she felt strong hands pick her up and carry her downstairs to the room she shared with Jamie. Her mind reeled as she was placed gently on their bed.

"You're going to be okay, Stella," a man's voice said as he patted her shoulder like she was a dog. *She was in a house with people she didn't know and he was petting her like a dog.* "I'll drive us down to Georgia tomorrow."

She heard him, but it sounded like he was in a tunnel. Stella looked up at the man petting her; it was their new roommate, Patrick. He was tall, with hard blue eyes, and his skin was the color of a mocha latte. His black hair was high and tight. His hand was rough on her skin. She nodded, laid her head on Jamie's pillow, and cried. Patrick had just broken the news that there had been a car accident involving a new ATF agent.

It was fatal.

It was Jamie.

She sobbed, not just cried, for a good portion of the night until she felt she had run out of tears. Lying in her bed with the weight of Cooper's head on her chest, she stared into the blackness. Every few minutes, Cooper's big, wet tongue would lick her and he would move a little closer to her face. By the time she tried to get out of bed, Cooper had pinned her down with the top half of his body and his big paws.

Her right arm was trapped under Cooper's massive belly, so she shoved him with her other hand. After the second shove, Cooper jumped off the bed.

Searching through her boxes, she found the only black dress she owned and a pair of heels. The only pair she could find were her red heels. *Jamie loved those heels.* She packed a bag and made her way to the couch where she sat for three hours until Patrick woke up. Cooper lay next to her on the couch, his head on her lap.

As the early morning sun peeked through the clouds, Patrick physically moved her into his car. Cooper stretched out in the backseat of Patrick's Audi. They set off for Savannah, where Jamie was raised. Gazing out the window, she looked into the side mirror. She was almost unrecognizable, her black hair wild and loose, her eyes bloodshot. The skin underneath her eyes looked bruised, as if she had been punched in the face; she certainly felt as if she had been. She squeezed her eyes closed and put her head against the window of Patrick's car. He didn't try to talk to her, which was good, because she wasn't capable of speaking. Images of their time together flashed through her brain sporadically, but the one memory that kept coming up over and over again was the day she first met Jamie.

It had been a few weeks before classes started her freshman year of college. She was enjoying a rare two-day break from softball practice. She and some teammates had gotten to the pool early that day and she had been dozing off for several hours, when she heard male voices. She looked up and saw him. He took her breath away without even trying. Mentally, she ran through a checklist of her appearance; an older seersucker bikini, not the greatest, but it gave her boobs a nice lift *and* she'd shaved everywhere.

Stella closed her eyes again, pretending to sleep. Listening to their conversation for a while, she realized that they were on the baseball team. She sat up, squeezed some sunscreen out of the bottle and stood to apply it seductively. Her black hair hung loose down past the string of her bikini top, so she wrapped it up in a messy bun. She rubbed more sunscreen on her back, awkwardly arching her back to reach the middle. Cassie, the first baseman on her softball team, giggled at the provocative show Stella was putting on for the boys. Stella winked at her.

The girls hadn't brought any beer to the pool, but they had plenty of vodka. Stella knocked back the rest of her drink and made herself another. She applied lip balm, slowly. The entire process took about five minutes, but the conversation between the guys stopped. As Stella lay back down on her stomach, she reached up and untied the back string of her bikini. Smiling, she turned her head to face Cassie. "You're bad..." Cassie mouthed. Stella nodded and then closed her eyes.

She felt a shadow across her back a few minutes later. Stella didn't open her eyes, but said, "Why is someone blocking my sun? I'm trying to get rid of my farmer's tan."

Cassie snorted. "That's not going to happen, Stella." All the softball players had horrible tan lines. Stella's arms looked like leather, but her stomach and chest were white as porcelain, as were her feet. It was heinous. All of them looked like they were wearing white shorts all the time.

"I don't know, I think it's kinda sexy. Like I know what you look like naked," Stella heard his slow, sexy southern drawl.

Her eyes popped open and she found herself staring at the guy with the drawl. One of the best-looking guys she'd ever seen in person. His hair was cut short and looked sandy blond in the sun. He had blue eyes and an actual six-pack. Stella had never seen a guy with a six-pack in person before, and it made her want to touch him. She laughed, noticing that he had the same farmer's tan that she and the softball players sported.

Stella cocked her head to the side and just looked at him.

"What?" Six-pack asked.

"I'm just following suit and picturing you naked," she said, then closed her eyes.

"Me too," Cassie agreed with a giggle.

"Now, I am too," one of his friends piped up loudly. "Damn it. Someone help me get that image out of my mind."

Six-pack leaned down to whisper into her ear. "I think you missed a spot." His fingers grazed the small of her back, just above her bikini bottoms, and her body tensed instantaneously at the spark she felt. Sexual chemistry crackled between them.

Stella used her sweetest voice. "Oh, really?" She cooed. "Could you get it for me?"

"Damn right, I can." He leaned over to grab the lotion, but she got to it first.

"Oh, I was talking to Cassie." She threw the bottle to Cassie. "Thanks, though."

Cassie snorted again. "It looks fine to me." Cassie yelled to the other guys, "Y'all got any beer over there you can share?!"

"Of course," one of the guys replied.

Cassie got up, sauntered over to the baseball players, grabbed a beer out of their cooler, and sat down with them. "Y'all play ball?"

Stella overheard the conversation and was interested. These were all baseball players and seemed to be pretty cool. Six-Pack's name was Jamie; and he was a sophomore. He was a pitcher. Confidence exuded from him and he seemed to be pretty smart and funny. Those were three mandatory traits for Stella before she would even look at a guy. She never fell for the type of guy who looked good, but annoyed the shit out of her as soon as he opened his mouth. *This Six-pack character could work.*

"Stella, you want a beer?" Cassie called.

"Sure." Stella turned just as Cassie threw the beer at her. She had two options, she could sit up and catch it, showing everyone her boobs, or the beer was going to hit her...somewhere.

"Fuck!" she called out as she rolled over to dodge the beer coming at her face. She fell off the chair, but managed to keep her hands covering her nipples.

For a moment, everyone was quiet. Then all of the occupants of the pool erupted in laughter. Stella turned forty shades of red and tried to figure out how to get up gracefully. Realizing there was no way to cover her nipples, get up, and grab her bikini top with only two hands, she gave up. Stella stood up, grabbed her bikini top, and with her chin raised, walked to the bathroom, showing everyone all she had.

Several hours later, everyone was good and drunk, playing Truth or Dare, and it was Stella's turn. She picked dare.

"Kiss me," Jamie said, leaning back in a lounge chair with a smug smile on his face.

Stella got up from where she was sitting and leaned over him. "You may regret this dare," she whispered in his ear, lips grazing his lobe. Stella kissed his neck, which made him tip his head back. She slowly kissed his top lip. He groaned and she went for the kill, parting his lips with hers. All of a sudden, his arms wrapped around her, pulling her on top of him in the chair. She forgot where she was, and that they had an audience, until she heard someone clear their throat.

Stella ripped her lips away from Jamie's and took a long breath. She put her fingers to her mouth and looked into Jamie's eyes. *Holy fuck. There's no going back from that.*

"I think you may be right," Jamie whispered, his arms wrapped around her. Stella thought for a minute he had read her thoughts. Then he said, "Best regret ever."

Stella smiled. She pulled herself out of his arms, separating their bodies. Suddenly, she felt too drunk, too high on the feeling she got from kissing this guy she just met, and too naked. She walked over to her bag was and checked her phone. She felt arms wrap around her again.

"You need to come with me. NOW," his lips whispered in her ear.

"And why's that?" Stella shivered and turned around so that she could look into his eyes.

"You're pretty much naked and I need to be the only one looking at you." He reached up and rubbed his thumb down her jawline. "I need to kiss you more."

If she hadn't been drunk, she wouldn't have gone home with him. But she *was* drunk, and she followed him home. Immediately.

CHAPTER THREE

Still Breathing

Cooper ran up and down the beach, chasing and barking at every bird that flew overhead. Stella sat in the sand, motionless, staring at the waves. Patrick had arranged for a rental house on Tybee Island, right outside Savannah, for the funeral. He also gave Stella a bottle of Zanax after he told her about Jamie. He'd thought of everything.

Cooper ran up to her and shook his wet fur, spraying saltwater all over her. She didn't even flinch. He made a couple circles around Stella and then dropped at her feet. She was still in the clothes she was wearing when she heard that Jamie was dead. Thankfully, Cooper didn't mind her stink.

"Stella!" Patrick yelled from a couple yards away. He was in his dark suit, looking very debonair. Glancing down at his watch, he tapped it once and said, "Let's go."

Slowly, she stood up and robotically motioned for Cooper to follow. She walked stoically to the house they were renting, or Patrick was renting. Patrick followed her, Cooper leading both of them up the stairs into the rented house. She walked to the room where her dress was hanging and mechanically put on her only black dress and her red heels, paying no attention to the sand that dotted her feet and legs.

Without speaking, Stella motioned for Cooper to follow her outside and opened the door to Patrick's silver Audi; letting Cooper jump in with fur still wet from the beach.

"Stella!" Patrick yelled as Cooper was jumping into the backseat. "Fuck," he muttered as Cooper made himself comfortable in the backseat. "You can't bring your fucking dog to a funeral."

Stella slid into the passenger seat and shut the door, staring forward. Patrick shook his head. She hadn't said a word since he told her about Jamie. On the way down to Savannah, Patrick used her cell phone to call her parents.

Patrick parked in one of the few remaining open spaces in front of the church. Stella put Cooper on the leash. He walked right by her side into the church.

"Ma'am! Ma'am!" A woman called after them. The woman chased after Stella and Cooper, her heels clicking quickly on the tile floor. "Ma'am, you can't bring a dog in the church."

Ignoring her, Stella kept walking and looked for a place to sit. Jamie's sister, Sara, motioned Stella to sit by her. Sara reached out and grabbed Stella's hand with a death grip. They didn't speak to each other, only held each other's hands.

Tears fell continuously throughout the funeral. *It's a closed casket, the accident must've been bad.* Stella never said a word. Sara released Stella's hand with a squeeze and silently joined the rest of Jamie's family. *Stella wasn't family, she was almost family. Apparently, almost family didn't count for much.* Inspecting her ring, she wondered if she'd be able to keep it. She and Cooper stayed seated as the rest of the church emptied. Stella stared at the closed casket. *How was this possible?*

She felt a hand on her shoulder. "Come on, Stella, they're doing the burial right away." Patrick stood in the aisle, waiting for her to move. *They can't do the burial without the casket.* She remained seated until six guys came to move Jamie. She recognized most of them from Jamie's college baseball team. It was only after the church was empty that Stella rose and pulled on Cooper's leash.

Patrick put his hand on her elbow and led her back to his car. At the cemetery, Stella and Cooper stood behind the seated guests and listened to the minister speak, pray, and then dismiss everyone. A collective sob erupted from the seats where Jamie's family and friends were all sitting, eyes red-rimmed.

So many people came up to her to offer sympathy, but she couldn't speak. Eventually, they all left her alone. When the service was over and all the attendees had gone, she and Cooper made their way up to the casket, watching as Jamie was lowered in the ground. *He's in the ground.*

Stella sunk to her knees next to the hole where Jamie had been, then lay on her side. She let out one quick sob, then nothing. *This cannot be real.* She felt like she didn't have any tears left. She lay on the ground next to the hole, her dress riding up; and Cooper next to her, his head on her side. She wasn't sure how much time had passed when Patrick picked her up, carried her over to his car, and put her in. He leaned in and pulled the seatbelt over her to latch it.

Stella didn't even realize her mom and dad had been at the funeral until she saw her father walking over to Patrick's car after the service. Her dad was talking, but she wasn't paying attention to her dad, she just stared out the front of the car. Stella's mom was standing a few feet back, crying. Jamie's parents didn't even try to talk to her, which was fine, since she had totally imploded and was physically incapable of speaking. There was nothing left. Her mind was completely turned off, and she felt like she was nothing but nerve endings.

"Stella, talk to me, baby." Stella's dad was stooped over her, smoothing her black hair. "It'll be okay. I promise."

As if the faucet in her eyes had been turned back on, tears began falling. Big wet drops landed on her dress and absorbed by the fabric. She didn't even try to wipe them away anymore. Her big green eyes were full of tears and devastation.

"Patrick, take my card." Her dad said. "If this keeps up, call or email me and I'll come up and get her." Patrick and Stella's father walked over to her mother and they spoke in hushed voices.

Her dad looked tired. Stella closed her eyes and concentrated on breathing, but she didn't really want to breathe. *Just breathe.* She couldn't wrap her brain around her situation. A few days ago she was happily engaged, optimistic and carefree. Now she was in a house with two guys she didn't know, in a city where she didn't know a soul; and she was all alone. *Alone.*

Her mother made her way to the car, her black hair perfectly coifed; she was clutching her pearls. She didn't speak to Stella, but smoothed her hair back and kissed her cheek. Then she turned and walked away.

She and Jamie had planned to get married in St. Simons Island off the coast of Georgia next summer. She'd already found her dress. It was simple and backless with exquisite beading on the torso, drawing attention to her narrow waist. The fabric was light, perfect for a beach wedding. Stella shook her head to clear the view of the dress she would never wear.

As the car made the drive back to Tybee Island, she closed her eyes and leaned her head back against the seat. Arctic air from the air conditioner blasted so hard from the vents it blew loose strands of black hair back. Once she felt the car stop, she opened her eyes. *Jamie's dead.* Stella let Cooper out of the backseat and walked up to the door. She stood there, waiting for Patrick to let her into the rental house.

The noise of her heels clicking across the tile floor of the main room vibrated through her chest. She opened the door to the room where her things were and collapsed onto the bed, heels still on her feet.

Patrick, with his military precision, shaved head, and cold demeanor, had moved her through the events of the day. Stella didn't understand why he would, he didn't know her at all. *Jamie's dead. Patrick's here.*

Cooper crawled into Stella's bed and laid his head right next to hers on the pillow, his big paw resting on her arm. Stella closed her eyes, but didn't sleep. She had lived through the day. Even though she thought at least a million times she was going to die, she was still breathing. She didn't know what came after this. Where would she go? She had no home. *Jamie had been her home.*

Chapter Four

Here's the Plan

Stella walked with Cooper down the stairs into the room she and Jamie shared for only one night. She slid down the wall, sat on the floor and glared at all the unlabelled boxes she would have to go through, all of his things. She sobbed again, even though she thought she was out of tears. *Could she please just run out of fucking tears!* She opened a box of Jamie's and pulled out his old college baseball jersey. Inhaling deeply, she smelled him. *Clementines.* Tearing off her clothes, she slipped it over her head and crawled into their bed. Sometime later she felt Cooper climb up on the platform bed and lay next to her.

Stella only got out of her bed to use the bathroom, which wasn't often since she didn't drink anything all day. She heard footsteps coming down the stairs, but didn't look up.

"Okay, I'm going to give you two more days of this shit before I take things into my own hands." She felt something hit the pillow; Patrick had thrown a protein bar and a bottle of water on her bed.

Stella didn't respond.

Two days later, true to his promise, Patrick returned downstairs after work. Throwing the covers off Stella, he picked her up, legs flailing. In two steps, he was in the bathroom, where he threw her unceremoniously into the bathtub. He turned on the water full blast, soaking her and finally forcing a reaction.

"Holy shit, Patrick!" she yelled as she put her hands up, attempting to block the water from her face. In less than thirty seconds, she was soaked from head to toe, including Jamie's baseball jersey.

"You stink and you haven't eaten in days. If you don't get your ass upstairs right now and eat what I cooked for dinner, I will call your fucking daddy. Is that how you want to be treated? Like a child who can't take care of herself?" With that, Patrick turned and walked up the stairs.

Stella was stunned, then pissed. She stomped up the stairs after him, soaking wet in nothing but Jamie's white baseball jersey. When she got to the kitchen, she glared at Patrick and stomped over to the table, sitting down next to a guy she had never seen.

"Well, hello there, hot stuff," the stranger said, looking over at Patrick. "I'm guessing this is our new roommate?"

"Yep," Patrick said, grabbing a towel and mopping up the water rolling off Stella's body.

"I'm Billy. Hopefully you'll attend all group dinners in a wet, white T-shirt." The guy took in her appearance and raked his hand through his shaggy, dirty-blond hair that reached just past his ears. He pushed his tortoiseshell glasses up the bridge of his nose. Dressed in what appeared to be a white undershirt shirt and suit pants, it was clear he had just gotten home from work. His eyes were a warm chocolate brown and full of humor.

"You know my fiancé just died, right?" Stella spouted at the stranger.

"Um," Billy Stevens looked down at his plate. "Yeah, sorry to hear about that."

"Whatever."

"What made you finally get out of your bed? It looks like Patrick threw you in the shower..."

"And threatened to call my 'daddy'," she made air quotes to emphasize the word daddy.

"Wow, Patrick, that's pretty dirty." Billy still looked amused.

"Well, she can't stay in her bed forever. She's supposed to start law school in a week."

"How the fuck do you know when I'm supposed to start law school?" she yelled belligerently.

Patrick put a plate of stir-fry and a beer in front of her on the table.

"Just to warn you both, now that I'm out of my bed, you may want to run and get more alcohol. I plan to drink until I pass out. Ready... go." Stella took the beer and swallowed it in two gulps.

"Holy shit, I'm in love," Billy exclaimed, eyes going wide.

Stella ignored him and motioned for Patrick to get her another beer, which he did.

"I guess functioning, even while drunk, is better than not functioning at all," Billy said, shrugging his shoulders.

Patrick took in Stella, his eyes raking over her body slowly. She looked at him, "What're you looking at?"

"Well, you're basically nude at the table with two dudes. What do you think I'm looking at?"

"You're the one who forced me out of my bed." She threw a piece of chicken to Cooper.

"So what's your plan? You've been laying in your bed for four days, certainly you've formulated a plan by now."

"A plan?" she asked with her mouth full of stir-fry.

"A plan to get through this mourning and missing Jamie shit." Patrick looked away and lowered his voice, "I mean…I understand this is hard for you and you loved him and all, but you've got to start getting back to life."

"My fiancé DIED LESS THAN A WEEK AGO, YOU ASS-HOLE!" She got up and threw her plate at the sink, breaking it, food flying everywhere.

Billy blew out the breath he'd been holding and Patrick pushed his chair away from the table. "You're acting like a child and you're not a child. Clean this shit up."

"No!" She yelled and walked back downstairs. She was almost back to her bed when Patrick grabbed her, threw her over his shoulder, and carried her back upstairs. As he put her down, she attempted to shove him. He didn't move.

"Clean it up now. We're not your fucking maids. We weren't put here on Earth to clean up after you. I know you're sad, mad, whatever…"

Billy walked over and started sweeping up the pieces of plate that had fallen to the floor.

"I'll get it," she sneered as she ripped the broom out of his hand.

Patrick sat on the counter while she cleaned. "You need a plan, El. A plan will help."

She looked at him. "How do you know what the fuck will help me? And my name is Stella."

"Everyone I know has a nickname," Patrick shrugged.

"What's Billy's?"

"Billy." Patrick looked at Billy. "His real name is William."

"My name is only two syllables. I really don't need a nickname." Stella wiped the dustpan off into the trashcan.

Billy handed her another beer. "I like El. Short and sweet." Billy commented.

"Just opposite of me..." Stella said.

"I like you already, El, you are one feisty bitch." Billy smiled and clinked his beer against hers, which was sitting on the kitchen counter.

"Watch it asshole, you don't know me," Stella fired back.

Patrick jumped down off the counter and sat back down in his seat at the kitchen table. "Here's the plan. First, we're going to go through all his things. You keep what you want, we give the rest to his family. Second, we'll drink with you until you don't want to drink anymore. Third, you go to law school and immerse yourself in all things law and get through it until you can act normal. Fourth, you'll do what I tell you to do."

Stella was staring at Patrick with her mouth open. "The only one of those I agree to is number two. We will drink. A LOT!"

CHAPTER FIVE

Drunk Facebooking

Stella had been drinking since she got out of bed, which was around noon. It was five. She booted up her computer and went back to reading the comments people had left on Jamie's Facebook page. *All these motherfuckers.* She knew Jamie was well-liked and widely known in college, but since he died, people had been coming out of the woodwork to share how broken up they were over his death. *No fucking shit.* After guzzling another beer, she threw the empty can near the trashcan, not even attempting to make it in the basket. The clang of the can hitting the tile made Cooper jump up and bark at the door.

"You're full of shit, Coop, that sound wasn't even near the door." Laughing, she clicked on one of the entries on the comment section of Jamie's wall where some douchebag had written a story about him and Jamie that occurred over ten years ago. She typed a comment: *hey d-bag, Jamie probly doesn't even remmdher your name.*

Clearly intoxicated, Stella clicked submit before thinking or checking her spelling. She scrolled down to see a post left by a cheerleader from college about how much she missed him.

Really, you miss him? Did you live with him? Were u negaged to jim. Cause I was bitch and I thinkn I miss him a little more

Again, she clicked submit. This continued for another thirty minutes. By the time Stella had finished another beer, she'd commented on over thirty different posts on Jamie's page.

Rage consumed her; all these people making it seem like Jamie was their person to miss, their friend. None of his real friends had commented on his webpage. His real friends were still reeling from the news of his death, still attempting to process the loss. The last thing they'd be doing is posting bullshit on a website.

The door slammed pulling her out of her manic attack on the webpage. Patrick walked up behind her, happy she wasn't in bed. His smile froze on his face when he realized what she'd been up to for the past hour. Stella started to slam her laptop screen down but Patrick grabbed it, stopping her.

"El, what're you doing?" he asked, staring at the screen.

"Nothing," she said. Getting up, she went to the fridge and grabbed another beer.

"You posted all these comments?"

Stella didn't answer him, she could hear pity in his voice. She turned up the beer and sent it hurling toward the garbage. Patrick sat at the table and started deleting all of Stella's rage-filled, grammatically-challenged posts. He wasn't quick enough on some of the posts; people were already responding in kind to Stella's drunken rants. Closing his eyes for a few seconds, he took a breath and deleted the remaining posts, and then deleted Stella's entire Facebook account.

"Why would you get online and make drunken comments to all these people?" Patrick rubbed his forehead with his hand.

"Why not? Those motherfuckers don't even know him. That one bitch saw him, like, one time and now all of a sudden she's going to '*miss him so much*'. People are fucking lunatics."

"You're acting like an asshole," Patrick said calmly. "You can't get drunk and put that kind of shit online. You can't get that back. It's out there. Based on those posts, you're a miserable person who thinks she's the only one who can mourn her dead fiancé. And you can't even spell. Plus, your grammar is horrific."

He powered down her laptop, wrapped the cord around it, picked it up without another word, he walked into his room and shut the door.

Stella felt someone sit on her bed. She glanced at the clock. "What?" she croaked.

"I wanted to catch you before you started drinking," Patrick said softly.

Stella pulled the sheet over her body. "What?"

"You start school in a couple days and you missed orientation. You haven't bought any books. You can't possibly be throwing away law school."

"Why do you care?" Stella was cantankerous on a constant basis since Jamie died.

"I just do." Patrick looked around the room at the boxes still packed all over the room.

She turned over in her bed, facing the bathroom. "I'm deferring," she said flatly.

"What?" Patrick didn't hear her.

"I'm deferring, okay?!" she yelled.

"You're not going? For how long?"

"I deferred for a year. Now leave me alone."

Patrick put his hand on her shoulder. She shrugged it off. "El, get dressed and come with me."

"Patrick, please leave me alone. I want to stay in my bed today," Stella begged.

"No can do. Today we're going to shoot things." He rose and headed up the stairs.

"Shoot things?" she called after him. He'd gotten her attention, but he didn't answer. She pulled on black yoga pants, a T-shirt, a hat, and flip-flops that she found in the first box she opened and walked upstairs.

Patrick pointed at her feet. "Closed-toed shoes, please."

She spun on her heel and stomped back down the stairs louder than necessary. When she got back upstairs, she rolled her eyes at him from under her hat, "Better?"

"Yep." Patrick grabbed his keys and patted Cooper on the head. "Be back later, man."

Stella guessed she had been ignoring Cooper lately. "He's a smart dog. Maybe he prefers you to me right now. Don't get used to it."

"El, we gotta get through this," he said as they walked to his car.

Stella opened the passenger door and sat down, silent. Arms crossed, she stared out the window and didn't respond.

After a twenty-minute trip in silence, Patrick pulled into the parking lot of a cement brick block building with a flashing neon sign. Before she read the sign, she looked at Patrick, "Are we shooting strippers?"

Patrick laughed heartily. "No, but that would be pretty fun. Just targets today, killer."

"Oh, it's a gun range." Stella got out of the car and watched Patrick pull a black duffel bag out of his trunk.

When they walked through the door, the man behind the counter smiled. "Hey, Patrick. Good to see you."

"You too, Ben." Patrick guided Stella between racks of paraphernalia and past glass cases lined with all sorts of guns. "We want to hit the range for a bit."

"You want to shoot any of mine?" Ben asked as he pulled out a set of earphones.

"Nope, I got it. I may buy some ammo though." Patrick pointed out a couple of boxes of bullets and Ben set them on the counter. After he paid, he led Stella around the corner and through a heavy, soundproof door into the range. He handed her the earphones and pulled his own out of his bag.

Patrick loaded the magazine of his Glock 37. He started to explain the gun's features, but she wasn't paying attention. He pushed her back a little and emptied the entire clip into the target at the end of the lane. He loaded the clip again and handed Stella the gun. "Don't point this at me or anyone else. Also, be ready, it has a bit of a kick."

Stella took the gun and walked to the center of the stall while Patrick pressed the button, bringing the target back to them to be swapped for a new one. She raised the gun to shoulder height, steadying her aim with her left hand. She hesitated to pull the trigger and Patrick leaned into her. "Just pull the trigger." She did and the gun exploded, recoiling so hard it almost hit her in the face. Adrenaline rushed through her body. She looked at Patrick.

"Shit," she said with a smile.

"Look at that! I knew I could get a smile out of you somehow." Patrick stood behind her while she fired the remaining rounds. He smiled as he pulled the target off the clips. "Nice aim!" he shouted, showing her the holes in the target centered on what would be a person's crotch.

"Ha." Stella blew her bangs out of her face, put the gun on the counter, and grabbed the target. "I believe I'll keep that."

CHAPTER SIX

Circling the Drain

She and Jamie were in his car, driving up GW Parkway, with the windows down. They were both smiling, windows down. Not a cloud was in the sky and a bright sun lit up Jamie's face. He rested his arm casually on the passenger seat behind her. He was wearing a light blue button-down and aviator sunglasses. The scent of clementines filled the car. Stella closed her eyes and simply drank in the warmth of the sun, his touch, and his smell. Her eyes shot open when she felt a wave of ice cold across her face. It was dark and Jamie was staring at her, not the road. She screamed as a Mack truck struck them head on. Jamie's arm fell lifelessly behind her, coming unattached at the shoulder. His body and face struck the windshield and slumped back into her lap. Blood was everywhere. Stunned, she froze covered in his blood. She couldn't stop screaming his name. She couldn't stop shaking...

"STELLA...STELLA!"

She looked around in a panic, trying to locate the voice yelling at her. Jamie was dead in her arms. *DEAD.*

"STELLA, PLEASE!" A slap across her face woke her up in an instant. She was drenched in sweat and still screaming. Her entire body shook violently. Patrick's eyes were full of concern and he pulled her into his arms. "Shh, it's going to be okay. Shh..." Patrick stroked her hair over and over like she was a frightened kitten.

Stella couldn't protest. She was back in the car with Jamie.

"Pat..." she croaked.

"Shh." Patrick pulled her into his chest tighter. "I'm here. You're okay."

Stella let herself collapse into his arms and howled until exhaustion took over and her muscles relaxed without protest. Stella didn't know how long she'd slept but when she woke, Patrick was still holding her tightly to his chest. It was the first time she had been able to get a few hours sleep without having a nightmare.

"Thank you," she whispered awkwardly.

Patrick nodded and sat up, putting his feet on the floor and staring into the closet with his elbows on his knees. Breaking his stare away from the empty closet, he put his head in his hands. "El, it'll get better."

"You going to hold me until it does, Patrick?" Stella got out of the bed and walked into the bathroom, not looking in Patrick's direction, and shut the door.

"If that's what you need," he answered. He rose from the bed and went upstairs.

Stella got into the shower, turned the water on as hot as it would go, and crumpled to the shower floor. She curled her body into a ball, feeling empty. Numbness spread across her brain and body. She welcomed the numbness. She stood up, washed her face and her hair for the first time in over a week. *This is better. Numb.* If Stella could just hang on to the numbness, she could make it through the day. This would be her life now, making it day by day without feeling. This was her plan. She had a plan.

Stella started drinking around 9:30 a.m. She sat on the couch, Cooper right next to her, throwing back beers like it was her job. Disgusted, she studied her new house. The den was a small, cramped room that barely fit the couch and a chair. It was painted a bright teal that reminded her of a sorority from college. The coffee table was covered in old fast food wrappers, dirty plates, and empty beer and soda cans. There were four pairs of shoes scattered on the floor. There was shit everywhere. *These fuckers are disgusting.*

The kitchen table was covered in newspapers, dirty plates, and books. She'd be damned if she was cleaning up after these pigs. She'd only been living with them a couple of weeks, and though most of her time was spent passed out, when she was conscious, the house was repulsive. Grabbing another beer, she walked down the stairs, promptly followed by Cooper.

She plugged in her iPod, selected the Dave Matthews Band, and started pulling clothes out of her boxes, hanging them in the closet, or putting them into drawers. There was plenty of space now that she wasn't sharing closet space with Jamie. She went back upstairs and brought down the whole six-pack so she wouldn't have to keep climbing up and down the stairs.

Cleaning out her boxes, she hung posters on the wall, put out pictures, and filled her bookcase. When she was finished with the boxes of books, she walked upstairs to get another six-pack of beer. Back downstairs, she sat on the floor and touched the spines of the books. Every time she closed her eyes she saw Jamie's face, laughing with her. She could still feel him touching her, loving her. *How could this have happened?* They were on the brink of everything they ever wanted. A wave of nausea hit her suddenly and she barely made it to the toilet before throwing up more than a few beers.

When her stomach was finally empty, she'd passed out on her bathroom floor, face flat on the tile. Stella felt a nudging against her face then something wet and warm on her cheek. Opening her eyes slowly, a big brown nose came into focus. Cooper was sitting next to her on the bathroom floor, licking her face.

"Hey, Coop." She sat up and leaned back against the bathroom wall. "Pretty fucking bad, huh?" already knowing the answer.

Stepping into the shower, she wobbled several times and had to brace herself against the wall. She stayed in the shower after bathing, trying to shake some of the cobwebs from her brain. Her knees were weak as she walked upstairs. Billy was at his usual station: the couch, with a video game controller in hand.

"Where's Patrick?" Stella asked from the kitchen, skipping any small talk or pleasantries with Billy. She stared into the fridge, trying to decide between water and beer.

"Not home yet," he said without looking up from his video game.

As if on cue, the door flew open and Cooper ran to greet Patrick.

"Hey, Coop." Patrick rubbed all over Cooper's fur. Cooper couldn't contain himself. He wiggled and danced around Patrick's feet in happiness.

"Okay, so you're both here." Stella shifted her weight from one foot to the other. "I can't stand the mess here. I know I'm not clean, but shit. I don't understand the point of putting empty cans on the counter right next to the trashcan, but not in the trashcan. I can't live this way. If we don't get a maid or something, I'll stab you both in your sleep." She grabbed a beer.

"Well, how do you fucking do," Patrick answered.

The more time went by, the more broken Stella felt. She couldn't seem to push herself to function, other than what was forced on her by Patrick. Insomnia had taken over her nights and she felt like she'd been awake since Jamie died, give or take a daytime catnap here or there, or when she was able to pass out from drinking. Everything reminded Stella of Jamie; she couldn't escape his memory. When she heard Patrick's footsteps upstairs, she glanced at the clock, swallowing the six-pack she started earlier in the day. She put the empty beer in her bathroom trashcan before Patrick could see her with it.

"El!" Patrick yelled from upstairs. "I work all day; the least you could do is make me dinner, woman."

Stella steeled herself, tried to put a somewhat pleasant expression on her face, and walked up the stairs. "Obviously, you have me mistaken for someone else."

He opened his bedroom door and threw his bag inside. "What do you want to eat?'

"Whatever..."

"Let's go, then, there's a bar I want to check out."

After several blocks, Stella glanced down at what she was wearing. If she cared, she would've been embarrassed by her stained tank top, yoga pants, and flip-flops. Her hair was piled in a knot on her head and she wore no makeup. As a matter of fact, she hadn't even opened her makeup bag since Jamie died.

"Oh, you look real good El," Patrick said sarcastically, as if he could tell that she finally realized how unkempt she appeared.

"Like I give a shit. You're the one who should be embarrassed." She pulled her bra straps up on her shoulders so that they'd be hidden by her tank top, surprised she even had on a bra.

"I'll never be embarrassed by you, El, but it would be nice if you put real clothes on." Patrick walked briskly toward the busy area of Old Town. "It's a casual place, you should be fine." Patrick took her hand as they walked into a bar called Finnegan's. He led her to a stool at the end of the bar.

"Well, this is progress, right?" Stella asked, thinking it was a good thing she already had six beers to get here.

"Progress." Patrick nodded in agreement. A woman walked up to them and Patrick ordered himself a Guinness and a Snakebite for Stella.

Stella briefly glanced around the bar. It was dark, with worn cherry wood everywhere. There were only a few patrons. The bar was shaped in an L, with tables and a stage in the middle of the room opposite the bar.

"Billy's meeting us here in a few minutes, which means he's probably had a rough day—which is saying something, because Billy never has a rough day."

"I'd like to switch my life for his." Stella didn't even look up when the bartender put her Pilsner glass in front of her. Patrick said thanks for both of them. The crisp taste of cider and lager mellowed her nerves as she took another sip.

Billy walked in and slumped onto the stool next to Stella. "Really shit day guys."

"What's up?" Patrick waved at one of the bartenders.

"Top secret clearance bullshit, but just know it sucks. I mean, give me a fucking break. They're talking to, like, everyone I have ever fucking known, including my ex-girlfriend." Billy looked at the male bartender standing in front of them and said, "Biggest beer you have. I don't care what it is."

"Hmmm...let's see what I can do." The bartender moved away from them and Patrick and Billy continued their conversation. When the bartender returned, he'd poured a dark beer into an actual vase. "So this is about five beers, but since you look like you'll be drinking several of these, I'll only charge you for one."

"Okay, I love this guy." Billy raised his vase at the bartender and took a sip.

"It's George."

CHAPTER SEVEN

Biggest Regret

Stella finally got out of bed around two in the afternoon. The house was quiet except for Cooper's nails clicking against the tile of the kitchen floor. He was hungry and pacing the length of the kitchen, waiting on her. She hadn't fed him yet. Slowly making her way to the stairs, something on the floor caught her eye. It was her phone. She'd left it there the day she'd gotten back from the funeral. That was over a month ago.

She pressed the power button as she walked up stairs. The beeping and chirping started instantly. She laid the phone down on the counter and went about feeding Cooper. The phone beeped again as she was setting down his bowl, notifying her of a voicemail. Stella walked over to her phone to see who left a message. It was a friend from home, checking in "to see how she was doing." *Really? How the fuck do you think I'm doing?*

She examined the screen of her phone. It showed 65 voice messages and 134 texts. She didn't have it in her to check either kind. Instead, she realized she needed to cut her toenails. She hadn't unpacked anything but her clothes, and she didn't know where her nail clippers were.

They always kept the clippers with Jamie's stuff. Stella sighed, walked back downstairs, and stared at all unpacked boxes. She opened the first box hesitantly. There was a picture of Jamie and Stella with several of their "couple friends" from school after a homecoming game. She couldn't remember which year it was. *That is what happiness looks like.* She looked back in the box, tears falling down her cheeks.

Her phone began ringing. She ignored it and began pulling more contents of the box. It was full of things she'd never seen. There were more pictures of him with other guys in baseball uniforms, from all different ages. A couple of ties were wadded up in the bottom of the box. His athletic cup was in the box. She held it away from her face with two fingers and flung it on the floor. There were a few pieces of loose paper. One piece was folded flat, as if it had fallen out of a book. It had her name on it. She unfolded the paper and read.

So Stella, we made it through four years of college together. I knew the minute I saw you that we would be good together. I was right. You are perfect for me. You are just the right combination of sweet and surly, smart and smartass. I love you with so much of my heart it is scary. We're so young, we shouldn't be feeling this so soon. I don't know if I can handle it. Our lives are so intertwined and I don't know how to separate them. I don't know where you end and where I begin. I'm moving to DC and taking a job there. I know, I'm a coward and can't tell you in person. I can't watch as I break your heart.

We'll go our separate ways, but know that you will be in my heart always. I wonder if you will be my biggest regret, the one that got away.

That was it. It was like he never finished the letter. Stella blinked, not feeling anything as she read this letter that Jamie intended to give to her, but never did. Instead, he'd proposed. He'd gotten down on one knee and asked her to marry him. *Why would he do that when all he wanted to do was go be by himself. Numb.* Stella sat on the floor and felt something inside her harden. *What the fuck ever, this shit doesn't change where I am.* She'd moved to DC instead of attending the UGA Law School for Jamie, and he'd died and left her. *Alone.*

Patrick and Stella were on the back porch drinking beer and staring off into the night sky. She'd had a minor setback when she finally turned on her phone; she listened to a months' worth of messages, and they were more than she could take. She'd returned a call to her best friend from college, Meghan, and the conversation had been a disaster. Words had escaped her and Meghan really hadn't been any better. Meghan was engaged and planning her wedding. As bad it sounded, Stella didn't care. She didn't want to hear about how great everything was for Meghan; it made her feel like an asshole. It was then that she made the decision to just plow forward. There was no need to talk to anyone from her past; they would simply remind her of Jamie and who she was with Jamie. That person didn't exist anymore. She wasn't anyone anymore.

Her parents called and left her messages every day for weeks, each message more heart-wrenching than the last. They were cut off, too. She couldn't handle talking about what they needed her to talk about.

"You know how me and Jamie became friends?" Patrick took a sip of beer and looked over to Stella.

"No," she said flatly, hoping that would be the end of it.

"We played ball together in the travel leagues in Savannah. He was so good. And it was just natural, you know." He looked off and sighed. "We've known each other for years, but reconnected a couple years ago when I saw him play in the College World Series for Georgia."

Stella sat silent. She was numb.

"I recruited him for the ATF, Stella, I'm so sorry," Patrick said sincerely.

"Why are you sorry?" Her head tilted slightly, puzzled by his apology.

"I just feel like this is my fault. If it weren't for me, you guys wouldn't be in this situation."

"First of all, there are no guys here, it's just me. And no one knew he would die in a car accident driving back here. I don't see how you think this is somehow your fault, but that's your shit to deal with." She chugged the rest of her beer and got up to get another one. "You want another?"

"Sure."

Stella walked to the cooler and grabbed two beers. "I know we are both dealing with this in our own way, Patrick, but if you're asking if I blame you, I don't. That's part of the problem with this entire situation. There's no one to blame but the other driver. And that guy died too."

"You know, you're nothing like I thought you'd be."

"Well, I guess I haven't given you a real good view of me." Stella twirled a section of her hair around her finger. "But you can't blame me for being a basket case. I'm nothing like I was a couple of months ago. I'm not how I was with Jamie. That girl's gone."

"I hope not."

"Pretty sure the happy-go-lucky, idealistic person I used to be has been replaced by a drinking, cussing mess. How do you like me now?" she said, dripping in sarcasm as she looked up into the sky.

"You'll be alright."

"Glad you think so…"

"I kinda like you anyway." Patrick laughed.

"Good to know you're a masochist." Stella peered over the fence into their neighbor's yard. Sitting in the backyard were four old toilets and a working Coke machine. "It looks like if we need a Coke or need to take a shit, all we need to do is go next door."

Patrick stood up and examined the yard. "Now I can't wait to meet them."

CHAPTER EIGHT

You Just Do

Stella still wasn't sleeping well; big fucking surprise. Seeing 11:59 turn to 12:00 on her clock, she sighed. It was now Jamie's birthday. Taking a drink from her glass of straight, room-temperature vodka, she looked around her room and she found what she was looking for under her desk. Crawling over, she stretched under the desk and grabbed the phone she'd thrown on the floor a couple days earlier. Patrick had taken her laptop to keep her from embarrassing herself online; he hadn't anticipated her using her cell phone to get online. When she found out he deleted her entire Facebook account she'd nearly hit the roof. Jamie had a public account, so she could still access his page under another name. She created a new account, using the name El Murphy.

Sitting on her knees, she pulled up his page on her cell phone and typed out a message.

You should be here with me, celebrating.

According to Patrick, he'd deleted her original account because scores of people were posting really hateful things to Jamie's page after Stella's alcohol-fueled comments. *Oops.*

She was out of tears, completely and totally dry from all the crying she'd been doing. Pushing herself up off the ground, she went upstairs and into the kitchen. Billy, still playing video games, looked at her but knew better than to talk to her. She pulled the bottle of vodka from the freezer and poured a good four fingers into a glass with ice. Moving to the cabinet, she pulled out a box of crackers and sat at the table.

"You know, you could at least come sit in here. I promise I won't talk to you."

Stella got up, poured a few more fingers into her glass, and sat on the couch next to Billy. Even sitting with someone, Stella always felt alone. For the past few months she'd been working on forgetting, and just being numb. It wasn't going well, but alcohol helped.

"Tell me something about him." Billy's eyes didn't move from the screen.

"No," she whispered. "Billy, it's so hard. I don't think I'm going to make it."

Billy paused his game and looked at her dry face and dead green eyes. She drained the rest of her glass and stood to get another. "El, you *are* making it. It might not be pretty, but you're making it. That's all you have to do for awhile."

She looked at his face. He'd been witness to her downward spiral, but somehow he sincerely had no judgment in his eyes. "Billy, how do I keep going? How do I keep getting up in the morning without him?"

Billy let out a deep breath. "Listen... I don't fucking know. You just do it. You drink too much, you pass out and you try not to think about him. You just do..."

"I can't even tell you how horrible that sounds. I've been drunk for a solid three months and it's not helping."

"That's where you're wrong El. The day I met you I thought you would leave here, go back home, and crawl into a hole somewhere, but you didn't. I think somewhere deep down you know you will keep going. You *deferred* law school, you didn't quit. You started eating again. You're getting better."

"It doesn't feel better."

"Just wait." Billy turned back to the television and restarted his game.

"For what?" Stella stared at the screen, watching the combat scene of the video game.

"I'm not sure."

"That's fucking helpful."

"You're alive; that's something."

Stella sighed and pushed his arm over so that she could lay her head in Billy's lap. She watched him play video games until 3:00 in the morning. When he got up to go to his room, she'd finally passed out.

After noon later that day, she couldn't stand to be alone anymore and walked to Finnegan's. She ordered a burger, fries, and beer. She made small talk with the bartender, Hazel, and was pretty lit by the time the bartenders changed shifts.

Stella blinked her big green eyes at the sight of him and twirled her engagement ring around her finger. It was one of the only things she had that was a part of Jamie. Patrick had gone through all Jamie's shit last weekend and made her pack it up and send almost everything home to Jamie's parents. Stella was picturing Jamie's face when George came over to where she slumped at the bar.

"You okay, Stella?"

"Nope," she said, looking past him. "Probably never again will I be okay."

"Can I get you something? A cab?" George rubbed his face and shaved head.

"What? No, I'm not done drinking, George." Stella shook her head to clear it and she held up her empty glass, her words slightly slurred. "I'm in need of another drink."

"They say that bartenders make good listeners. You can talk to me."

"I'm not a good talker. I don't plan on falling apart today, just drinking to pass out, and didn't want to drink alone." Her phone beeped to alert her of another text message; she now had twenty. Stella ignored them and looked at her ring again.

"Bad breakup?" George ventured.

"Not even fucking close." She squeezed her eyes closed.

"You know we met before, right? At the dog park, your first "real day" here. Your dog played with Brutus?" George said, hoping it would ring a bell.

Stella opened her eyes and tried to remember that day. She couldn't. All she remembered was that night; Patrick telling her about Jamie. Her face was blank.

"You were so... I'm sorry about whatever's happened to you, Stella."

"George, call me El. Apparently all my friends call me that now. As a friend, I'm asking you to change the fucking subject." Stella downed the rest of her beer. "Another one, please."

"Sure." George took one more look at Stella and went to pour her another beer.

"So... George. What's your story?" Stella said when he brought her the beer.

"What do you mean, my story?" George was wiping down the counter behind the bar. He smiled at her even though he could tell she was wasted. He was trying to figure out what to do with her when Patrick walked through the door.

"Patrick," Stella said, conveying neither excitement nor animosity.

"El. You okay?"

"Oh, just fucking peachy, right, George?"

"Patrick, what can I get you?" George shook his head at Patrick, attempting to show him Stella was not okay.

"I've just come to collect this one." Patrick put his arm around her waist and stood her up, her weight leaning against him. "Can I get the bill?"

"Of course." George moved down the bar to get the final tally of Stella's drinks.

"But... I don't want to leave. George was just about to tell me his life story. I'm sure it's way better than mine."

"He can tell you another time, when you're not loaded. You wouldn't remember if he told you now anyway." Patrick brushed his hand across her head, smoothing the hair out of her face.

Stella leaned into his arms, as if she would topple over if not for him holding her. "Patrick, I feel like I'm being tortured. When is this all going to end? I seriously can't handle it. My brain feels like it's being punished. My heart is demolished and there's no hope of it returning. What's the point?" Stella grabbed at both of his shoulders, but missed. "What's the fucking point?" she muttered softly and fell into him.

"Patrick, I would've called you earlier, but I didn't know how to get in touch with you." George handed him the bill.

"Not your problem, George, but I'll write my number on this receipt in case this happens again."

"Is she okay?"

"What do you think?" Patrick awkwardly carried Stella out the door.

George watched them stumble all the way to the door, shaking his head.

CHAPTER NINE

Have a Heart

"**A**re you sure you want to do this?"

"Yep." She leaned back in Patrick's car and looked out the window as they drove over the Key Bridge into Georgetown. They were going to get the tattoo she'd been wanting. He helped her design what would go on her left shoulder blade. It would look like a hole in her back, with the pieces of her broken heart crumbled on the bottom like rubble. She found it an accurate depiction. Patrick put his arm on the back of her seat and she leaned into him.

"Well, it's a cool design, I guess. But you know, you still have a heart. You're still alive, even if you don't feel like it now."

"Whatever."

They pulled into a parking spot off a side street and walked along the cobblestone sidewalk until they got to the tattoo parlor. Patrick had used this shop for all six of his tattoos. He was such a good customer that he and the owner had become friends. He would only get tattooed by an artist named Richard, so naturally, it was Richard who was doing her tattoo.

Sweat dripped down Richard's forehead as he was concentrated on Stella's tattoo. He had black spiky hair and a full beard, with deep brown eyes and huge round spacers stretching a hole in each ear. Stella was sure he was covered in tattoos, but she could only see the ones on his arms. Her favorite one was a bright red heart on the inside of his left forearm with an intricate knife sticking out, blood, the same bright red, pooling at his wrist. It was quite graphic. She wondered who had broken Richard's heart.

Today was the third and last tattoo appointment. She'd had to wait an entire month since the last visit for the coloring to heal before putting the finishing touches on it. This third trip was really just to fill in some of the detail because Stella could only handle a couple of hours of needles at a time. The finished product was amazing and disturbing at the same time. Looking at her back, she saw a hole at her left shoulder blade, detail of bones poking out all the way through to where her heart would be. Instead of seeing a heart, Richard had drawn what looked like tattered remains of a heart. It was beautifully grotesque.

Patrick sat in a leather chair next to where Stella lay on her stomach in a sports bra, shorts, and flip-flops. "Richard, I really think this is one of the best and most intricate tattoos I've ever seen. Looks good, man."

Richard wiped blood droplets off the tattoo and blew out a breath, examining his work. "Perfect."

Stella lifted her head and released her hands from the white-knuckled grip she had on the handles of the chair. "Done?"

"Yep." Richard walked over to the drawers next to his chair and took out a cigarette.

"Let me get a smoke and then I'll rub you down."

"Looking forward to it," Stella joked.

Cory, the shop manager, piped up, "I can rub her down while you smoke."

"Don't think about touching Stella," Richard rebuffed.

Cory put his hands up, "Fine, fine, I was just trying to help."

"I bet," Patrick muttered under his breath.

"How's it look?" Stella asked.

"Exactly like we thought it would, it's awesome in a gross way." Patrick smiled and got out of his chair to examine her finished tattoo. "It certainly makes a statement."

"I can't wait to see it finished." Even after the second trip the tattoo had been amazing to see, she wondered how the finishing details would change the look of it stretching across her back.

"Patience grasshopper, you know how Richard is..." Patrick smirked.

Stella laid her head back down on the chair. Her desire to get this tattoo was two-fold. It served as both a memory of Jamie and a warning sign to stay away from the girl-with-the-disgusting-tattoo-that-takes-up-half-her-back.

"Okay, okay..." Richard walked in and stood her up in front of a floor-length mirror and gave her a handheld one so she could see her back. "Whatcha think?"

"It really is perfect, Richard, thank you so much." It was exactly how she had pictured it. A depiction of her lack of heart, destroyed when Jamie died. Now everyone would know.

"Lay back down for a minute and I'll get you out of here." Richard washed his hands and then rubbed salve all over Stella's left shoulder blade, covering her entire tattoo in a thick coat of ointment, and then a patch of white gauze and medical tape. "Alright kid, good doing business with ya."

Stella hugged him.

"I got a favor to ask."

"Anything," Stella answered.

"I want to get a picture of this one for the display. It really is one of the best I've done. You okay with that?"

"Not a problem, Richard. I'll come back in when it heals."

CHAPTER TEN

My Person

"No, I'm not going to my parents' house."

Patrick and Stella were running with wool caps on; Patrick held Cooper's leash as they ran through Old Town in the early morning a week after Thanksgiving.

"Come on, El. It's Christmas." Patrick's breath billowed out in front of him.

"No, I can't be around them. I just can't." Stella closed her eyes for a few steps and felt the ice sting her lungs. "I'm barely making it here, Patrick. I can't handle the scrutiny of the people from home, even if they don't mean it. They don't know me anymore and I can't pretend for them. I don't fucking care about Christmas or presents or joy."

They kept pace together as they ran several blocks in silence. Stella had been thinking about this since Thanksgiving. Again, life went on for everyone else. In DC, at least, she could deal with it because no one knew who she was before. Before, when she loved Christmas, and she would make Jamie drive her to a Christmas tree farm to pick out a tree for her apartment. The day after Thanksgiving, they would explore the entire farm before deciding on a perfect tree. Jamie would effortlessly throw it in the back of his truck. Before, he would unload the tree and she would decorate it. Every time she broke an ornament she had to take off a piece of clothing. Before, she bought him the best, most thoughtful Christmas presents because she was so thankful to have him. Before, she brought him to her parents' house for Christmas Eve. They would wake, eat breakfast casserole, and open presents. Then they would drive to his parents' house for Christmas Day and Christmas dinner. Before, she couldn't stop smiling. *Before...*

She'd made the right decision, she thought, *the decision that would hold her together.* She was held together by a thread. Not even strong fishing wire, but the kind of thread that could fray and break in the wind. A thread that could unravel at any moment, scattering and smashing all the pieces of her that she was trying desperately to keep together.

She was a horrible actress, even before. Her emotions always gave her away. Jamie used to tell her she was the worst liar. Now, her insides were exposed, bare for all to see. Her face was hollow and sallow, which mirrored how she felt in her chest.

Her self-awareness had increased exponentially in the last few months. As she cautiously began to put her life back together, she was made painfully aware of her weaknesses. She had to be careful, or all the tentative progress she'd been making would be erased effortlessly by a thoughtless stranger, or even a caring family member. When she stuck to Billy, Patrick, and Finnegan's, she was safe. She could make it through each day.

When she got home from her run, she composed an email she hoped would convey her love for her parents but also her inability to come home.

Mom and Dad,

I know this is a horrible thing to do, but I can't come home for Christmas. I don't think I'll make it, emotionally. It has nothing to do with either of you. I'm barely able to put one foot in front of the other these days. Nothing I want you to see, but I'm trying, I really am. I can't be happy right now. I love you both. Thanks for understanding. I'm sure Patrick's told you he is staying with me.

Stella

Christmas morning she got up, made coffee, and got out the bottle of Bailey's she'd purchased the day before. She cooked the casserole last night and popped it in the oven to warm while she waited for Patrick. Stella moved soundlessly to the couch to watch the Christmas Day parade, Cooper's head in her lap.

Look at all the happy people, she thought. *What she would give to be back to that, happy and oblivious to the shit that life could throw?* She was hard, numb. The hardness had come about recently, spreading slowly through her brain and chest. She worried that if she were hit hard enough she would just crack.

Patrick opened the door and was met with the smell of coffee and breakfast casserole. Smiling, he walked over to Stella, staring at the television, and kissed her forehead. "Morning."

"Merry Christmas," she said, devoid of any Christmas spirit.

"Back at you."

"Thank you, Patrick. Thank you for being my person." Stella nudged Cooper off her lap and checked the oven. She slipped on Billy's pig-shaped oven mitt.

"Your person?" Patrick poured himself coffee and added Bailey's.

"You're my person. You got my back, and front, for that matter." She set the casserole down on the counter. "You're spending Christmas with me, when you should be at home. I'm selfish and I want you here. So the least I can do is thank you."

"Your person, huh?" Patrick ruffled her hair.

"My person," Stella confirmed, looking up at him. "I wouldn't have made it without you."

"Sure you would've." Patrick smelled the casserole, his mouth watered.

"No, that's where you're wrong." She cut a corner piece for him and put it on a plate. After she put the plate down, she went downstairs and got his present.

He looked at her, stopping mid-chew. "We're doing presents? Fuck." He put down his fork.

"Patrick, you've already done so much for me. Think of it as a thank-you, not a Christmas present."

He ripped the paper open. Patrick's eyes widened. "Stella..." He looked from the gift to her face and back to the gift.

"Thank you," she said, putting a piece of casserole on her plate. She sat down to finish watching the parade.

"This is too much," he said pulling out the brand new Glock 23 and inspecting it. "How did you know I wanted this?"

"You're my person," she answered, without even looking away from the parade.

CHAPTER ELEVEN

Working Girl

Patrick made his way down to her room, which was dark as usual. "El?" He turned on the light. "What are you doing?"

"Get your fucking eyes checked if you can't see me still sleeping!" Stella yelled from under the pillow she had over her face. She was still in a heap. Cooper jumped up, tail wagging, and went over to Patrick. "Traitor!" she called after her dog.

"He just needs to pee and it looks like you aren't getting up anytime soon." Patrick walked back to the door and let Cooper out into the backyard. He lay down in the bed beside her.

"It's been five months, Stella; you stink and you can't pay rent. Billy and I can't keep covering you."

"Well, nothing like honesty first thing in the morning, huh?" She didn't move the pillow from her face.

"It's afternoon." Patrick pulled the pillow from her face. "You've got to start living again."

"I can't."

"You have to." Patrick looked over at what used to be Stella. "Jamie would hate this."

"Well, he's not here, is he?"

"No, I guess it's up to me then. *I* hate this. Please tell me what to do, Stella."

"You can't fix this." She rolled onto her side so that she was looking at him. "You can't fix me."

"I bet I can." Patrick sat up and swung his legs off her platform bed. "Get dressed, I'm taking you to your new job."

She stared at him, dumbfounded. "New job?"

"Yep, it's perfect, you'll love it," he said in a fake tone.

She stood up reluctantly and stretched. Since Jamie died she'd been sleeping in his college baseball jersey.

Patrick reached over and swatted her butt. "Wear something cute," he laughed and then walked upstairs.

After her meeting with the manager of Cosi restaurant in Old Town, who just happened to be a friend of Patrick's, and getting all the details of her new job, Stella and Patrick walked to Finnegan's. She sat on a barstool and stared into her Black and Tan. Patrick was talking; what he was talking about, she had no idea. What she did notice was that the hottie bartender kept looking at her. She could feel his eyes on her. His eyes were greenish grey, reminding her of smoke. They were intense. His features were almost perfect, tainted only by a nose that looked like it might have been broken a time or two. Although it had been awhile, Stella recognized the look he was sending her. Stella didn't know what she thought about that look.

Interrupting Patrick, she leaned into his ear. "Why is the bartender staring at me?"

Patrick tilted his face and looked at the bartender. "George always looks at you, El."

"He does?" She looked back at her glass, now half-empty, unconsciously running her fingers up and down the glass.

"Yes, he does. So do lots of other guys in the bar, but this is the first time you've noticed." Patrick sat up straight, stretching his back. "So, you want to grab dinner before we go home?"

"Sure," she said, smiling and then draining her glass. She stood on the lower rung of the barstool and leaned up over the bar. "Hey barkeep, can we get our check?"

He smiled and nodded at her as he set someone else's drink down on the bar. It was like Stella was seeing George for the first time. He was probably around Patrick's age, a few years older than her. He had tattoos on his forearms, numbers maybe. He wore a white long sleeve button-down with sleeves pushed up to elbows that had obviously seen better days, but the fabric stretched over his chest, subtly giving away the muscles underneath. He was wearing a red Nationals baseball cap and gray New Balance tennis shoes; she noticed because Jamie had worn the same pair.

"You guys done?" he asked Patrick.

Stella redirected George's attention to her. "Here," she said as she slid her debit card across the bar to cover the bill. Stella put on her navy pea coat and pulled a wool cap down over her messy hair.

"El..." Patrick chastised.

"What? You always pay, I have a job now. I can contribute." Stella sat back down and fussed with her bag on her lap.

"You working, Stella?" George inquired politely.

"Right down the road actually, I just got a job at Cosi." She looked pointedly at Patrick. "I think I'll weigh about 300 pounds after working there awhile."

"Oh, that's one of my favorite lunch spots." George took her card and walked over to the computer. Stella watched his ass as he walked away. It was nice.

When George came back with her receipt, Stella said, "Maybe I'll see you there." She signed her receipt, added a pretty hefty tip, and put her card back in her bag.

"Oh, you'll definitely see me there." George smiled a smile that was so big it took over half of his face, showcasing two delicious dimples.

She smiled at him, looking him in the eyes for the first time since she started going to Finnegan's. George seemed a little taken aback, and looked to Patrick, who put his arm around her shoulders. "See you, George."

"Yep," George called over his shoulder, making his way down the bar.

CHAPTER TWELVE

Progress?

Physically, Stella was still alive, but barely. She had finally looked through the documents Jamie had scattered all over their desk. Jamie had opened a bank account with the right of survivorship to her. To her surprise, the account contained several thousand dollars. She'd been able to pay Billy and Patrick back and still had some left to cover rent for awhile. Stella felt like she could only deal with life right now by staying where she was. She still refused to listen to voicemails or read text messages. No one here knew her with Jamie, how she was before he died. Hell, she didn't even remember who she was before he died. *Had she always cussed so much?* She was still staying in bed more than necessary and crying at least three times a day. But it *was* progress. She was moving forward, even if it was one tiny step at a time. Patrick was almost livid that she wasn't making more progress, but he was trying to let her grieve in her own way.

Although she still suffered from insomnia, she started reading like crazy to fill the sleepless hours. Patrick had given her a Kindle and she read three or four books a week. When she read, she was able to shut off her brain and lose herself in the lives of the characters. Drifting through life with no real purpose or feeling wasn't ideal, but she was making it. She couldn't escape the memories of Jamie, or the memories of their four years together; it was eating her alive. She knew she was getting off easy. She was in a city where they hadn't yet made any memories, and had no history. The pain could've been worse.

Stella had started eating again, and hadn't stopped. She'd gained about fifteen pounds in the last two months, which she'd anticipated when she started at Cosi, but she'd gained most of the weight from eating smores everyday and she was forced to join a gym.

Patrick drove her to the gym every morning and they went their separate ways at the door for their workouts. He was the perfect person to make her do what she didn't want to, like get up at 6:00 in the morning to do squats.

Stella was pushing through her workout, sweat dripping off her face. Jay-Z pounded through her earbuds; she let her mind wander. Wiping her face and chest with a gym towel, she remembered her graduation from college and the trip with Jamie that followed. They hadn't gone anywhere that special, but drove to Savannah for a few days before Jamie left her to go to DC that summer. Jamie had shown her where he grew up, his favorite restaurants, and the baseball field where he fell in love with the game.

She was so young then, so innocent, and totally in love. They had walked down River Street holding hands, kissing as much as possible, in public or not, and making love several times a day. It was her favorite time with Jamie.

On their last day in Savannah, he took her to The Old Pink House, a well-known historic restaurant on a square just off River Street. They ate and drank wine. When dessert was served, she noticed a grey velvet box in the center of the plate. She looked at Jamie and knew he was asking her to marry him before he could even speak with words.

He took her hand gently and kissed it. "Stella, I am so in love with you. I need you to know how much. You mean so much to me. I know moving to DC and starting our careers will be tough and we were planning on waiting, but I just can't. I can't wait for you to be mine officially." He got down on one knee, still holding her hand, and asked, "Stella Murphy, will you make me the happiest man on earth and agree to put up with me the rest of my life?"

She wiped a tear from her eye. "Of course." They left the dessert on the plate, got the check, and hurried back to the hotel.

Stella's stomach clenched from the memory. She did lunges, which hurt so badly that she couldn't think anything of other than the physical pain while doing them.

It was her birthday. She didn't care, but Billy and Patrick insisted on taking her out to dinner and to Finnegan's. Stella dressed in jeans, t-shirt, and flip-flops. It was one month before the wedding that she never got to finish planning. Blowing her bangs out of her face, she looked into the mirror. *It's fine; I can make it through today.* She walked upstairs and poured herself a tall vodka on the rocks and sat on the couch, twisting the engagement ring still on her finger while she waited for Patrick to get home.

Stella was already on glass number three when he arrived. "Happy Birthday," he yelled.

"Fucking happy," she responded.

"Come on let's go. Billy's already there and you're already drunk."

"I'm not drunk yet," she protested.

The night was blur, she drank so much that she really had no grasp of conversations or events. At one point, she fell off the back of her barstool. That's when Patrick got frustrated and brought her home. Somehow she made it down the stairs to her room, pulled her clothes off, and passed out on the bathroom floor.

The night was clear and dark. Stars shone like diamonds in the sky. She and Jamie were walking on the beach, hand in hand. Stella was barefoot, wearing her wedding dress and Jamie was in a seersucker suit. She heard a loud crash and tried to find where it had come from. A car was barreling down the sand back from the street and onto the beach. She pulled on Jamie's arm to get him out of the way, but the car hit them both. Jamie was unconscious, his body twisted and trapped under the car, and Stella was pinned, still holding his hand. The front left tire of the car rested on her chest; she couldn't breathe.

She screamed and woke with a start. She hadn't had a nightmare in awhile. Stella pushed herself off the chilly tile floor and walked upstairs. She opened Patrick's door and crawled into his bed. His eyes still closed, he turned toward her back and wrapped his arms around her. Feeling her nightmare let go, she let go too, and fell into a restless sleep.

Stella bent over behind the glass case arranging in the best-looking cookies she had ever seen. It was after the lunch rush and time to refill the dessert case, then she would go on break. "Hi, there," she heard, and stood up quickly.

"Oh...hi." It was George. He wasn't lying when he said he came in to Cosi for lunch every day.

She'd started looking forward to his lunch break.

"I want one of those cookies," he smiled, putting his plate down on the glass counter by the register.

"I know, they look delicious." She grabbed one, bagged it, and pulled her gloves off as she moved to the register.

"You're practically drooling." George pulled out his wallet and gave her cash to cover his lunch and cookie.

"It's hard not to. I've eaten at least one of everything." She tucked a stray hair from her braid behind her ear. "Enjoy it," she said and walked to the back to clock for her break.

She ordered a turkey and brie, her favorite sandwich, and sat at a table near George. She pulled out her Kindle and was ready to read about a girl escaping her past by going to college, who fell in love with a beautiful bad boy.

"Stella, come sit with me. Keep me company." He nodded at the chair across the table.

"Okay." Stella picked up her things, put her Kindle back in its case and made her way to George's table.

George pushed the chair out with his foot. "Turkey and Brie," he said, "that's a good one."

"My favorite, but *so* not good for me." Stella pointed at the tattoos on his arms. "Do you mind me asking what the dates are?"

"People really shouldn't have tattoos if they don't want people asking what they mean, should they?" He smiled. "5/24/48 is my dad's birthdate and 9/12/11 is the day he died."

"I'm so sorry," Stella said, looking down at her sandwich.

George pushed his cookie toward her. "I bought this for you."

"What? Why?" She eyed the cookie.

"Because you really were drooling just looking at it." George rubbed his hand over his shaved head.

"You have any more?" Stella picked a small piece of the cookie off the side and popped it in her mouth. It was the perfect mix of white chocolate and macadamia nut, drizzled with melted peanut butter.

"Any more what?" George stared at her dramatic reaction to the cookie. "Must be good."

"Oh my shit, it's *so* good." She pushed it back toward his plate. "Try it."

His shoulders were shaking with laughter. "Oh my shit?"

"Umm... taste it." She pushed the cookie closer to his hand.

He broke off a piece of the cookie and popped it in his mouth. "That is good. I'm not sure what qualifies as 'oh my shit,' but I'll take your word for it."

They ate and carried on with small talk. George didn't have any other tattoos. She told him she had one on her back. Stella looked at her cell phone. "My break's up. I'll see you later."

"Yep." George was still working on his lunch.

Stella walked over to the trashcan. "George?"

He looked up at her. "Yes?"

"Thanks for the drool-worthy cookie."

She finished her shift at Cosi and was walking home when her mind drifted back to the cookie. She couldn't remember the last time she had actually enjoyed a cookie that much; or anything for that matter. She could still taste it in her mouth.

CHAPTER THIRTEEN

Lucky Shit

She was a step behind Patrick as they ran across the bridge from Arlington Cemetery into DC and past the Lincoln Memorial. Today they were running ten miles. She'd been working up to such a distance for a while. After Jamie died, she'd given up running along with everything else. It was something she loved, but couldn't bear to do; they used to run together every day.

She pushed her sunglasses up her nose and adjusted her earbud. She was proud that she was keeping pace with Patrick. They ran to the Washington Monument and then turned around. As they started the last mile of their run, Stella began feeling a little stronger than when she started. It was a long run and it hurt in the beginning, but it seemed she hit her stride. Patrick turned and smiled at her as she trailed him for the last half mile.

As he motioned for her to pick it up, he tripped and fell. When Stella bent over to give him a hand she felt something warm sliding over her bare shoulder and down her right arm. "Fucking hell!" She examined her arm and the trail of bird shit now streaking it. Stella bent forward, laughing so hard she couldn't help Patrick to his feet. She sat down and gave in to the laughter. When she looked up, Patrick was looking at her with alarm. "What?" she said, breathless from her run and from the laughter.

"I've never heard you laugh before," Patrick said gently.

"Really, never?" Stella was stunned. She'd known Patrick for almost ten months and he'd never heard her laugh.

"Nope." Patrick got up, but leaned over to touch his toes in a stretch. He grabbed a quad and stretched it. "I like it. Your laugh is ridiculous."

"Jamie used to say that all the time, too. My laugh was so funny it made him laugh." Stella looked at the bird shit sliding down her arm. Flicking her arm, she tried to shake some of the shit off.

"I may've heard a polite fake laugh at some point, but that was a real laugh. I like it. You need to laugh more, obviously."

"There really hasn't been too much for me to laugh about this past year." She got up and started walking back to Patrick's car.

Patrick nudged her shoulder. "You know, they say that a bird shitting on you is good luck."

Laughter burst out of Stella once again, which made Patrick laugh, too. "They only say that so you won't feel that bad about a bird shitting on you. There's really nothing lucky about getting shit on...period."

Stella turned her old red Honda Accord onto GW Parkway and thought of two things simultaneously. First, Jamie had been gone for a year. Second, she hadn't talked to her dad in almost as long. She reached for her phone and took a deep breath. Stella punched her dad's number and waited.

"Stella?" Her eyes pricked with tears just hearing his voice. "Are you alright?"

"Hey, Dad," she barely whispered.

"Wow, it's good to hear your voice, baby girl."

"I'm sorry it's been so long, I just couldn't..."

"Oh, Stella, it's okay. I'm just glad to hear your voice."

The phone was silent for a couple of beats. "It's my first day of law school today."

"I know."

"How?" Stella was taken aback that her dad had any information about what she was doing.

"Patrick has kept your mother and me informed about your life since you haven't been able to."

"Oh really?" It took a minute for Stella to go from pissed to understanding Patrick's motive and let the irritation pass over her. "Well, I just thought you might want to know." She was about to hang up.

"Mom and I have been so worried..." Her dad's voice broke.

"Hey, have you seen the show about the rednecks in Georgia where the little girl is in pageants or something?" Stella changed the subject to something neutral.

Her dad laughed and she realized how much she had missed him over the last year. "Yes, your mom and I were watching the other day."

They talked about everything from Sugar Bear to the problems with the two-party political system. She told him about her job and all the books she'd been reading. He told her about all the things going on with him and with her mom. Life in their world was the same as it had been last year. Her life was drastically different. That was the biggest lesson she learned this year; it doesn't matter if you're falling apart, shit keeps moving. The world didn't stop because she did.

After they hung up with a promise to talk again soon, she closed her eyes while stopped in traffic. She smiled, feeling a little more settled than she had in quite some time. This next chapter in her life was a complete unknown, but she was moving forward. It was progress.

Stella pulled into the parking lot assigned to first-year law students. It was on the main campus instead of the law school campus. Everything about law school so far had been unpleasant. The application process, now the parking: it was like they were hazing first-year students. In the future, she would either have to catch the bus or walk the mile from the lot to school. Checking her watch, she realized she better just park and start walking. After a brisk fifteen-minute walk, she made it to American University, Washington College of Law. Smiling when she saw the Starbucks across the street, she bet the law students kept the owner of that coffee shop loaded.

As she walked through the law school doors, sweat started dripping down her back. Having worn layered tank tops, she shed one in the bathroom and used it to wipe the sweat from her face and back. She took the elevator to the third floor for her first class. She walked in and surveyed the room. There were a few other students there already and she took a seat in the back row.

Pulling out her laptop and her Property book, she released a breath she didn't realize she had been holding. This was it. She was starting over.

A girl with caramel-colored hair opened the door and looked around. She made her way to a seat at the table next to Stella and pulled out her things. "Hi. I'm Millie. I mean, it's really Camille Rodriguez, but I go by Millie." She smiled at Stella and held out her hand. Stella shook it. "Where are you from? I'm from Arizona, but I moved up here this summer. I love DC. How about you? Have you been to..."

Stella tuned out at this point. The girl was talking a mile a minute, not even waiting for a response to the questions she asked. The class was almost full. She'd be with these people for the entire year. For the first year, the students were put into sections and would attend all classes as a group with the same students.

"... so, what's your name?"

"Stella," she replied shortly.

"I like it." Millie reached out and touched the back of Stella's shoulder. "Killer tattoo. Did you get that here?"

"Yep; Needles and Skin parlor in Georgetown. I highly recommend Richard."

"It's kinda gross, though," Millie said, examining her shoulder more closely.

"Yeah, it kinda is." Stella smiled. She liked Millie right then. She had gotten all manner of reactions to her tattoo, but Millie's was her favorite.

Millie's skin was immaculate; she wore very little makeup, if any. She was striking in a very natural way, and was maybe twenty-two. Her hair reached to the middle of her back. Millie flipped her Property book open to the first case they were to read, according to the class syllabus, and looked at Stella. "You're weird." She said. "I like you."

Before Stella could respond, their professor came in and immediately began an hour-long lecture that confused every student in the class. Stella wasn't sure the professor had stopped lecturing long enough to take a breath, and after class her brain hurt. She was definitely heading to Starbucks. She packed up her things.

"I'm hitting up Starbucks, you want to go?" Millie asked, standing there waiting for Stella.

"Sure, I was headed there anyway."

"Good." Millie began telling Stella all the gossip she'd heard about their Civil Practice professor and how famous he was in the legal community.

They ordered coffee and sat at a small table outside. *This feels... almost normal.*

"So, Stella, do you live around here?"

"No, I live in Old Town." Stella had her sunglasses on and was taking in the sight of all the law students.

"Where's that?"

"Alexandria."

"Why do you live out there?"

"I live with two guys I know." Stella answered shortly.

"Oh, are they students too?" Millie took a sip of her coffee and spit it out violently. "Oh my...shit, I think I burned my tongue!"

Stella burst out laughing.

"It's not funny, I think I have, like, third-degree burns on my tongue. I'll never enjoy wine or chocolate again."

"No, it's not that. I say 'oh my shit' all the time and my friends make fun of me."

"Well, I wasn't really trying to phrase it that way, but I think it works..." Millie stuck her tongue out, trying to look at it and show it to Stella at the same time. "Is it burned?"

"Obviously," Stella answered with another laugh.

"So you live with two guys, how's that?"

"It's fine. I've lived with them for a little over a year, so I guess it works."

"We'll have to go out sometime."

"That'd be cool. Where do you live?"

"I live down Mass in Tenleytown." Tenleytown was a neighborhood filled with law school students, mainly because it was so close to campus. It was mostly rental houses and condos, sort of an oasis in the city. The streets were tree-lined and it mirrored the suburbs.

"You live by yourself?" Stella pulled out an apple and bit into it.

"No, there's no way I could afford that."

"Me either. I know you aren't supposed to work your first year, but that's harsh."

"Well, they say you have so much work for school, there's no way you could handle both." Millie looked at her cell phone. "There's a happy hour for our section on Thursday, you in?"

"Not sure yet." Stella didn't want to plan on going to happy hour just yet. She still really only socialized with Billy and Patrick at Finnegan's.

They finished their coffee and headed back across the street to their Civil Procedure class. When they sat in the back row together Stella leaned over and whispered, "By the way, my friends call me El."

CHAPTER FOURTEEN

The Plot Thickens

Stella pulled into the parking lot in time to see the bus driving away. *Fuck.* She was going to be sweaty and late again. After practically jogging to the law school, she rushed into Contracts class, skidding into another student. Stella's bag fell to the floor and books scattered everywhere. "Shit," she muttered under her breath.

"Shit, I'm sorry."

Stella kept picking up her stuff, not even responding.

"It's Stella, right?"

She looked up. "Yeah." She stood and quickly said, "I'm about to be late."

"I know. We're in the same section." The guy smiled warmly at her. "I'm Davis." He was blond and fair-skinned with perfect features. His teeth were white and straight. His lips were so uncharacteristically red, she wondered if he was wearing lipstick.

"Hi." Stella moved quickly through the door and into the classroom.

"Um, are you going to happy hour tonight?" he called out to her back.

Stella almost ignored the question entirely, but responded without turning around. "Don't know." She smiled as she hopped up the stairs of the room to the back row where she and Millie sat. Breathing heavily, she sat down and opened her laptop.

"Hey, bitch." Millie was typing while she talked. "Davis looked like you kicked his kitten. What did you say?"

"Nothing." Stella was calming down now, since she'd made it to class before the professor. Tardiness was not a trait she appreciated in anyone, least of all herself.

"Well, you must've said *something*." Millie stopped typing and looked at her. "Your social skills aren't that great."

"Agreed." Stella pulled out her book and logged onto campus Wi-Fi.

"Well, what were y'all talking about?"

"Fuck, you're relentless. I bumped into him and spilled my bag. He introduced himself and asked if I was going to happy hour," Stella said without taking a breath. "Happy?"

"So you aren't going?"

"I don't know," Stella said slowly.

"You don't find him attractive?"

Their professor walked into the class. "No." Stella shook her head. "Not my type."

"You're engaged, not dead, right?" Millie started typing again. "What is your type? I guess it's not perfect-looking," Millie muttered sarcastically.

Stella was stuck; men weren't even on her radar and Millie still thought she was engaged. She was still wearing her ring, so it made sense. "Okay...So I'm not engaged anymore," Stella whispered with her eyes glued forward on their professor.

"And the plot thickens," Millie said before the professor began her lecture about the necessary elements of a contract.

Stella was on a couch at the bar with several people from her law school section. The idea of the first year section was helpful, she heard, because people could form study groups that lasted the entire year.

This sort of socializing was difficult for her now. She kept quiet and just observed the interaction between the other law students. She'd determined that law students, in general, were weird. Some were weird in a bad way, some in a good way, but the whole lot was peculiar.

Millie leaned over to Stella and pulled her up to her feet. "Let's go dance." Millie motioned to the dance floor.

"There's no one dancing," Stella said flatly.

"Perfect way to get the party started, don't ya think?" Millie pulled Stella by the hand all the way to the dance floor and started dancing.

Millie swayed her hips casually to the beat of a song by Jay-Z while throwing her hands in the air and screaming out the lyrics about having problems.

Stella made her dance by herself for a while, but gave in after a few beats, and started dancing. Soon, several members of their section were dancing around them.

Stella kept perfect time with the beat of the music and danced with Millie or by herself. Looking around the dance floor, she saw most of the law students were standing around talking, not dancing. She took a break to get a beer. She motioned to Millie that she would get one for her as well and sauntered over to the bar to order two beers. Her shirt was soaked with sweat; she was glad she had worn a black halter top. Someone leaned into the bar next to her and held his hand up at the bartender.

The guy turned to look at Stella, his eyes travelling to the tattoo on her back. "Damn, girl, is that a real tattoo?"

Stella grimaced. People asked her that all the time; it was a stupid question. "No, it's fake," she answered sarcastically. She recoiled when the guy touched her, rubbing his finger across her tattoo.

"Oh, sorry," the guy said, pulling his hand from her back.

"You touch me again and I'll break your fucking hand." She smiled at him condescendingly and took her drinks back to the dance floor.

CHAPTER FIFTEEN

Fine

She was in the back of the restaurant, eating a salad and reading for class when George walked to the back and put down his plate. She didn't even look up until he slid the chair out so he could join her. Stella's hair was in a bun and she was twirling pieces that had fallen out with her hand while she read.

She smiled briefly when she finally noticed him. "Ah, we meet again." Stella turned down the corner of her Civil Practice and closed it.

George took a huge bite of his sandwich. "That's a mighty big book, Stella."

"It's what chicks with big minds read." She checked the time on her cell. She had fifteen minutes before she had to go back to work.

"I love a girl with a big mind." George smiled again.

Stella went back to work on her salad, and the two sat pleasantly silent for a few minutes. "So, George," she finally said. "You are totally obsessed with Cosi sandwiches." Stella didn't look up from her salad; she had pretty much seen him every day for the last year, either at her job or his.

"Pretty much." He opened his bag of chips and she almost salivated. "You want one?"

"I wish." Stella looked at her salad. All she ever ate these days were salads. "I gained some weight over the last year and I'm trying to get it off. Patrick's making me go to the gym with him every morning at six. It's obnoxious."

"That's a bit tough. You should tell him to fuck off. He should like you for you." George didn't look at her when he said this, but examined his food.

Stella smiled a little. "George. You're too funny; *he* isn't making me lose weight. I could give a shit what Patrick thinks about my looks." She laughed again. "I asked for his help, he's good at making me do shit I don't want to do."

"So, how long have y'all been engaged?"

Stella actually spit food out of her mouth. "No!" She grabbed a napkin and put it over her face while she laughed.

"Why is it so funny? You're always together at the bar. Always. The way he looks at you just made me think…" He stared intensely at her face, but pointed to her engagement ring. "I know if I was engaged to you I wouldn't let any other guy act like Patrick acts around you."

Stella's eyes clouded over, but she refused to cry. "He's protective, but it's like I'm his little sister." Stella thought about it; she guessed she was always with Patrick. "He's my roommate." Her voice shook a little.

"Oh…well, I guess that clears up the whole *you're always with each other* thing." George was rambling. "Where's your fiancé? I thought you moved up here together?"

"Wow, George, you ask a lot of questions." Stella looked at her cell for the time. "We did move here together."

"Well, why haven't I met him?" George leaned, still staring at her.

"George, I'm not engaged anymore…" Stella let out a long breath, relieved she hadn't started crying.

"Oh." He looked at her ring again. "Why are you wearing your ring then?"

"None of your business, George." Stella pushed herself back from the table and threw the remainder of her lunch in the trash, walking as fast as she could to the employee kitchen.

"So, I've been ordering pizza since last Tuesday. If finals aren't over soon, I'll probably die from stress eating…or just stress," Millie lamented. Millie and Stella were taking a break from studying and having coffee at Starbucks across the street.

"Millie, this isn't the end of the world. It's not life or death, they're only fucking tests. You're studying and preparing, so you'll be fine. You make a B, you'll be fine." Stella took a tentative sip of her gingerbread latte and sighed.

"I've wanted to do this my whole life. My entire future depends on me making good grades, actually depends on how I do on ONE test."

"Peter said this is what law school does. It beats you down to build you back up, kinda like the armed forces." Stella took another sip of coffee and pulled her wool cap down over her ears.

Peter was a Constitutional Law professor at the school. She'd met him a few weeks ago while eating lunch in the cafeteria on the top floor of the law school. Millie had run home so Stella was eating by herself, and reading cases. He'd dropped his tray on her table and immediately started talking to her, making it impossible to ignore him. They'd talked for a couple hours until her next class. He'd changed her perspective on many aspects of law school.

"Why are you so calm? Why aren't you freaking out? Look...look!" Millie urged pointing at her eye. "My eye won't stop twitching and I haven't had a solid shit in two weeks."

"Um, gross." It took all Stella had not to spit her coffee at Millie. "First of all, too much information. Second, I'm already as down as I can get. All law school can do is build me up. Third, you can't let this shit control you."

"Your mouth is moving but I don't understand the words coming out." Millie looked at her cell to check the time. "I honestly think I may be losing my fucking mind."

"You'll be fine. Although, you do look a little crazy." Stella looked around at the mass of law students sitting outside in the thirty-degree weather just to smoke, get coffee, or just get out of the library. She pointed at Millie's feet. "You *are* wearing two different tennis shoes."

"That's so fucking condescending. I know I'll be fine, you asshole, I'm just freaking out like every other first year except for you." Millie looked down at her feet and cringed. "This is a fashion statement."

"What's it saying?" Stella couldn't hide her grin.

Millie flipped her the bird.

"Well, look, my life has been a little different than most of the first year law students. I'm sure I'll freak out at some point and get mad at you for telling me I'll be fine."

"I've got to go finish my outline for civil procedure. That final is open book so I'm not as worried about it."

"If your eye doesn't stop twitching soon, I'm going to get nervous."

"Shut up, I can't help it."

"Last final is Friday, how do we celebrate?"

"I'm going home on Saturday, so it can't be too much... Finnegan's?"

"Any place I can walk home from after drinking is fine with me."

"Besides, there are always yummy conservative men there."

"What's yummy about that?" Stella looked at Millie's smiling face; her eye had stopped twitching.

"I love a conservative man, El. Military is even better."

"Okay I guess everyone has a type."

"What's your type, El? You never even look at guys." Millie smiled at a girl in their section as they made their way to the library.

Stella opened the door and put her finger to her mouth. "Saved by the silent library," she mouthed and walked over to the carrel where her laptop was and put her earbuds back in her ears with a smile.

CHAPTER SIXTEEN

Christmas Pie

Stella, Millie, and Billy walked up to the bar where Patrick was sitting. It was almost happy hour and Millie and Stella had just finished their first set of finals in law school. Stella was exhausted and ordered two beers to start.

Millie had a cranberry vodka. "I can't stay too long, I'm leaving in the morning." Millie drank half her drink in one gulp. "When are you leaving, El?"

Stella felt all three sets of eyes on her. "I'm staying here."

"Damn, you hate your parents or what?" Millie took another gulp of her drink and flagged down a bartender for another one.

Stella was already on her second beer. "No, I don't hate them," she said softly. "We don't really know each other anymore."

"Whatever, weirdo. What about you, Patrick? You going home for the holidays?"

His blue eyes softened when he looked at Millie. "Yep."

Stella raised her brows at Patrick; this was the first she was hearing about this. "When you headed home?"

"Christmas Eve."

Stella examined his face; she knew he would go back earlier if she left. They would talk later. Stella caught sight of George and waved him over. "Yo, I need two more!"

George nodded at her and started pouring her two draft beers. He walked over to where she was sitting on a barstool. "You look a little tired, El."

Stella took one of the beers and took a large gulp. "You're fucking observant."

"That's why I get paid the big bucks." George winked at her. "You know, you have the tolerance of a 300-pound man."

Stella held her glass up in a "cheers" motion. "Proud of it."

Stella refused Patrick's request that she come home with him for Christmas. Millie asked her, too. She was fine being alone with Cooper on Christmas. She was running with Cooper on the afternoon of Christmas Eve when she ran into George as he made his way into Finnegan's, his hands full of boxes.

"Hey," she said, out of breath. "Let me get the door for you." Stella ran over and held the door as he walked in, the heat warming her frozen face. She shut the door and started to run off.

"El?" She heard George call to her as she made her way toward Queen Street. She turned and smiled. She waved and jogged back over to where George was standing, his hand shielding his eyes from the bright afternoon sun. He had on a navy pea coat and a grey wool cap pulled down to his eyes.

"Merry Christmas," she said.

"Merry Christmas. What're you doing here?" He reached out to touch her arm.

"Oh, I'm staying here for Christmas." Cooper began smelling George. "Cooper, stop that. So sorry."

"That's okay, I love dogs. My dog died a few months ago. I'm still broken up over it."

"Oh God, I'm sorry, George." She pulled at Cooper's collar.

"So, is Patrick staying with you for Christmas?"

"No, he left yesterday," she said, inching away.

"No one should be by themselves on Christmas." George smiled.

"It's okay. I won't be by myself."

"Oh, well, okay. If you get bored, we have a big buffet tonight. Since we all have to work Christmas Eve, we do it up. You should come by."

"Maybe," she said. "I gotta go. Thanks for the invitation, George. If I don't see you, have a great holiday."

"Hopefully I'll see you tonight," he called after her.

When she walked into Finnegan's, she was shocked by the number of people there; it was Christmas Eve. She took the only barstool left, unwrapping her scarf from around her neck as she craned to see who was bartending. She waved at Hazel. "Guinness!" Stella shouted over the crowd. She felt an arm go around her shoulder.

"You came." George leaned over and gave her a kiss on her cheek.

Stella, taken aback, scooted away from George's touch. Then she saw his rosy cheeks and glassy eyes. He was drunk. "Hey, George."

"Hey," he said, moving a customer out of the way to slide up the bar next to Stella. "Get me another Bass, Hazel." He turned his body to face Stella's, showing her his puzzled eyes.

"Thought you were busy?"

"Plans fell through," she lied easily.

"I'm glad." He leaned down close to where she was sitting. "You look beautiful."

Stella blushed. He smelled amazing, like rosemary and mint. "Thanks, George, so do you." *What? That didn't make any sense.*

He chuckled. "You want to sit with me at my table? Eat with me." George grabbed his beer, then took her hand and led her back to where he was sitting. "Let me get you a plate."

George handed her a plate and led her to the buffet. After she loaded her plate with all sorts of amazing food, she made her way to the table in the back.

She smiled at George. "This looks incredible."

"It is." He looked around. "Finnegan's has been open on Christmas Eve every year since it opened. Look at how many people would rather be here than with their families."

"It's crazy." Stella took a bite of the Shepherd's Pie.

"I'd give anything to have my dad back, but I guess this is better than nothing."

She shook her head, confused. "What?"

"Nothing." He smiled at her. "It's hard at Christmas without him, you know?"

"I sure do," she said softly.

"So how were finals?" George asked, changing the subject.

"They're over. I'm glad. I think Millie lost her mind a couple of times. I threw up before every final."

"Shit." George leaned back in his chair, gazing at her.

"I have a nervous stomach. If I get really stressed, I vomit; always have."

George reached over and wiped at something off Stella's lip with his thumb; a buzz started where he touched and traveled all the way to her toes. She cocked her head in a question.

"You had a little of the pie on your mouth," he said, staring at her lips.

"Thanks," she replied, feeling very uncomfortable all of a sudden. His touch had been unexpected. Maybe that's why there was a buzzing throughout her body. She was quiet as they finished dinner. After dessert she politely excused herself, thanking George profusely for inviting her, and made her way home.

Christmas morning she got up and made coffee, filled her cup with Bailey's and then sat down in front of the television to watch the Christmas parades. Cooper sat down right in front of her, his face searching hers hopefully.

"I don't have any food for you." She smiled, leaned over and put her chin on the top of his head. When she sat up again, she showed him her hands. "See, no food." His big paw landed on her knee, showing he wanted her to pet him. "Okay…" Stella got up and picked up his new bowl. Patrick had gotten him a new aluminum bowl with spikes circling the entire thing. He'd said Cooper needed to be more "badass."

"You're badass enough, right?" She filled the bowl with dog food and put it on the floor. Her phone beeped, indicating a text message. Turning on The Lumineers, she began cooking an omelet and turkey bacon. Cooper hovered, hoping she'd drop scraps.

Her phone made a motorcycle noise; her dad was calling. She picked up her phone and realized he wanted to video chat with her. He and her mom were squeezed together to fit onto the phone's screen. Hitting the accept button, she smiled. "Hey, y'all."

"Merry Christmas," they recited together.

"Merry Christmas to you, too."

"Since you couldn't be here in person, I told your father, 'let's do that video thing.' I want to see my baby on Christmas."

"Here I am," she answered.

"You look like shit," her dad said.

"Thanks," she replied looking down at Jamie's baseball jersey.

"Where's Patrick?" Her mother craned her neck like she might be able to see Stella's kitchen.

Stella hadn't anticipated them asking about Patrick; she'd told them he was at the house with her again this year. "He's in the bathroom," she answered.

"Well, tell him we asked about him." Her mother straightened her hair as she looked at the screen. "This phone makes me look weird, doesn't it?"

"A little," Stella answered hesitantly, trying to figure out the right answer.

"You look fine," her dad responded. "Stella, are you eating? Patrick said you were eating. You need to eat."

"I'm eating fine. I went to a Christmas buffet last night and ate my weight in Shepherd's Pie, so I've been carrying on the holiday tradition."

"Well, look at this..." her mother pointed to a few boxes sitting on the table in front of them. "These were under the tree for you. I kept thinking you would come home."

"Sorry." Stella looked over at her omelet, it was starting to burn.

"Its fine, baby girl, we just wanted to see your face this morning." Her dad chastised her mother with his tone, she could tell this was a fight they had already had.

"Okay, I've got to go," she said. "Love y'all."

"Love you, too," her dad responded.

"Come home soon, baby," her mother said at the same time.

Her dad was shooting her mother the death glare as they hung up.

CHAPTER SEVENTEEN

I'm Not Puking

Stella was hard at it with school and work, and before she knew it, it was St. Patrick's Day. Millie and Patrick were sitting next to each other at the bar waiting on drinks, while Billy and Stella remained at the table. St. Patrick's Day happened to fall on a Friday and the four had been at Finnegan's since 5:30. The band playing traditional Irish music had the entire bar singing along. They were singing "The Unicorn Song." Stella had become very familiar with the song because every Saturday night right after midnight the band played it. "The Unicorn Song" required the crowd to stand up and do the body motions along with the song. It was hilarious to see grown men singing about unicorns and other animals. She was shocked to find out the song was actually a Shel Silverstein poem set to music.

Stella leaned into the table, her face a few inches from Billy's. "I'm hammered."

"It's only midnight!" Billy laughed and leaned back in his chair. "You're gonna puke tonight."

"Bullshit," she said, and looked over to see Millie and Patrick making their way back to the table with drinks. "I can out-drink all of you, probably most people at this bar."

"Sadly, that's a true statement." Billy winked at her and took his beer from Patrick. "Let's put a wager on it. The one who pukes first has to take us all out to dinner tomorrow night."

"I'm not puking," Patrick said.

"Well, then you don't have to worry about it, do you." Billy ran his hand through his hair and pulled his glasses off, hanging them in the collar of his shirt. "The rules are as follows: (1) Everyone drinks the same amount. The first one finished forces everyone to get another round. (2) You bow out, you lose. (3) You pass out, you lose. (4) You puke…"

"You lose," Stella finished for him. "Millie's out. She's a 'normal' girl, she can't hang."

"Excuse me, I can drink with the best of ' em." Millie pouted, offended that Stella didn't think she could hold her liquor.

"Mill, this isn't about you being able to drink or hold your liquor. This is about being able to drink as much as me *and* hold your liquor."

Millie had seen Stella drink several bottles of wine by herself in one night without even getting a hangover the next day. "Okay, I'm out."

"Good," Patrick said. "I'm in, and I'll win."

The three of them kept up with each other until 3:30 in the morning, when Stella decided she wanted to go for a swim. As she got up, she teetered on her heels and then walked to the bathroom. She heard Millie come in after her, giggling.

"I'm *so* drunk," Millie commented. "I still look okay though," she said, looking at herself in the mirror.

Stella exited the stall and looked at Millie in the mirror. "I hope you groomed yourself today. We're going skinny dipping."

A squeal escaped Millie's lips. "I've never been skinny dipping! Where's there a pool?"

"There's a hotel with an indoor pool a couple of blocks from here," Stella opened the door. "We'll have to sneak in," she whispered.

They walked to the bar. "George, we need our tab. We're going swimming ," Millie said looking around cautiously. "Naked."

George's eyes crinkled with laughter "That should be fun, Millie."

"I've never been before…shhh, don't tell anyone."

"Mill, just act like you've done it before. Haven't you learned anything in law school? Perception is 95 percent of the game." Stella released a loud hiccup and then put her hand to her mouth. Millie burst out laughing. Stella put her debit card on the receipt and winked at George, ignoring the hiccup. "Right, George?"

"Something like that," he replied.

Stella and Millie waved goodbye to him as they grabbed Billy and Patrick on their way to the door. "It's this way," Stella said, gesturing for the group to follow.

"What's this way? Our house is this way." Billy motioned towards their house, confused. Stella put her arm through the gap between his arm and his body, linking their arms together to steady herself. "We Are Going Skinny Dipping," Stella said smiling. She hiccupped again and started laughing.

"We are?" Patrick asked with a giggle. Everyone stopped walking and turned to look at him.

"Did you just giggle?" Millie asked, shock on her face.

"You may be the one to puke tonight…" Stella winked at Billy as they laughed at their usually stoic roommate.

"No puking, just naked swimming with beautiful people," Patrick said with a wide grin.

"Thanks, Patrick," Billy said laughing.

When they got to the boutique hotel on King Street, Stella shushed them and told them to follow her lead. She walked confidently up to the clerk at the desk.

"Hi, I'm drunk and I lost my room key," Stella said cheerfully.

The clerk took in the four of them, trying to stifle a grin. "Okay, give me your ID and I'll get you another key."

"Oh wait, aren't you Missy's dad?"

The clerk examined her. "Yes?"

Stella pointed at herself. "Cooper."

His entire demeanor changed. "You mean the runner with the huge tattoo?"

She awkwardly pulled her collar down in the back to show him her tattoo. "The one and only." She turned to face Millie, Patrick, and Billy. "Cooper loves Missy, his dog," she stage whispered. She racked her brain trying to come up with his name before turning around and realizing it was on his nametag. "Steve!" She smiled. "Can I ask a favor?"

"Of course," he replied.

"I'm here with a friend of mine and we just want to get him back to his room. He lost his entire wallet and he's so hammered he doesn't know what room he's in. He knows it's on the fifth floor in the very back of the hotel." She smiled. "He said the window was useless." She whispered the last part, as if trying to preserve the reputation of the hotel.

"Let me check." He started looking on the computer. "How's Cooper doing?"

"Great, he's obsessed with the cookies at the dog bakery around the corner, but that's why we run." She chuckled and so did Steve.

"520?" he said, looking at Billy.

Billy nodded his head. "That's it." He hit himself in the forehead with his palm to overdramatically show what an idiot he was.

"Okay, Mr. Williams, I'll just need you to sign this saying we issued you another key."

"Sure." He walked over and signed a name so messy no one would be able to tell what it said.

Steve handed the key to Billy and looked back at Stella. "It's so good to see you; I didn't recognize you without spandex on."

Stella giggled playfully and said, "That sounds dirty, Steve."

He blushed and watched them make their way onto the elevator.

"I'm glad you wear spandex all the time," Patrick slurred, nodding appreciatively.

"Me too," agreed Billy.

Millie giggled and pointed at the sign showing the way to the indoor pool. They used the key to get into the pool area and started taking their clothes off. Stella pulled off her shirt, jeans, bra, and underwear hastily and jumped in the pool.

"Hey!" scolded Billy, "I didn't even get to see anything." He and Patrick both turned to Millie, who was demurely taking her jeans off and folding them on a pool lounger.

"What?" Millie blushed. "I'll make you both turn around if you don't stop staring."

Patrick and Billy busied themselves with their own clothes. Patrick jumped in the water splashing Stella, and Billy eased down the stairs.

"Not bad, fellas," Stella said enthusiastically of Patrick and Billy's physiques.

Stella was trying to dunk Patrick under the water when Millie attempted to run and jump into the pool. She had just yelled "CANNONBALL!" when she tripped and fell before reaching the water. Everyone erupted in laughter; Millie started crying she was laughing so hard. Then she crawled the couple of feet to the pool and rolled in unceremoniously.

The next morning, Stella woke with Millie in bed next to her, both with their hair slicked back to their heads. Her head pounded. She walked to the bathroom quietly for some pain medication. She hadn't been this hungover in a very long time. After swimming last night, they had lain on the lounge chairs talking until the morning, all partially dressed. When Steve woke them up, scolding them for passing out in the closed pool, Stella had been draped over Billy. Millie and Patrick spooned on the lounge chair next to them. Stella had apologized profusely while pulling on her jeans. All of them were still drunk and silent for most of the way home. She still wasn't sure how they'd made it home. Her memory took her up and until Billy had put his arm around her shoulder and held her upright as they'd exited the pool. Patrick had puked in the trashcan and then followed them out, dragging Millie by the hand. As soon as they got home they all respectively passed out again.

"Holy shit," Millie groaned from the bed. "Did I throw up?"

"Patrick." Stella replied and smiled.

"Ugh, I feel horrid."

"You look it, too."

"Oh my God, did you notice Patrick last night? Naked?" Millie pulled the pillow over her face.

"Yes," Stella responded and got back in bed.

"He is the hottest man I've ever seen naked."

"Really? That's pretty sad." She laughed.

"No. I'm serious. How can you not think he has one of the hottest naked bodies you've ever seen?" Millie turned and looked at Stella. "I mean, seriously hot. Did you see he has that arrow muscle?"

"What?" Stella was confused.

"You know, the muscles that point to his dick, the *arrow to his dick*. Good God," she groaned. "I almost jumped him last night."

"I'm glad you didn't. It would've been a little gauche." Stella had her arm draped over her eyes.

"Did you just say gauche?" She laughed. "You're so weird."

Stella laughed briefly, but stopped because it made her headache worse.

"He *will* be mine." Millie put her feet on the floor. "We need food that's really bad for us. Let's go."

The last three months of her first year of law school were a blur of reading and studying. She and Millie had worked out a schedule to study with the group for a couple hours a day, then by themselves. Stella had created a "finals" playlist full of soothing music on her phone, and listened while she studied.

After her last final, which had been that morning, she'd come back to the house to lay outside in the sun. For five hours, she alternated between sleeping and reading a fiction book she'd been pining after for the last year. At around four, she opened a bottle of white wine that had been cooling in the fridge, turned up Mumford & Sons, and started cooking. She was making dinner tonight for the boys.

Singing and swaying to the music, she cut the vegetables. Cooper, knowing their old routine, came into the kitchen and looked at her expectantly. Stella smiled. "What? You want to dance?" she asked. She used to always cook dinner for Jamie while listening to music and dancing around the kitchen. Back then, Cooper would hear the music and stand on his hind legs, big paws on her chest, and let her guide him around the kitchen. That was when she was happy. They hadn't danced in awhile. Stella patted her chest and Cooper obliged. They danced around the room for a few minutes before Patrick came into the kitchen, unnoticed because the volume of the music.

Cooper ran over to Patrick wagged the entire back half of his body in hello. "Hey man, you got pretty good moves for a fat guy," Patrick said directly to Cooper. He looked up at Stella. "What you cooking?"

"Whatever I want and you'll like it," she replied.

"I'm sure I will." Patrick moved past her and into his room.

She began making the stuffing for the eggplant that was roasting. Singing to herself, she stiffened when she felt arms around her waist pulling her into a hug. "What?" she asked.

"It's just that seeing you a little bit happy or lackadaisical makes me feel all warm and cozy inside." Patrick laughed. Letting go of her, he grabbed her wine, taking a huge gulp.

"You're weird," she said, nudging his arm and forcing him to back up. Cooper stood in between them and looked hopefully at Stella for a scrap. "You don't eat eggplant, Coop."

Once Billy got home, she set the table and they sat down to eggplant rollatini, salad, and garlic bread.

"Damn. This is so good." Billy wiped his mouth with a paper towel. "I was going to eat Frito pie for dinner."

"What the fuck is Frito pie?" Stella asked.

"You've never heard of Frito pie?" Billy acted utterly appalled and offended by her lack of knowledge.

"Um, no." She looked from Billy to Patrick, who was smirking.

"Frito pie is one of the most delicious meals I can make myself." Billy looked to the left and the right, then whispered, "I've got a secret recipe."

"I don't want your recipe. I just want to know what it is."

"It's basically chili dumped on corn chips," Patrick answered. "It's disgusting."

"How dare you?" Billy feigned outrage. "My secret recipe includes cheese, jalapenos and salsa."

"Sorry to offend, but that sounds gross," Stella said. She took a bite of her eggplant and set her fork down. "Listen, I know we haven't seen each other that much this year because I've been so busy with school, but I just wanted to say thanks for helping out with Cooper when I haven't been around."

"Not a problem," Patrick said.

"Who's Cooper?" Billy asked and then laughed.

At the sound of his name, Cooper looked up from his position under the table, his tail swishing from side to side.

Stella looked around at her family, the two people that helped her get through the last couple of years, and at Cooper, now the love of her life. All of a sudden it hit her like a bullet.

Of course "happy" was relative. She was in law school and it was kicking her ass, but she was enjoying it. For the past 21 months she was sure she would never enjoy anything again. People like to throw around the old adage that *time heals all wounds*. That adage sucked because it felt condescending when someone else used it towards you. And it isn't exactly helpful. She felt ready to admit that time makes things *tolerable*. Time gives you perspective on events that shake your world to the core. Time allows you to move forward. But time doesn't change the pain that sits in your gut. It doesn't impact the trickle of sweat and fear that traces your spine when the phone rings in the middle of the night. Time doesn't alter how that pain changed your entire personality. In fact, time, which had made things tolerable, had actually allowed her to appreciate how precarious life was and gave her a little perspective. Maybe she needed to simply be enjoying life a little more. *Maybe.*

CHAPTER EIGHTEEN

Anniversaries and Outlines

Jamie had been dead for two years; she couldn't believe it. The image of him smiling before he kissed her their last night together hadn't faded, but she wasn't having nightmares anymore. Now she could go an hour without his memory invading her thoughts. Running helped keep her sane. It was when she did her best thinking. That or she ran so fast and with the music so loud she couldn't think at all.

For two years, she couldn't stand the quiet. Stella always had her television or music on, even when she studied. It drove Millie crazy. She also found that she was no longer a fan of being by herself. The quiet made her head pound and she would get queasy with the quietness reverberating in her head. The quiet was so loud it made her hands shake; it made her think she was losing her mind. The only time she appreciated time alone was working out and studying.

Her second year in law school would start today, and looked to be even more daunting than the first. Evidence was one of the hardest courses in law school and it was required in order to graduate. Her professor was notorious for his Socratic method. He routinely made students stand up in class to interrogate them about cases or the Federal Rules of Evidence, which he had literally written. Millie was in her class, so at least she would have a study partner. She was also taking Administrative Law, Tax Law, and a seminar discussing the International Criminal Court. She was hoping to get an internship with the Department of Justice the following summer.

Recently, Stella had quit her job at Cosi. She just didn't think she could manage it all this year. Reading a hundred pages a night, minimum, had been difficult last year while she was working, but working had been a necessity. She'd taken out more student loans this year so she wouldn't need the extra money.

She smiled as her phone rang the motorcycle ring tone. "Hi, Dad."

"You ready?" her father asked, knowing her answer.

"Of course," she answered without hesitation. This had been the opening line for them every first day of a law school year. They talked for a while about politics and her mother's latest obsession, scrapbooking. She hung up when she pulled into the parking garage, promising to call again later.

Stella walked into the student lounge and saw Millie sitting on a couch with Davis. She smiled at them as she approached.

"Stella, it's good to see you." Davis said from the couch. Millie raised her eyebrows at Stella.

"You too, Davis. How was your summer?" she asked politely.

"Great, I went back to Arizona and worked for my Dad's law firm. It was awesome."

Stella wondered how working at a law firm your first year of law school would be awesome, but held her tongue.

"Millie tells me we're in a couple of classes together. We already have a study group," he said, looking at Millie again.

"You bet," Millie answered enthusiastically.

"Well, we should get going. I don't want to be late the first day." Stella turned.

"Oh, and I already have an outline for Evidence that I heard is killer. I don't mind sharing with my study partners, the two most beautiful girls in class."

Stella turned on her heel, her face registering shock and a little bit of awe. "You have an outline?"

"Yep," he smiled. "I'll email it to you both. Let's go."

Outlines were how all law students studied for finals and getting an Evidence outline was like winning the law school lottery. Maybe her luck was looking up. She put her arm through Millie's and walked with her two study partners to class.

CHAPTER NINETEEN

Home Again

She'd finally agreed to come home. Standing in baggage claim, she waited for her mother to pick her up from Atlanta Hartsfield International Airport. Her parents were having everyone over for Thanksgiving this year and begged Stella to come. It had been over two years since she'd been home. Her mother argued that so much had happened, Jamie wouldn't even be a topic of conversation. Stella convinced herself that even if Jamie's name came up, she could handle it now. Patrick was watching Cooper while she was gone.

Making her way outside, she scanned the pick-up/drop-off lanes for her mother's maroon Mercedes. Her mother pulled up to the curb, jumped out and she ran around the front of the car to embrace Stella. Miranda Murphy held onto her, clutching her tightly, for what seemed like an eternity to Stella. Stella interrupted, "Mom?"

Her mother looked perfect, as usual. Her stylish bob was shiny and had recently been dyed back to its natural color, black. She was on trend with her skinny jeans, riding boots, and black turtleneck sweater. The only exception being the tears streaming down her face. "I'm so ecstatic to see you." She gushed. "I've wanted to hug you for two years. Thank you, Stella. Thank you for coming home."

Stella knew that her self-imposed exile from the state of Georgia had been hard on her parents, but she really didn't know how hard until she saw her mother's face. "I'm glad I was able to swing it this year," she said, trying to keep it casual.

"Let's put your bags in the back. I can't wait to hear all about what has been going on. I know this year you've been so busy, but you really should call me more often." They loaded her bags in the back and got in the car. The ride to downtown Norcross was about forty-five minutes due to her mother's lead foot and the surprising lack of the typical Atlanta traffic. Her mother talked the entire way.

Stella's dad was at the house when they arrived; he lifted her up off her feet a bit when he hugged her. "Baby girl," he greeted.

"Good to see you too, Dad," Stella said, grabbing her bag and making her way further into the house. "The house looks great."

"Thanks, we've been working on all the flowers. Your dad's been planting almost every weekend. It's his new hobby." Miranda put her arm on her husband's shoulder, patting him teasingly.

"Gardening?" Stella looked at her dad with an eyebrow raised.

"Whatever." He waved her off, changing the subject. "You want something to drink?"

"Of course," Stella answered as she walked up the stairs to her designated guest room. Her parents had moved into this house after Stella left for college, so she didn't really have a room there that felt like hers.

She walked into the soft sage-green room where she usually stayed. There were photos on the bookcases she'd forgotten were there. She picked up a wooden frame with a picture of her and Jamie, smiling and in love, showing off Stella's engagement ring. She frowned and put it down. Fear spread through her stomach and she felt extremely hot all of a sudden. *Could she do this?* She walked around the bed to the pictures of things that had happened in the last two years: cousin's weddings and baby showers. She'd ignored all of those family events and gatherings. Now she felt a little guilty.

Stella and her mother got up early on Thanksgiving Day, turned on music, made mimosas, and started cooking. They made the turkey, dressing, mac & cheese, and about ten other casserole-type dishes. Her extended family started arriving around 11:00 and lunch was set for 1:00. Everyone seemed sincerely happy and excited to see her. No one mentioned Jamie's name, just that they had all missed her since she'd left for law school.

The only tense moment occurred when one of her favorite cousins' girlfriend pointed at her ring and said, "I didn't know you were engaged." The entire room fell silent, waiting to see if Stella would break. She responded that she wasn't engaged, then asked her cousin when he was going to propose, sending the conversation in a totally different direction. There was news of new babies, new husbands, and new girl-friends to fill the space that Stella dreaded. She smiled the entire day, barring those few seconds, happy she'd decided to spend Thanksgiving with her family.

Later that night, she and her parents sat on the back porch for wine and dessert. The weather was pleasant in Atlanta and they were enjoying the fresh air.

"See. Stella, that went perfectly. No one even asked you about Jamie. I hope you enjoyed yourself." Miranda took a bite of chocolate pecan pie with ice cream and groaned. "I'm sure I gained ten pounds today."

Stella inwardly cringed at her mother's denial of the "the whole en-gagement question," but wasn't surprised she'd ignored it. "I did enjoy myself today. I guess it's okay take a step out of my protective bubble every once in a while."

"Stella, Patrick told me that you've been so busy this semester that he hardly sees you." Her dad took a sip of his wine and looked at her. "School okay?"

"Just busy as shit, it seems like August was yesterday. I have no idea where the semester went. I only have one more week of classes, then we start studying for finals." She put down her wine glass and closed her eyes.

"So, you think you can make it back for Christmas?" her mother asked hopefully.

"I'm not sure. Let me think about it. I was planning on spending Christmas Eve with a friend."

She'd never seen her mother's head whip around so quickly. "A male friend?"

Oh shit. "Yes," Stella answered honestly.

"Like a boyfriend?" Stella's dad asked quietly, looking over at Stella twisting her engagement ring around her finger.

"No, not anything like that," Stella said with a smile. "He works at the bar that we go to all the time. They have this huge blowout with a buffet every Christmas Eve since they all have to work. You'd be amazed by the number of people that come."

"But you have family to spend the holidays with, Stella, please. Will you just think about it?" Stella's mother took another bite of her pie.

"Of course." Stella would think about it, but a couple weeks ago George asked if she would be eating with him again this year. She'd agreed.

Stella's mother dropped her off at the airport the Saturday after Thanksgiving. Stella needed to get back to get her reading done for the week. They hugged; her mother cried.

"I've missed you so much. I know you're handling things like you need to, but please come home more often. I need to see you more."

"Yes, ma'am." Stella smiled. She turned to go, but then turned back around and leaned in to kiss her mother's cheek. "You know I love you. I'm doing what I can. I promise."

Millie flew back on Saturday, too, so they met at Finnegan's for a few drinks before they had to spend all of Sunday reading.

"How was your Thanksgiving?" Millie asked with trepidation.

"It went fine." Stella motioned for George to come over to their end of the bar. "Hey, George. How was your Thanksgiving?"

George smiled his megawatt smile and said, "Much better now that I see your pretty faces."

"Flattery will get you nowhere, George." Stella grinned back at him.

"I probably ate my weight in turkey on Thursday," he said, rubbing his belly.

"Oh, I'm so sure you ate that much. I can see your abs through your shirt," Millie guffawed. "I, on the other hand, ate an entire pumpkin pie myself."

"I'm really happy to see you girls, you've ignored Finnegan's for months. I was starting to get my feelings hurt."

"It's not you, George, it's us. Law school is kicking our collective ass," Stella replied and took a long gulp of beer.

"Okay, my ego is very precious and needs to be stroked on a continual basis." He smiled at them and then moved down the bar to help other customers.

"I bet you would stroke something on him continually," Millie laughed.

"Shut up," Stella said petulantly, but nodded her head anyway.

CHAPTER TWENTY

Southern Women

Stella was hunched over her excessively highlighted Evidence book while Professor Lightman started his lecture on hearsay within hearsay. It was all so confusing, she had taken to drawing diagrams.

"Stella Murphy." *Fuck.* Her head popped up and she saw her professor looking around for her. "A good Irish name."

Stella bounced out of her seat, "Yes, sir."

"Okay so, hearsay within hearsay, pretty easy, right?" he asked, grinning at her.

"If you say so," Stella muttered.

"Tell us a little about this case, Ms. Murphy."

Stella recited the fact pattern and then went into detail about the hearsay problem. The prosecutor wanted to submit a business record with handwritten notes from another employee containing statements the defendant made admitting to the criminal act. She was grilled by Professor Lightman, but had an answer for every question. After what felt like thirty minutes in the spotlight she finally sat down.

Professor Lightman walked over to the lectern and pointed at Stella. "You see, class, you must watch out for Southern women. They may sound sweet and innocent, but they'll kick your ass in court. Good job, Ms. Murphy."

A smile slowly spread across her face as she stared down into her book.

The next week, Stella, Millie, and Davis sat in their reserved room in the back of the library to schedule study sessions and share the outlines they completed. It was necessary for all the members in a study group to have confidence in each other. If they didn't, there was no point in having each other draft outlines for studying. Davis had taken the Evidence outline he received before the semester started and updated it to reflect the new cases they covered and information he believed was important. Stella was actually impressed; Davis was pretty smart.

"This outline is awesome, Davis, thanks." Stella paged through it and caught sight of a picture of her attempting to kiss the professor's ass, literally. "Very cute." She laughed.

"Okay, so here's the schedule. I've color-coded the next two weeks of us getting together to study and what classes we will cover which day. Blue is Administrative, red is Evidence, and yellow is Tax." Millie said, throwing the calendar on the table in front of each of them. "Oh yeah, the black bar on the day of our last exam is Finnegan's."

"Millie, you're a freak." Stella scratched her head and looked at all the time allotted for studying over the next two weeks. "Did you schedule in time for me to vomit and work out?"

"I left that for you to fit in yourself." Looking at Davis, Millie explained, "El has a really weak stomach, you might as well know now. It comes up from time to time during finals."

"Oh, you made a funny," Stella looked over at Davis, who was trying to stifle a laugh. "You won't be laughing if I throw up on you. It's the real deal." Davis held his hands up in surrender. "You should also know that Millie goes insane."

"It's to be expected, ladies. I won't bore you with how awesome I am around finals; you'll just have to see the magic happen."

CHAPTER TWENTY-ONE

A Good One

S tella stepped inside Finnegan's and took in the scores of people gathered and talking jovially. George stepped through the crowd, making his way over to hug Stella. His dimples were on display. "Merry Christmas, El."

"Merry Christmas," she replied. Looking down at her tight black sweater dress and knee high boots, she was glad she had put a little effort into her appearance.

"I'm glad you came. You hungry?" George was wearing a red v-neck sweater, a green and white checkered button-down underneath, and khaki corduroys and looked delicious.

"Of course." Stella followed him to the buffet. "This looks fantastic."

They made their way down the vast line of food to the dessert table. "Look," George pointed. "I made a chocolate pecan pie, just for you. To remind you of home."

Stella was dumbstruck. "Why would you do that for me?" She stared into George's eyes, the green sparkling above the gray.

George smiled wildly, drawing her eyes to his dimples and then to his lips. "Why not?"

They sat at the same table as last year and had a comfortable conversation, steering clear of anything heavy. George hadn't been hitting the bottle as much this Christmas Eve as last, she could tell.

"Let me get drinks. I'll be right back." George got up and walked behind the bar.

An older woman, maybe in her early fifties, made her way over to Stella's table. Stella had just taken a big bite of pie when the woman sat down and scrutinized her. After a few awkward moments, Stella swallowed and asked, "Can I help you with something?"

"You seeing him?"

"Excuse me?"

"You two dating?" The woman gestured to George behind the bar.

"Uh, no, ma'am," Stella replied, glancing at George and hoping he would hurry back.

"He's a good boy," the woman said. "You better be good to him."

George emerged from behind the bar wearing an amused expression. "Ms. Hershel, I see you met my friend Stella. Let me help you back to your seat." He put down the beers and guided Ms. Hershel back to her table.

When he sat back down, Stella was already halfway done with her dinner. She had eaten her piece of chocolate pecan pie first. They ate without chatting for a while. When she was done with her beer, she stood up to get another. "I'll be right back."

Waiting at the bar, she glanced back at George. He was staring at her. She met his eyes and smiled. She kept her eyes locked on his until she sat down across from him. It was several seconds before Stella tore her eyes from those green speckles. They turned up their drinks. George reached over and ran his thumb over her knuckles. Her breath caught. Buzzing started at her knuckles and traveled through her body. She looked at her hand.

Reluctantly, Stella looked into his eyes again. "I guess I better go, George. Thank you so much for inviting me. I enjoyed it."

He responded, staring back. "Let me walk you home, El." He walked her all the way to her house, told her Merry Christmas, and again turned on his heel to leave.

She called out to his back, "You know, Ms. Hershel was right!"

George looked over his shoulder, inquisitive. "About what?"

"You're one of the good ones."

CHAPTER TWENTY-TWO

El

Thanks to the study sessions, Stella aced all her finals the first semester of her second year. It's true what they say about law school. The first year they scare you to death. The second year they work you to death. It's said that the third year, they bore you to death, but she hadn't experienced that yet. She was just a few weeks into the second semester and already behind in her reading.

Stella and Millie met to complain over beer, fish and chips at Finnegan's, which had turned into a drunken bitch fest. They'd sat at a two-top table instead of the bar and complained all night. Millie got a cab back to her place and Stella walked home. After she began her walk home, she turned around and went back into Finnegan's. She sat back down at the bar.

George sauntered over to her and leaned on his forearms, his face inches from hers. "You came back."

Stella's breath caught in her throat for a second, then she nodded and managed to stutter. "Yes."

"You need something?" George's eyebrow raised; he never broke their eye contact.

"Just one more beer, I think."

He blinked at her and then stood up. "That I can do." He walked over and poured her another Bass while smiling at another customer. It was a blonde. A pretty blonde. Stella felt something bloom inside her, it was jealousy. She was jealous of the blonde flirting with George. *Fuck her.* She quickly looked away and wondered where that had come from.

"El?" George sat her beer down in front of her and again leaned on his forearms, positioning his face close to hers.

She closed her eyes inhaled deeply, his scent of mint and beer filling her nose. "El?" He asked.

"Oh, yes?" Her eyes popped open and she was instantly mortified that she'd just done that; smelled him so obviously.

"I asked if I can do anything else for you?" He touched her hand gently. "You okay?"

She pulled her hand back, embarrassed that she felt his touch throughout her body. "When do you get off work?"

His head tilted in a question. "I close," he answered. "Why?"

"Oh, I was just wondering." She was horrible at doing whatever it was she was trying to do. Was it flirting? Stella turned up her beer and finished it in two gulps. She laid cash on the table and smiled. "I should get going." Stella took off down the bar and George followed her.

"You're not going to say goodnight?" he teased.

"Night!" she waved without looking at him as she raced out of the door.

"Be careful!" He called, his eyes never leaving her back.

Sometime later that night, she walked upstairs and grabbed a bottle of water and guzzled it while standing at the sink. Stella stared at her reflection in the window and didn't recognize herself. She ran her hand through her hair and sighed. Stella looked in the pantry to see if there was anything she wanted to eat. She wasn't hungry, but her body was buzzing with an unfamiliar feeling. Stella went back downstairs and peeled off her clothes, snuggled into her bed, and fell asleep. She dreamed of George and not Jamie for the first time.

Stella hadn't noticed exactly when, but sometime within the last year George had begun calling her El. She liked it.

Chapter Twenty-Three

Personal Space

During the winter semester, Stella had been on several interviews for her internship this summer. Finally, right before spring break, she heard back from the General Counsel's Office for the U.S. Marshals Service. They offered her an internship for an entire year, not just for the summer. She was excited that she would get credit for doing actual work instead of sitting in class. The amount of work that her second year of law school had required had taken up so much time, she really felt like the year was over in the blink of an eye.

Along with her internship this summer, she was taking one seminar class that covered Administrative Law in more depth. She was working for a government agency and wanted to know as much as possible about how the agencies worked together and the applicable laws.

She continued to run; Cooper mandated it. Because Stella was so busy and hardly home, Cooper had taken to sitting in her lap and sleeping on her pillow with her at night. Stella missed Cooper, too, but she knew he wouldn't be neglected with Billy and Patrick in the house.

Patrick and Billy had both gotten girlfriends, and both girls gave Stella the evil eye when introduced. Stella had a visceral dislike for Patrick's girlfriend, Lisa, immediately. Lisa was very possessive and she was just plain obnoxious. The last time Stella had gone in Patrick's bedroom she noticed that Lisa had replaced a picture of Stella and Patrick from last summer with one of him and Lisa. She was often snarky for no reason. Stella didn't understand why Patrick even liked her, let alone why he was dating her.

Millie was devastated about Patrick. When Stella told her about Lisa, she immediately went to Finnegan's and hooked up with some random dude in a bowtie. Stella was still making fun of her for that.

During their spring break, Millie and Stella decided they needed to dance it out. They went to one of their favorite dance clubs and danced with each other and with many guys over the course of the night. Stella was wearing a light blue, racerback, tank top that hung low on each side, exposing her back and her purple bra. She was slick with sweat from hours of dancing. Millie was wearing a strapless dress and heels, which looked very uncomfortable. Stella threw her hands up and pulsed to the music and a new faceless man pumped to the beat behind her. She needed another drink and leaned into Millie yelling, "Drink?"

Millie nodded and continued to dance. Stella made her way past the throng of people on the dance floor to the bar and ordered drinks. When she turned around, she ran directly into a guy. "Shit," she yelled as she spilled her drinks on herself. "Fuck." She turned around and put her drinks down on the bar and grabbed a bunch of cocktail napkins.

"Sorry," the guy breathed in her ear.

She was stilled by his proximity. "Excuse me, can you back away from my personal space?" Stella said as she continued to attempt to mop up her spilled cranberry and vodka off her light blue tank top. "Fuck," she sighed, resigned she might as well throw the shirt in the trash.

"Looks like you could use a little help." The guy took a napkin and started wiping off drink from Stella's shirt, touching her breasts.

"Fucker..." Stella hissed. "Stop touching me now." Stella took a step back, her voice getting louder.

Millie was just making her way over the bar and took in the scene. She acted drunk and took her drink from Stella, fake tripping into the guy and spilling the rest of the drink on his shirt. "Oh MY SHIT, I'm so sorry!" She looked at Stella and tried not to laugh. "I'm so drunk." She fell into Stella and then whispered, "This is a good time to go."

The guy was so busy cussing and wiping off his shirt, he didn't even notice them leave.

"Millie, that was perfect. Perfect timing and perfect aim." They locked arms together and walked out into the early spring night.

Millie pulled her phone out of her purse; she had a message. "Patrick wants us to meet him at Finnegan's."

"Why?" Stella whined.

"Your guess is a good as mine."

"My shirt has cranberry all over it."

"You wear T-shirts with holes in them to Finnegan's," Millie reminded her as she flagged down a cab.

"Fine." Stella got into the cab first and slid across the seat.

Once they got to Finnegan's, it was obvious why they had been summoned. Patrick and a bunch of other patrons were playing beer pong in the back part of the bar. She smiled and was genuinely amused by the sight. Then she looked over to the bar and waved at George. He motioned her over.

"I'll be right there," she told Millie, who headed to the beer pong tables, her heels clicking on the hardwood floor of the bar.

"Beer pong? I like it," she said as she shimmied her way up to the bar near George.

"Glad you approve." He smiled at her. "You look like you got a little something on your shirt there, miss. Would you like a free Finnegan's shirt to wear?"

"Really?" Stella asked enthusiastically looking down at her shirt. "That'd be great. This jerk bumped into me at this club Millie and I went to and..." Stella pointed to her shirt " it's obvious what happened next."

"Sure, come with me. There are shirts in the office." Stella followed him to the end of the bar and then around to the office, which was across from the bathrooms. He opened the door and then started rummaging around the boxes. "Here's one." He was about to throw it to her when he noticed her tattoo on her left shoulder blade. "Holy fuck, that's a tattoo."

She turned around and watched his expression. "Yep, it is."

"Tell me about it." George's eyes were full of curiosity.

Stella took a deep breath and then took a step closer to him. She pulled off her shirt and stood there. George took in her body in very slowly.

"You're beautiful," he whispered.

"Shirt." She held out her hand.

"Oh...yeah," George stammered as if he had forgotten why they were in there. He held it up to her.

"Thanks," she pulled the white shirt on with the Finnegan's logo on over her purple bra.

"Go to dinner with me," George blurted suddenly.

"I don't date," Stella replied matter-of-factly, and then turned to walk out the door.

"You don't date?" he called to her back.

Stella turned back to face him. "Nope. In my effort to make the world a better place, I have precluded myself from dating." Stella walked over to where George was standing. "Let me be clear, George, I like you, but I don't date. If you want to date someone, you can get that somewhere else." Stella leaned into him and whispered in his ear, "If you'd be interested in something else. That, I do." That statement wasn't entirely true since she hadn't had sex with anyone since Jamie, but she was about as sexually frustrated as one human could get.

The alarm on his face was priceless; then his lips turned up at the edges.

CHAPTER TWENTY-FOUR

Well Played

Finnegan's kept the beer pong tables up for several weeks and made teams sign up for a tournament. She, Millie, Patrick, and Billy had entered the tournament. Billy and Stella were a team and beating everyone, but so were Millie and Patrick. They were prepared for a battle to the death, or at least until one of them passed out.

Stella and Millie had started their scheduled study groups getting ready for finals. One of her classes without Millie was National Security Law and her study group had just finished meeting. Millie was waiting for her in the student lounge, reading a novel.

"How do you have the energy to read anything other than to study right now?" Stella asked as she slumped down next to Millie on the couch.

"I'm a well-rounded person, El, you know that. Plus, this book is so good. It's by one of my favorite authors." Millie shut the book and looked at Stella with a serious expression. "I believe it's my duty as your best friend to get you laid."

"Excuse me." Stella started laughing. "Believe me, if I wanted to get laid, I could. Shit, Billy would probably have sex with me."

"Confident much?" Millie said, standing up.

"Not confident…honest. If a girl wants to get laid, she can. Period. That's the truth." Stella followed Millie through the cafeteria and to the elevators. They waited with a bunch of other law students to get on the elevator.

"Then why haven't you?" Millie stage-whispered.

"Not talking about that here." Stella stared at the numbers as they stopped at the main floor and most of the occupants got out. She and Millie stayed in to go to the garage where her car was parked. They had carpooled.

"I mean. I think it'd make you a better person. You know, put you in a better mood."

"I'm sure it would." Stella was so sexually frustrated, she'd been having some wild dreams about George.

"Maybe we'll meet someone this summer for you to use for his body."

"Maybe…" Stella was pretty sure she wasn't ready for any sort of complications, so using a guy for his body sounded perfect.

"You know who's super hot?" Millie walked out of the elevator toward Stella's car.

"I'm sure I have no idea."

"George."

Stella kept looking ahead, hoping she wasn't giving anything away. "We're friends."

"That's a good thing."

Getting in the car, Stella finally looked at Millie. "You know that's not true, why are you lying?"

Millie laughed. "Because George is fucking hot and he's single."

"How do you know he's single?" Stella steered her car out of the garage onto Massachusetts Avenue and toward Millie's house. "Anyway, that doesn't mean anything, Millie."

"But it does; he looks at you like he wants to eat you." She giggled.

"He does not…" Stella protested, but she had caught him looking at her lately like she was a steak.

"Yes, he does," Millie insisted. "Now, this is a good thing, because you can get laid."

"I can go to any bar tonight and get laid," Stella said defiantly.

"Prove it."

"Fine, good thing we're going to a bar tonight." Stella turned onto Millie's street. "I do want to remind you that you aren't going to bully me into getting laid. The goal is to see whether someone would be willing to fuck me."

"You're so gruff, fine. Someone willing."

Stella walked upstairs in a tight halter dress that stopped at mid-thigh. It was red and she was wearing nude strappy sandals with a high heel. Billy looked amused when she walked into the den.

"How are you going to play beer pong in that?"

"Very well," she responded and sat down, crossing her legs demurely.

"Can't you change? You'll distract me with all…" he waved his hand over her chest and then down to her ass, "that."

"Well go ahead and look, because the goal will be to distract all of our opponents, which, may I remind you, are mostly men."

Billy laughed. "You're a fucking evil genius. I love it."

Patrick and Millie came out of Patrick's room and stopped abruptly when they saw Stella.

"Last minute strategy session for the game?" she asked.

"What're you wearing?" Patrick asked, not amused.

"Well, *this* is called a dress and these are shoes," she said sarcastically, pointing to each item.

Millie looked at her own tank top, jeans, and flip-flops. "Well played, ma'am. Well played."

When they walked into Finnegan's, it was like time stopped and she saw at least ten guys sitting at or around the bar stop what they were doing and look at her. She smirked at Millie, "This is going to be like taking candy from a baby."

Patrick laughed. "What does that expression even mean? Don't babies like candy?"

Millie leaned into her ear. "It would be if you weren't still wearing your engagement ring."

Stella's eyes went wide. "Guys will have sex with me anyway," she said, but she knew Millie was right. "Fuck." Then she walked up to Patrick, "Hey Patrick, I don't want my ring getting nasty with all the beer. Could you hold onto it for tonight?" she asked, looking pointedly at Millie.

"Well, I didn't see that one coming." Millie pouted and then went to the bar to get the schedule of their game.

Billy patted the stool at the bar next to his. "Let's go over strategy."

"I think I've got it covered." She smiled as she waved at George, his eyes going wide when he saw her.

"Um, did you forget we were playing Patrick and Millie? They've both seen you naked on numerous occasions. I don't think this strategy will work for that game."

"Calm down. We'll win if we keep playing like we have been."

"Hey, Billy, Stella." George had moved to right in front of them at the bar. "Can I get you something?"

"Hey, George," Stella greeted and leaned into the bar giving him a clear shot of her cleavage. "Can you make a Cosmo?"

"Sure." His face turned red and then he looked at Billy.

"Harp," Billy said.

"Be right back," George replied, taking off.

Taking her drink, she made her way back toward the beer pong tables and waited on their game. She was really bad at this flirting thing. She didn't see any guys in the crowd she was even remotely interested in talking to, let alone having sex with, but she also didn't want to lose her bet with Millie.

As she was waiting, she played with the strap on one of her shoes and watched the match. She laughed as the four guys took shots of beer one after another. She felt eyes on her before she saw who they belonged to. When Stella looked up, George was staring at her like he was undressing her with his eyes. She smiled and he smiled bigger. She wanted to lick his dimples. Stella took him in as he walked over to her where she sat. His broad shoulders were stressing the tight T-shirt he was wearing. It was light blue and made his eyes look more grey than usual.

George sat next to her, casually putting his arm behind her. "What's with the dress?"

"Nothing, what's up with your tight shirt?" she said, touching his chest casually.

He looked down and started laughing. "Nothing."

They sat together for a few minutes, watching the match in comfortable silence. Then he leaned into whisper in her ear, his breath warm but causing goosebumps to spread quickly through her body. His lips on her ear did things to her she thought were long gone. "Where's your ring?" he asked.

Stella closed her eyes and said, "Gone."

"Why?" He tucked a strand of hair behind her ear.

"George," she barely breathed into his ear before Billy came and grabbed her, pulling her to the table so they could begin their match. Stella's body was buzzing in a way she hadn't felt in years. She turned up her drink and downed the entire Cosmo, looking back at George and giving him a weak smile.

Millie threw her ball first and it landed in the cup right in front of Billy. He drank first. Patrick hit another, Stella drank. They hit every cup until there was only one left. Billy was cussing, furious. Millie missed the last shot. It was Billy's turn now. Stella and Billy hit every cup, Billy hitting the side of the last cup, causing them both to gasp. After what seemed to be an eternity, the ball fell in the last cup. They won! Billy picked up Stella and ran around the bar with her. She was trying to keep her dress from riding up; they looked ridiculous. Patrick was pissed, he didn't like to lose.

Patrick walked over to them and threw his arms around them both. "Next time," he said.

Mille drank the last shot of beer and hobbled over to where they were sitting. "So, I'm drunk. How's everyone else?"

"I need more to drink," Stella complained. When she looked up, George was standing there with a round of beer for everyone.

"For the victors, you drink for free the rest of the night." He smiled at Stella. "You two, these are on the house but you will have to pay for the rest."

"Thanks George," Millie purred.

"Go ahead and bring another round, George, this is going to be a long night of me drinking to forget." Stella said glancing at her empty ring finger.

Patrick, Millie, and Billy looked at her and she looked at her finger. George heard her, but he had already turned around.

CHAPTER TWENTY-FIVE

The Challenge

"Hey, George, you remember when you asked me out on a date?" Stella yelled over the music in the bar.

"No, not really," George answered, but his face blushed, remembering.

"I was wondering if you were ready for anything else yet." Stella was drunker than usual. She'd been drinking since lunch with Millie and they were both worse for wear.

"Whatcha talkin' about, El?" Millie giggled and closed her eyes.

"Millie, I told George, awhile ago, that I don't date, but I'd be interested in doing other things with him and he's failed to get back to me on that."

"George, that's just rude." Millie leaned back a little on her barstool and shouted, "My friend needs some assistance in the sex department! Who wants to sign up?"

They both burst out in loud, obnoxious laughter. George's face turned bright red and he moved to the opposite side of the bar. That is, until he saw a guy approach them, followed by another. They were actually flirting with these guys! George walked out from behind the bar and grabbed Stella by her elbow.

"Uh oh, Millie..." Stella laughed, "I think I'm in trouble."

George dragged her behind him.

"Maybe he'll spank you!" Millie yelled and burst out laughing.

George pushed her into the office and shut the door. He walked in and circled the desk. "You can't seriously want to go home with one of those pricks."

"Why not?" Stella looked around at the office. "It's not like I'm with anyone, George." She walked over to where he was standing.

"You're not like that, El." George stared into her eyes.

"Oh, George, you don't know what I'm like." She dragged a hand across his chest. "I'd be more than willing to show you."

"El, you think I don't know you. I know you very well. I know you're pushing me, you want me to want you, but you don't want to give in." George pushed her hair off her face and kissed her hungrily.

She gasped, separating her mouth from his. "George...I didn't know you had it in you." She smiled and rubbed her hand over the crotch of his jeans. "You up for the challenge?" she chided.

He attacked her, pushing her back against the wall and pulling her legs around his waist. He kissed her neck, her mouth, and pushed her shirt down to kiss her cleavage. Stella's breath was rapid and her heart was beating fast. "Are you?" George set her down and walked out of the office.

"Holy shit." Stella rolled over in her bed, her head feeling like there were spikes on her brain. Every time she moved her head, even infinitesimally, pain erupted in her head. Her mouth felt like it had been stuffed with some sort of really nasty-smelling cloth. She worked her mouth up and down and tried to steady herself while she pushed herself up off the bed. She closed her eyes and an image flashed in her mind; she and George kissing in the bar's office. *Wow!* She had no idea George would trigger such feelings in her; she wasn't sure she even had those feelings after Jamie or maybe it had just been so long she didn't remember what those feelings were like.

She turned the water on in her bathroom and drank directly from the sink. Stella hadn't been this hungover in a very long time. She put both of her fingers to her mouth, remembering the kiss, or more like a mauling. Her lips were still red from the kisses, and swollen. He'd been so mad she was going to leave with another guy from the bar. She'd never been interested in leaving the bar with anyone other than Patrick or Billy before last night, which was a little sad if she thought about it.

She pulled Jamie's jersey over her naked body and walked to the back door to let Cooper out. The jersey and the ring were the only things of her life with Jamie that she saw on a regular basis. *She'd gotten through it*, she sighed. She hadn't put the ring back on since she took it off at Finnegan's. It was in the box with all her memories of Jamie. George was nothing like Jamie. Chastising herself, she was so not ready for relationship material. George, based on their encounter last night, would clearly be open to having sex.

She opened the fridge and drank orange juice out of the carton. She heard a chuckle from the den.

"You're as bad as we are!" Billy called from in front of his video game. "Had a little too much fun last night, El?"

"You could say that." Stella ran a hand through her hair and grabbed her phone off the table there was a message.

glad u left with Millie. 2 b continued

She smiled and put her fingertips to her lips and traced her bottom lip.

"So where did y'all go?"

Stella sat down next to Billy and sat as ladylike as possible with only a shirt on. "We went to happy hour in Adams Morgan, but ended up at Finnegan's, of course."

"What's with the gooey look this morning?"

Stella stared at the video game. "You mean the hungover look, I think you should recognize that, as long as we've lived together." Stella smiled and looked at Billy. "Where's Patrick?"

"Lisa...I know your hungover look, but you have a gooey lovey look in your eyes I've never seen before."

Stella busted out laughing. "A lovey look?" she asked incredulously. "I don't do lovey." She made finger quotes around "lovey."

"Well, your hungover ass face is doing something," Billy retorted.

Stella snorted. "Ass face?"

"...and you're being funny and almost pleasant." Billy smiled. "I'm confused by your change in attitude today. I've only known one you and you're switching it up."

"Shut up, Billy, I'm always funny." Stella threw a pillow at him.

"Oh, you think you're funny..." Billy paused his game and looked pointedly at her. "I like it, El. I hope you continue to be pleasant, because I like your smile and I haven't seen it nearly enough." He re-started his game and Stella smiled to herself.

The next weekend, Stella limped over to the bathroom in Finnegan's. She and Patrick had run ten miles that morning and she was already sore, which was a bad sign. She, Billy, and Patrick had starting drinking early this Friday and it was starting to relieve some of the pain she felt in her legs. As she pushed the door to the bathroom open, she was pulled by the arm into another door across the small hall.

Shrieking in surprise, she almost fell into whoever had a death grip on her right arm. She was pushed up against the wall in the little office and George was pressed against her entire body. Her body responded immediately and a slow smile crept across her face.

"Well, hello there, George. You need something?" Her face was inches from his. Stella gazed into his eyes and saw only desire before he kissed her.

George had both of his hands wrapped around her jaw with his thumbs close to her mouth. Then he moved his left hand through her hair and parted her lips with his. She moaned into his mouth and leaned her head back. George took that opportunity to kiss her exposed neck.

Out of breath Stella whispered near his ear, "So does this mean you're interested?"

He nipped at her top lip before he answered, "That would be a yes." His hands were now roaming all over her body, igniting it like she hadn't felt in years. "If I weren't working I would take you home immediately," he growled.

"What's wrong with here?" she teased and pulled his earlobe with her teeth.

"Oh, no. This is going to be slow and deliberate."

She smiled at him, putting his arms on the wall framing her face. "I'm a fan of both, but I'll allow it." She blew her bangs out of her eyes. "I like this side of you, George." She ducked under his arm blocking her against the wall. "Very sexy." She opened the door and walked backward out of the little office, trying to appear like the adventure hadn't affected her. It was clear from his pants that George had been. "You may want to stay in here a minute." She laughed, pointing at his crotch, and limped her way to the bathroom.

The rest of the night dragged as Stella's stomach twisted with anticipation. She told Patrick and Billy to leave without her. George assured Patrick he would get her home safely and he winked at her as he said it. She was so nervous she drank a little more than she intended. As she waited for George to finish his duties at the bar, she texted Millie.

So tonite- me and George

U & G what?

He's going home with me

Good you need a lay—don't fuck it up

How encouraging

It's like riding a bike

I used to be good at that once too

Don't worry

Nervous

Don't be. Call me with details tomorrow… never mind I'm coming over

George walked over to where she was slouched at the table. "Sorry you had to wait, love." He put his hand through her hair and looked into her eyes. "You ready?" he asked.

"I'm the one who's been waiting for you," she replied, accepting his hand as he pulled her out of the chair.

"No, love, I've been waiting for you for over a year." He smiled and guided her outside.

After a self-conscious walk to Stella's house, they barely made it into her room before she literally ripped his shirt off. He growled and picked her up. Stella wrapped her legs around him and explored his mouth with hers.

"El?"

She was breathless as he threw her on her bed. "Let me do this how I want, okay?" George was looking at her so intensely it made her pause for a minute.

"You kiss me like that again and you can do whatever you want with me."

A grin spread slowly across his beautiful face. He lifted her shirt and kissed her stomach, pulling her shirt over her head. She struggled with his belt.

"I've dreamed about this." George put his hands on her face and kissed her so gently it took her breath.

"George…" she sighed.

He quieted her with his lips, pushing harder against her. "Shh," he hushed her with his mouth. Then George pulled her pants off and began kissing every inch of her body, starting with her ankle and going all the way up her leg to where she was throbbing for him. She wanted him so badly.

"George."

"Quiet, El. Let me love you."

She was so caught up in the moment and her wants and needs that she didn't correct him.

CHAPTER TWENTY-SIX

Trouble

Stella woke up smelling of sex and alcohol, quite a powerful combination. "Shit," she muttered as she rolled over and hit a solid chest. *George.* "Fuck," she said and laid her head back on the pillow.

"Do you wake up every morning full of such sunshine?" He shifted and draped an arm over her.

"Pretty much," she replied and turned her head, looking into his gorgeous eyes, which were a little more green this morning.

"So, you're regretting inviting me back to your place, huh?" He smiled and kissed the corner of her mouth.

"No, just so we're clear. I don't do this with everyone."

"I know. I've known you for almost three years." He kissed her forehead. "As you told me last night, and I agreed, we'll be exclusively fucking until we are not. We will respect each other enough to inform the other so as not to have to share," he recited.

"I said all that?" She winced. He nodded. "You agreed to that?"

"Anything to get you in the sack, love," he laughed.

"Well, I guess that's that." She sat up and swung her feet off the side of the bed.

George reached out and touched her tattoo. She froze and then pulled out of his reach. Walking around the bed, she smiled. "Shower?"

"If you're inviting me, hell yes." He walked into the bathroom after her.

"Can you give me a minute?" She glanced at the toilet.

"Oh, sure." He stepped back and watched as the door shut between them.

She slumped down on the toilet. *Well, I guess that's that. Right.* This was a very dangerous situation, she knew. She liked George, a little too much for her liking. She flushed and opened the door, then stepped into the waiting shower.

"So," he said, while peeing with her in the same room. "What's the tattoo about?"

She stepped under the showerhead and said, "It's the remains of my heart." She looked at him over her shoulder and smiled. "You regret coming back with me?"

"Not even a little." He shook his head, looking at her left shoulder blade, where there were black pieces of rubble about where Stella's heart would be located, and his heart broke a little.

Several nights later, Stella woke with a start in the middle of the night and felt his heat missing. He was gone. *Isn't that what she had told him she needed?* She chastised herself. She ran a hand over where he had been when she fell asleep, taking in his scent and felt something. Sitting up, she picked up what felt like paper and went in to the bathroom. Flipping the light on, she read what he left her.

El,

I would have enjoyed staying with you, but I'll honor your wishes and leave. I've kissed you bye and I look forward to tomorrow night when I will be able to kiss you again.

G

Walking back to her bed, Stella sighed and fell into bed, enjoying George's lingering scent. She reached over to her phone, put her earbuds into her ears, and stared into the blackness until she fell into a restless sleep.

Patrick walked midway down the stairs and yelled, "El, get your ass up! It's time to go."

Stella rolled over naked in her bed. "No."

"We're running in two minutes." Patrick made his way into the cave of her room and saw her stretched out, naked. "Shit. Sorry."

"It would be okay if you didn't come down here whenever you wanted, but knocked like a normal person," she groaned. She and George had been up until 3:00.

"Well, you could sleep in pajamas like a normal person." Patrick didn't move, still looking at her lean body tangled in the sheets.

"I don't believe in pajamas," she said, "and I'm not running today."

"You need to run." Patrick called as he headed up the stairs. "Gotta get the booze out."

"Coop and I will go later." She rubbed her face and blew her bangs out of her face. "Alright, I'm going back to sleep. Let Coop out," she yelled.

Patrick stopped at the back door and let Cooper out, "So George, huh?"

Without even moving from bed, Stella replied, "You saw that, huh?"

"Yep. It was quite the shock to see a man leaving your room. You could've given us a heads-up."

"Whatever…" Stella called.

"I like George," Patrick said as he shut the back door and went up the rest of the stairs.

She breathed hard as she made her way down King Street, she and Cooper dodging in and out of the crowds. At the next intersection, she took a left and then and immediate right and ran down the less crowded road down to the Potomac. Music pounded in her ears and her thoughts drifted to George. He'd surprised her, being so gentle yet intense. She wasn't sure how to deal with that intensity; she was hoping the sex would just be adequate so she could just do him a couple of times and not really care about not doing it anymore. Unfortunately, that wasn't the case. He was fantastic; brilliant at turning her on and excellent at giving her what she needed for her body to completely unravel.

She turned left and ran toward the dog park. Slowing her pace, she leaned down, letting Cooper off the leash. The Potomac was packed with boats moving up and down the river. Walking lazily over to the bench close to the dog park overlooking the river, she stood behind it. Stella leaned down and said, "Funny meeting you here."

George turned and took her in. She had her hair pulled into a messy bun and was wearing black spandex capri pants and a halter sports tank. Her tattoo was glistening with sweat, but he thought she had never been more beautiful. "Damn," he muttered.

"What, you aren't happy to see me?" Stella glanced over at Cooper to make sure he was behaving, but he was just lying on the ground catching his breath.

"It's not that. I just haven't seen you so hot before." George smiled.

"Well, that's what happens when one runs, you know." She moved around the bench and before she could sit next to him, he pulled her on his lap.

Putting his hand on her tattoo, he looked into her eyes. "I wasn't talking about that sort of hot." George pulled her to him and kissed her senseless.

"Good God." Stella pushed her bangs out of her face. She was breathing heavily and extremely turned on.

"There's more of that if you're interested." He kissed her neck.

"Um," she wavered, "I think we've given enough of a show." She moved over to his right, but he kept her legs on his lap. "So, whatcha been up to today?"

"Had to leave this beautiful woman's arms last night. I cried myself to sleep, then I came here to stare at the water and contemplate life," he smirked.

"That sounds rough; she sounds like a bitch." She looked over to where Cooper was playing tug with a dog half his size. "Coop, careful!" she yelled. Her back was to George, but she felt a familiar palm on her left shoulder blade. She turned to look at him, "What are you thinking?"

"I think I'm in trouble." His smile was a little sad and melted her a bit.

"I think I may be, too."

The weekend after she and George had sex for the first time, Stella was checking herself in the mirror when Millie came down to her room.

"What's up with the primping?" Millie asked.

"What do you mean? I'm just getting ready." She pulled on a sapphire-colored thin sweater over her skinny jeans and gray ankle booties.

"Hot booties, when did you get those? I want to borrow them." Millie inspected her.

"Just picked them up the other day. You like?" Stella gave one more look in the mirror and moved toward the stairs.

"Wait a second. What's going on?" Millie grabbed Stella's wrist gently.

Stella had spent time straightening and then curling her normal unruly hair. It was not quite straight, not quite wavy. "What do you mean? We're going out, I'm dressed. Now, let's go." Stella pulled her arm back and headed up the stairs.

"Um, we've been going to this bar for over two years and you've never looked like that," Millie said with a question in her voice as she followed Stella up the stairs.

"I'm wearing jeans and a sweater. You act like I'm wearing a bikini," Stella said amused.

"Oh my shit, he got you." Millie smiled. Stella hadn't had the opportunity to tell Millie what happened after they texted last weekend. Millie ended up not coming over and they both have been insane with classes. "I like George."

"I know, I know, everyone likes George." She blew her bangs out of her face. "I look normal."

"You don't look normal, you look hot." Millie replied.

"Whoa..." Billy said when Stella entered the kitchen.

"What the fuck?" she asked exasperated.

"You look hot, is all." He admitted.

"Right," Millie agreed.

"I'm wearing normal clothes; what's all the shit about?"

"You don't usually wear clothes like that out, El. It looks good. We're glad to see you putting in some effort into what you look like again." Millie pulled two beers out of the fridge.

Patrick and Lisa came out of his room and he took in the room. "Everyone ready?"

"Yes, let's go." Millie grabbed Stella's hand and they walked out the front door, finishing their beers.

The entire group walked down King Street until they got to the right intersection, then took a left and walked into the bar. Because Lisa was there, they grabbed a table, which was unusual for them. Stella took a secret glance at George. He was giving her a 100-watt smile. She smiled, blushed and looked back at the table.

"Aww shit," Mille said, looking at Stella's face. "The bartender's really got you."

"Um no, I've got him doing exactly what I want him to," she said and she leaned into Millie. "And he *is* fantastic at it." She actually giggled and was so shocked by herself that Millie started laughing hysterically.

Millie took a glance over Stella's shoulder to look at George. "He's staring a hole into your back right now. Go get me a drink."

"I'll get the first round," Stella said. "Regular for everybody?" Everyone at the table nodded, except for Lisa. "What do you want, Lisa?"

"What kind of wine do they have?" Lisa was looking at the table for the menu.

"Oh for fuck's sake, it's an Irish bar. I wouldn't drink the wine they serve here."

"Just get me whatever they have in white wine, Stella," she said, throwing daggers at Stella with her eyes.

Stella walked over to the bar and leaned in, looking at George and Hazel. Hazel started down her way, but George walked past her, telling her he'd get it. He smirked at her. "Hi. What can I do for you, El?" His tone was teasing.

"Many, many things, George." Now his smile was so big she saw the dimple on his right cheek. "But, for now, I just need drinks. The regular for everyone, except the hanger-on wants white wine. Give her the cheapest, nastiest you've got."

George laughed and started collecting the drinks. She took the drinks over to the table two by two. At the last round, he caught her hand. "I missed you last night."

She turned. "We'll catch up tonight."

"Count on it," he said over the music.

Chapter Twenty-Seven

Picnic

She leaned over the bar put her cheek on his, whispering, "Hey." Her breath warm, her lips grazing his ear.

"Meet me in the office in five minutes," he answered gruffly.

Stella adjusted her halter top and pulled her jeans up. Her blush started on her chest and spread slowly across her face. "Okay."

After a few minutes, she made her way toward the bathroom. George appeared a minute later and pushed her into the office, covering her mouth with his. His hands were all over her; she felt a slow burn across her body. Stella was a little sore since she hadn't had sex in so long, but it was a feeling reminding her of their nights together and she welcomed it. She breathed in his scent; spice and sweat. The combination was enough to send her over the edge.

"Oh, you're good with doing this here tonight?" she asked as he unbuttoned her pants and pulled them down to her knees.

He pulled down her panties and made his way down her body. "We aren't doing anything."

Later, Stella stretched her arms over her head and leaned from side to side, her shirt inching up her stomach and exposing a little skin.

George leaned over the bar. "You better stop teasing me," he whispered.

She pulled her shirt down and glanced around. "I wasn't trying to tease you," she said innocently.

"Hey, tomorrow's my day off. Let's go to the Cherry Blossom Festival." George's eyes lit up when he spoke.

"Um," Stella didn't know, that sounded an awful lot like a date.

"Oh come on, El." George rolled his eyes. "How about this? I'll be sitting at a bench behind the Roosevelt Memorial, overlooking the Tidal Basin, in front of the Jefferson Memorial at noon tomorrow. I hope you can make it." He pushed himself off the bar and walked to the other side, not giving her a chance to respond.

About that time, Patrick and Billy entered the bar and took up the two seats on either side of her. "What up, fools?" she asked.

"Yo," Billy answered, giving her a one-arm hug. Neither Patrick nor Billy had seen much of Stella this year due to her hectic schedule with school and work. They had to arrange this night of drinking.

"You look good," Patrick said, kissing her cheek.

Stella glanced at George, hoping she didn't give off the just-fucked glow.

"It'll be nice to blow off a little steam tonight. I'm feeling a little crazy with school. I'm having to go to school, work, and read like 200 pages a night. It's impossible." Stella took a drink. "How's Lisa?"

"Oh, let's not waste time on the unpleasant," Billy interjected.

"Shut up, dude," Patrick said, leaning in to look Billy in the eye.

"I'm just saying; she's the same." He smiled and winked at Stella.

"How'd you get permission to come out tonight?"

"She's coming over later," Patrick answered, looking down.

"Of course," Stella said.

They drank at the bar for several hours before they left to meet Lisa at their house. Billy was working on a big anti-trust investigation and would be in Houston for the rest of the month. He was leaving tomorrow. Patrick's job was clicking along, nothing that exciting to talk about. If she had to describe it to other people, her life was hectic but boring. Billy and Patrick's eyes glazed over when she started talking about all the papers she was working on and the legal issues that she was addressing at work. When they got up to leave, she waved at George.

Sunday, a few minutes after noon, she finally found a parking spot around the memorials. She cursed being late and had to jog over to the Roosevelt Memorial to make sure she got there before George thought she stood him up.

This time of year in DC was gorgeous. The Japanese cherry trees on the Mall were all blooming and it was a canopy of light pink petals. The festival ran for a week and had food, drinks, art, and music.

When she saw George sitting on a bench looking out at the Tidal Basin surrounding the Jefferson Memorial, she smiled to herself. He was wearing loose-fitting jeans, flip-flops and a Nationals T-shirt, but he looked perfect. He looked up at her when he heard her approach.

"I wondered if you were going to show." George patted the bench next to him.

Sitting, she took in the paddle boats coasting along in the Tidal Basin and the crowds of families and other people enjoying the view of the historic trees.

"I brought us a little lunch," he said, smiling and lifting a picnic basket.

"You have a picnic basket?" She laughed.

"Sure, don't you?" George asked sarcastically.

"Nope."

"I thought everyone had them, at least that's what my sisters tell me." George blushed a little.

"I don't know anyone with a picnic basket." She laughed.

"Now you do. If you ever need one, you can borrow mine." He gave her his full-on dimpled smile.

"Do you have a blanket, too?"

"Of course, what self-respecting adult would have a basket and no blanket?" he asked indignantly.

"But of course," she replied. "Come, George, feed me grapes on your picnic blanket."

George's face looked crestfallen. "I was hoping you would feed me grapes."

"Whatever you want," she replied.

George grabbed the basket and her hand and led her over to where the cherry trees were thick in the small area between the Jefferson and Korean Memorial. The ground was covered in what looked like pink snow. George spread the blanket and they sat side by side, their thighs touching. He started pulling out food in little containers and placing them on the blanket.

"What if I didn't show? This is a lot of food." Stella pointed at the plethora of containers scattering the blanket.

He genuinely laughed. "I'm sure I could've talked some pretty little thing into sharing with me." He shrugged his shoulders and his voice dropped lower. "I didn't know what you liked."

"I like most food," she answered, popping opening a container. Holding the orange spread up to her nose she giggled, "What do you know about pimento cheese?"

"I appreciate Southern delicacies." He unscrewed the pinot noir he brought and pulled out solo cups. Filling up the cups, he looked around mischievously. "You know alcohol isn't allowed on the Mall."

"I've broken that law before." She winced, sort of remembering her alcohol-filled first Fourth of July on the Mall. It was embarrassing to remember; Patrick had to escort her out of the family-friendly event due to her excessive cussing.

"I'm not surprised." He took a sip and lay back on his elbows, his long legs crossed in front of him. "So, El, how's school?"

"Ugh, anything but that," she said, waving off his question. "My life sucks right now..." his eyes went wide, "...with the exception of this." She pointed at them both several times.

"Glad I'm the only bright light in your life right now." He opened the rest of the containers.

"Tell me about what's going on in the real world. I haven't seen the news in weeks."

He laughed and pulled out the *Washington Post* from his basket. "Looks like you're in luck."

She lay on her back, watching the blossoms floating on the wind as George read her the newspaper while stroking her hair. Every once in a while she would glance at him and smile, perfectly content.

CHAPTER TWENTY-EIGHT

A Good Lay

Stella woke in the morning with a familiar warmth on her left shoulder; she sighed and turned over, placing George's hand on her right boob instead.

George opened one eye and peered at her. "Hi," he said sheepishly.

"You broke our rule." Stella was still holding his hand on her boob, looking into his grey green eyes.

"Your rule," George answered.

"George, we agreed." Her brain was going a mile a minute.

"No, El we didn't." George pulled her closer and caressed her breast and kissed her.

"George, I don't think we ought to go there."

"So, I can spend the night from now on?" George pushed.

"No." Stella still grasped his hand, not letting go.

"El...*we* are going there. I want to wake up with you and be able to see the sleep in your eyes, desire evident in your body. Just like now." He reached down in between her legs and she gasped, her head going back, exposing her neck.

"This is so hard." Stella was turned on, but she was fighting her brain that was telling her to cut this off immediately.

"Well something's hard..." he started laughing, "but it's not me and you, love." He kissed her forehead. "We have something. We don't have to label it or call it anything. I just want to spend the entire night with you."

"I know what you're doing. You just keep pushing." Stella blew her bangs out of her face. "Why do you even want to bother with me?"

"I have faith in you. You and I *will* end up together, I knew a long time ago. You just haven't figured it out yet. You make me laugh and you're crazy smart. You like football. Your boobs look like that." He pointed to her breasts, then flipped her over. "And your ass is awesome."

She laughed. "You're ridiculous." She turned to face away from him. "I don't know how to do this, George. I've been numb for so long, I don't even know how to feel things."

He nuzzled her neck. "Oh, I know I can make you feel things."

"'nother one." Stella raised her hand and pointed her finger at George.

"El, I think you've had enough, love, don't you?" George, the bartender, walked over to the slumped figure at the end of his bar. "It's Tuesday, don't you have work tomorrow?"

"So," Stella blurted. "Come on, George, one more and then I'll walk home." Stella had been sitting on the barstool for three hours, drinking by herself.

"What has gotten you so down, love?"

"Pour me another one and then we can talk about it." She smiled and could see he was melting.

George had to be talked into the last three drinks. He pushed the Crown and ginger ale over to her and leaned against the bar, putting his face level with hers. "What's going on?"

"I got my grades from last semester." She put her head down on the bar and said something incoherent.

"What?" George leaned closer; he could smell the coconut fragrance from her and smiled unconsciously.

"I got a C in Intellectual Property," she wailed.

George shot up off the bar and looked at her, dazed. Then he leaned his head back and offered her the biggest laugh she had seen from him in awhile. "For fuck's sake, El. I thought your dog died or you were pregnant or something."

"Um, I hope you wouldn't think I would drink this much if I was pregnant," she laughed.

"Whatever, you know what I mean. Shit." George continued to laugh as he took more drink orders and moved to the other side of the bar. Then he called to her, "Forgot to tell you I called your mom..." He laughed some more.

"NO!" She put her head back on the bar, where it actually felt much better. A few minutes passed before she felt a very large hand on her head.

"El? You okay?"

She looked under her arm and saw Patrick and his girlfriend, Lisa, standing off to her left. It was difficult, but she raised her head. "Shit. I'm so sorry George called y'all."

"Come on," Patrick said, running his hand through his hair and throwing some cash on the bar. "Thanks, George."

"Stella, why are drinking by yourself? On a Tuesday? That seems a bit much." Lisa picked up Stella's purse and headed out the door. She didn't even wait for an answer.

"I made a C in Intellectual Property," she whispered.

"It's okay, El." Patrick put his arm around her shoulder and led her toward the door.

Stella looked back and yelled, "George, you shit! I'm finding a new place to drink by myself."

"I hope not, El." He winked at her.

She let Patrick lead her to his car and climbed in the back. Immediately Lisa started talking. "Patrick, you know, Stella is a big girl. She doesn't need you to rescue her all the time." Lisa looked towards the backseat to see if Stella had passed out yet. Continuing on her tangent, Stella tuned her out for most of the car ride home.

"For once, I agree with Lisa," Stella forced out and then looked out the window and blocked out the argument she'd caused in the front seat. As soon as they pulled in the driveway, she tried to get out of the backseat, but was locked in.

"Damn it, unlock the door, I think I'm going to vomit." The locks immediately released and Stella opened the door.

Just the getting outside made her feel better; Patrick went around to help her out of the car.

"Shit, I'm not that drunk. I can walk." She pulled her arm from his grasp and walked, staggered was more like it, up the stairs to the front door.

"Hey, Billy, you didn't join the come-get-me party?" Stella asked as she shuffled through the den into the kitchen.

"Drink some water, El!" Patrick called from the front of the house.

"There was a party?" Billy looked up from the video game he was playing.

"Oh sure," Patrick said, sitting on the loveseat in the den. "El didn't invite anyone to it."

"Bring me a beer!" Billy yelled from the den as he saw Stella at the fridge.

She moved toward the den with two beers. Threw Billy's at him and then fell into the overstuffed chair where Cooper was laying. She opened her own beer and laid her head back on the chair. "This day sucks."

"Well, at least you didn't have to walk home," Patrick said tilting his head to look at her.

"That was my plan; drink a lot, walk it off on the way home."

"Great plan," Lisa said, popping off the couch. "I'm going to bed, you coming?" She looked over her shoulder at Patrick.

"Yeah, give me a minute," he answered gruffly.

Lisa sighed and then made her way back to the back room.

"El, making a C in the class is not the end of the world."

"I'm aware..." Her eyes closed as the day's stress and alcohol settled in. She was sort of embarrassed she was letting a grade get to her. Closing her eyes, she remembered her computer totally cutting off thirty minutes prior to her final being due and she hadn't backed up her exam. *Fucking stupid shit.*

"You'll be fine," Patrick said.

"El, you're like the smartest person I know," Billy said, not taking his eyes off the television.

"That's not saying much for you," she replied. "Enough of this shit; this is why I wanted to drink alone." She stood up and drained her beer. "Come on, Coop." Cooper jumped off the chair and followed her as she went through the kitchen. She pulled her shirt off and pants off on the way, throwing both in the laundry room off the kitchen.

Turning the corner, she heard Lisa grumble, "You know you can wait until you get in your room to undress."

"You could stay at your own damn place," she said loud enough for both Lisa and Patrick to hear. She went downstairs into her bedroom and sunk into her bed.

Sometime in the middle of the night she felt him get into bed with her and snuggle into her back. "If I knew you were going to make regular use of that key I would've made you work harder for it."

"Sure you would've, love." He pulled her as close as she could get to him, pressing her back into his chest. He loved that she slept nude all the time.

Buzzing woke her up and she looked at the clock. "Motherfucker," she groaned. "I thought you were going to let me sleep late, asshole." She pushed herself up and reached up and over George, who hadn't moved to see his phone vibrating continuously. As she picked it up, her body situated right on top of George, he reached for her, pulling her down on him.

"I don't remember saying that," he said, kissing the underside of her breast.

She was stretching in the mirrored area of Washington Sports Club, the gym where she and Patrick were both members and worked out together six days out of the week. He'd yelled down this morning saying he was leaving and she barely slid into the car at 7:00 as he took off.

"Why are you in a mood this morning?" Stella asked. He'd barely let her shut the door before he was backing out of the driveway.

"I don't have to time to waste waiting on your ass."

"Just my ass?" She laughed. "You can wait on the rest of me, though, right?"

"You know what I mean, shit."

She looked at him from the passenger side of his black Audi. His black hair was still military short and his green eyes were looking forward. He was scowling. "Lisa gave you shit about last night?"

"You told her she should stay at her own place..." He looked at her with disdain.

"Give me a fucking break, she's in our house, not hers. She doesn't like it, she can leave."

"Then I wouldn't get laid and I'd be in an even worse mood." He finally glanced over at her and smiled. "I had to work a little extra for it last night after that comment."

"So sorry to make you have to work for it," she laughed and pulled up her sports bra so that it wasn't showing as much cleavage.

"Whatever; you know I don't mind coming and picking you up from wherever. It was strange for George to call, though, right? You weren't even that drunk."

"Maybe he was tired of me taking up space at his bar. I don't know. I was too drunk to care." She wrapped her hair into a messy bun with a rubberband and put her armband on so that she could listen to music on her phone while she worked out. "Lisa's annoying, by the way."

"Not that great of a lay either..." Patrick mumbled.

"Cold bastard this morning," Stella commented. "Things not working out?"

"Whatever." He threw his car into park and jumped out, not wanting to talk about it.

Stella inspected his face; normally she tried to stay out of Patrick's personal business. "Why do you even bother, you don't even like her?"

"She's an easy lay, I guess." Patrick slung his workout bag on his shoulder.

"What the fuck, Patrick? You could fuck any one you want. You should at least like who you're fucking." She shook her head in disgust and went into the female locker room.

CHAPTER TWENTY-NINE

I Know You

Stepping off the escalator at the Pentagon City Metro stop, she hurried the couple of blocks to the nondescript office building where the General Counsel for the U.S. Marshals was housed. Stella was wearing a navy suit with a cream shell underneath and red heels. She signed in and made her way up to the seventh floor. As she pushed the doors open to the lobby, she took in the three other law students that were waiting. Checking her watch to make sure she wasn't late, she smiled at receptionist.

The receptionist was a well-put-together African American women with perfect red lipstick. "Gary will be with you all in a few minutes, okay?"

Stella sat down next to a girl about her age with curly red hair and freckles. "Hi, I'm Stella," she said in a friendly tone.

"Sarah," the redhead replied. Sarah was wearing a black suit, black heels, and pearls.

"Nice to meet you." Stella looked over to the two guys sitting in the chairs opposite of hers.

"Jeff," a guy with dark hair and glasses said.

"Brian," the other guy responded. They both wore black suits and blue shirts, Jeff a red tie and Brian a yellow tie.

After a few minutes, Gary Mathews opened the code-enforced door to the offices behind the receptionist and smiled. He had spiky gray hair and a mustache. "Hey, guys. Come on back and let's get started." He motioned them in and held the door as they filed inside the offices.

The morning was filled with paperwork, getting ID cards, and settling into their offices. Stella had one of four cubicles in the office with the three other interns. They would be handling the backlog of citizen claims against the U.S. Marshals allowed under the Federal Torts Claims Act. This was the law that allowed private citizens to recoup money for property damaged by a marshal. Gary had given them each thirty cases to start, with plenty more where those came from once they had a resolution for the initial claims. Everyone she came in contact with at the office was nice and relatively normal; most attorneys were anything but normal, so she was a little surprised by the overall collegial atmosphere of the office.

When she took her seat on the Metro for her short trip home, she knew she would enjoy her job with the Marshals.

Stella and George had been driving each other crazy at least three nights a week for several months. It worked well for Stella because she was so busy with work and law school she didn't have time to deal with typical relationship bullshit. Stella trusted that George wasn't with anyone else. He simply didn't have time. She hoped he trusted her.

Billy and Patrick were at work. Stella had taken the week of July 4th off work. Initially, she planned on a quick trip to Atlanta, but cancelled at the last minute. Her phone buzzed, it was George.

Can I come over?

Stella replied.

Sure

George told her he would be there in five minutes. *He was presumptuous.* Stella heard him knock on the door. As soon as she opened it, he was kissing her, holding her face in his hands. It took her a minute to kiss him back. They moved through the house, not separating. Then he picked her up, putting her legs around his waist and walked down the stairs. He threw her on the bed and ripped his shirt off.

Stella smiled. "Someone's happy to see me."

"Take your clothes off," George almost growled.

After they were done, George was tracing her tattoo and humming. "Come somewhere with me."

"Where," she asked.

"It's a surprise."

"I don't like surprises," she answered and then turned over.

"You'll like this one, it involves a pool." His eyes twinkled. "And alcohol."

Stella jumped up. "You sold me on pool."

She put on a string bikini, shorts, a tank top, and her knee-high boots. Stella smiled; because she loved riding on the back of bikes. Her dad had a Harley and she used to ride with him all the time. They put her bag in one of the bike's side bags. She swung her leg over and grabbed George's waist.

Stella leaned in and whispered/yelled in George's ear, "I love having you in between my legs."

He turned, grinning at her and answered, "You keep that up and we'll never leave here."

Stella threw her hands up in surrender. The ride lasted a little more than an hour and Stella closed her eyes and felt the warmth of the sun on her arms on the way. She was surprised to see them pull into a house out in the country, somewhere in Virginia. George punched in a code and the gates opened to let them in. He pulled up in front of what looked like an old plantation house.

George stopped the bike and put the kickstand down. He got off first, turned to help her take her helmet off, then pulled her off the bike and into his arms. "Having your legs around me like that for so long did things to me." He nuzzled her neck.

"Me too," she answered. Looking up at the house, she asked, "What is this place?"

"Friend of my dad's place, they're gone for the week. They said we could stay here."

"For how long?"

"All week if you want." George took her hand and walked her around the side of the house to the pool area.

She dropped his hand and ran to the pool. "I've missed pools…" She turned around, tore off her shirt and looked at him, "You sure you want to stay with me for a couple of days?"

"There isn't anything I want more," he said smiling.

"But I only have these clothes to wear."

"I'm hoping you won't be wearing clothes."

They ran to the grocery store and picked up a few essentials, then made their way to the pool. Stella was lying on a float in the middle of the pool and George was talking to Hazel about closing the bar tonight. All of a sudden, she felt the side of her float lift and she was thrown into the water. She emerged from the water gasping for air and lifted by strong arms.

"Fuck, George," Stella sputtered, trying to get all the hair out of her face.

"You know," George started, but then Stella pushed him under water with all of her weight. He pulled her down with him and kissed her. They drifted to the surface, still kissing.

"At least I know how I can shut you up now," she smiled.

"All you have to do is ask. I'm happy to shut up." George covered her mouth with his.

Stella lay on her stomach, getting sun with no top on. George was making them lunch. Her phone buzzed, it was Patrick.

Where are you?

Stella had gotten so caught up she hadn't told Patrick where she was. She replied:

With George back tomorrow morning, I think

She put her phone back when it buzzed again. Shielding her eyes she read Patrick's reply:

U scared the fuck out of me

She texted back her smartass reply:

Sorry dad

U can watch coop, right? I didn't know I'd be gone

Patrick replied:

Always coming to your rescue

She frowned:

Thanks

"Who you texting?" George asked, carrying out a tray with meat, cheese, bread, and white wine.

"I think I've died and gone to heaven," Stella said, taking in the feast.

"I'm there too, with you laying around practically naked." He set the tray down in between the two lounge chairs. "Who you texting?"

"Patrick; he was pissed I didn't tell him where I was." Stella threw her phone under her towel so it wouldn't get too hot.

"So you guys are really just friends?" George didn't look at her as he opened the wine and poured two glasses. "You never...you know?"

"Um, no. We haven't." She grabbed an olive and popped it in her mouth.

"But, he's seen you naked."

"Well, that's true," she said, thinking the best way to respond to this. "I don't really care who sees me naked."

"What do you mean?"

Stella blushed, but she didn't know why. "I get drunk and get naked." She shrugged her shoulders.

"You get naked?" He raised his eyebrows.

"Yep," she answered and put blue cheese on a cracker.

"Like, just sit around naked?"

"Could be," she answered.

"Billy's seen you naked?"

"Yep." She took a gulp of her wine.

"Millie?"

She nodded her head.

"And here I was, thinking I was special." George took a drink of the wine. "That's pretty good."

"Oh, but you *are* special, George." Stella got up and walked over to him, kissing him on his jaw line. "I let you see me naked when I'm sober."

George bent to her and kissed her caressing her breasts. "Only me, right?"

"Only you," she whispered.

"I don't like that other guys have seen you naked. It kinda makes me crazy."

"George, my roommates have seen me passed out naked on my bathroom floor." Stella walked back to her lounge chair and sat down. "Not too attractive, believe me. They don't see me like you see me. They see me as their drunken sister. They've seen me at my worst."

"I want to see you at your worst. I want to see you all the time." George reached out and held her hand.

"You've seen me at my worst, just not the entire picture. The first year I met you was the worst time of my life. I'm amazed anyone that knew me then wants to talk to me. Patrick basically saved my life."

"I want to know everything about you, Stella." George leaned in and kissed her gently.

"No, you don't." Stella grabbed salami and cheese, stuffing it in her mouth.

"Oh, but I do. I want to know about your dreams, your nightmares, and most of all, I want to know when you're going to admit you love me."

She pushed herself off the lounge chair and pulled on her tank top at the same time. "You think you know me! You don't know shit about me, George. If you did, you would know that I won't admit to loving you because I can't." She ran to the house to get away from him.

George caught her by her arm, "If you didn't care about me you wouldn't be so pissed off," he said gently.

"Of course I care about you." Stella was so frustrated a tear fell down her face. "I can't give you what you want. I don't have a heart to give you," she said, beating on her chest. "Take me home, George."

"No can do, love, I've been drinking," he said smiling. "You think you're the only one who has had loss, pain and despair? That's ridiculous. You're a smart girl, El, you know that's not true. You don't have a monopoly on baggage or pain."

George calm demeanor pissed Stella off even more. "Don't fucking condescend to me." She snatched her arm out of his reach and grabbed an unopened bottle of wine and the corkscrew on her way through the kitchen.

"This is what happens when you love someone, Stella. You argue, fight, yell, and then make up. You can convince yourself all you want, but I know you."

"I CAN'T!" she cried and ran upstairs. She locked herself in a guest bedroom. Taking a quick look around she sighed; no television. *Shit!* She opened the bottle and turned it up.

George knocked on the door. "I'm going to sit here, with my back to this door, love, until you come make out... I mean, make up with me," he said, amused.

"Fuck you!" she yelled and slid down the door with her bottle of wine. She tipped it up. "You know, George, if you did know me, you would know how stubborn I am."

"You know me and you know how stubborn I am, so this should be fun." He turned up his own drink.

Hours later, Stella woke up after drinking the entire bottle of wine and passing out. It was quiet and dark and she needed to pee. She opened the door and saw George slumped on the wall next to the door.

She padded down the hall to the bathroom, relieved to have made it without peeing herself. When she opened the door she ran smack into George's solid chest.

"You ready to make out yet?" he smiled sleepily.

"You mean make up, right?" Stella asked, not looking at him.

"No, I mean make out." He ran his hand over her hair, then down her back, leaving his hand on her tattoo.

"I can't give you what you want," Stella whispered.

"I disagree." He kissed her lips gently.

"I'm not whole. I can't love you like you should be loved." Tears falling down her face, she buried her face in his chest.

"Hey." George pulled her back so that she was looking at him. "I'm stubborn and patient."

"I ..."

He kissed her, not leaving it up to debate. George cradled her and carried her up to the room they were sharing.

She woke up in his arms and felt sad. Somehow, she felt it was the beginning of the end; George was well aware she couldn't be who he wanted.

"Stop overthinking it, my smart girl." George turned her to face him. "We're good."

"You're good with having 50 percent of me?" Stella rubbed her thumb over his jaw. "This is all so unforeseeable."

"I love it when you talk lawyer to me." He kissed her. "I'll settle for 75 percent for now."

CHAPTER THIRTY

Only Me

The week before her last year of law school started, they had a big lunch for the other interns that were finishing their summer stint with the Marshals. Linda Morgan, the General Counsel, had addressed all of them. Stella was impressed that a woman was in the position of General Counsel of the department. However, she was stunned when Ms. Morgan got glassy-eyed at the table talking about the sacrifices she made to obtain the position. It was evident she was bitter that she pursued her career instead of a family. Because Stella was so young and there wasn't a prospect of family for her, she hadn't even thought about the sacrifices women made to advance their careers. If she and Jamie had gotten married, she guessed those sorts of issues would be on her mind.

She'd grown to really like Sarah; they were pretty opposite on most things, but Sarah was so honest and genuine she was hard not to like. Sarah had been in DC only for the summer; she attended University of Virginia law school and was already back. All four of them had gotten close, eating lunch together and working in the same office for nine hours a day. Stella liked the casual, sarcastic banter that was steady from the time they got there until they left in the evening. She was going to miss having them around. She didn't know if she was going to enjoy the office as much without them.

Each of the other interns had left their remaining open files on her desk and her chair with witty notes on them for her entertainment. She'd also found little post-it notes from Sarah on everything in her cubicle. Smiling, she piled them all in a drawer in her desk.

Jamie had been gone for three years. She was starting her last year of law school and it was all very surreal. The sound of a motorcycle revving coming from her phone made her smile. "Hi, Dad."

"You ready?"

"Of course," she answered. She and her dad spoke most mornings, but especially the first day of school every year.

"What classes you taking this semester?"

"Working for the Marshals gives me credits for a class and I'm taking a Seminar on Secrecy in Government and a clinic in Administrative Law," she answered. A clinic was a class in law school that was more practical that a typical class. Professors usually had practicing attorneys come in to each class and then there was a mock trial at the end of the semester.

"Well, I'm not going to pretend to know what any of those classes will entail. I'm sure you'll do fine." He cleared his throat.

"So, you'll never guess who I ran into the other day."

"Who's that?" Stella was driving up Massachusetts Avenue and appreciating all the embassies on both sides of the road.

"Sara."

"Sara who?"

"Jamie's sister."

Stella remained quiet.

"You okay?"

"Sure."

"She asked about you. I told her you were still in school. She said she tried to contact you a couple of times, but you've never responded."

"Dad…"

"I'm just saying, Stella. She cares about how you're doing."

"I'm glad you told her I was fine then." Stella cleared her throat. "Listen, I'm pulling into the school. We'll talk later," she said, cutting off the conversation.

After several weeks of attending her last year of law school, Stella could agree that the third year of law school was a huge snorefest. Her classes were interesting, but they were all papers, so no big pressure to keep up with reading or stress about a final. She was still working for the

Marshals and that kept her occupied most of the time. Stella felt almost normal. One Saturday, Patrick and Billy invited some of their friends over for the Penn State football game that night and she was trying to figure out if she was going to make herself scarce or what. She was checking her email when she heard her name called from the stairs. Stella put her laptop down and walked over to stairs.

Walking down the stairs was Cory, the manager at the tattoo parlor where she and Patrick get their tattoos. He had a tight Penn State shirt on with jeans hanging low on his hips. "Hey, Stella." He kissed her on the cheek.

"Hey, Cory. What's up?"

"I was wondering if I could take that picture of your tat? We've been trying to get it forever." He pointed at his camera and looked around, trying to find a good background.

"Oh, sure." She'd told Richard they could put up a picture of her tattoo after she got it done and hadn't found the time to go back.

"You got any clear wall space?" Her room was covered with poster and pictures. "I love *Fight Club*," he said as he passed the movie poster on her wall.

"Um, just over the bed," she blushed. Cory was good looking and had quite the reputation as being a ladies' man.

"Okay, let's go over there." Cory walked the length of the room into the cubby where her unmade bed was positioned. "This will work."

"Okay." Stella was a little uncomfortable, but followed him.

"Take your shirt and bra off." He was messing with his camera and didn't see the look on her face until he looked up. "Oh come on, I won't bite." Cory smiled.

"Okay, just hurry. I don't want to be down here shirtless for too long."

"I've never heard that one before." Cory laughed and started clicking the camera, attempting to get lighting and flash right.

Stella pulled her sweater over her head; she wasn't wearing a bra. "Where do you want me?"

"Wow, Stella." Cory cleared his throat. "Get on the bed and face the wall."

She gave him a look of caution. Covering her boobs, she got on her knees and faced the wall.

"Okay, take your pants off."

Stella burst out laughing. "Negative. Take your fucking picture and hurry up."

"Kay, seriously... Turn your entire body to face the wall, but look over your left shoulder. Don't look at the camera though."

Stella did as he asked and looked to the side. She held her left hand over her nipples and right hand straight down. Cory moved around, taking a million shots and giving her instructions.

"El?" She hadn't heard George come down the stairs, but he was staring at her with murder in his eyes.

"George..." she breathed. "What're you doing here?"

"Sorry to interrupt," he growled with teeth gritted together.

Cory, seeing the look George was giving him, held his hands up. "Oh no, man, wrong idea."

"The idea that you're taking a picture of El with no top on is wrong?" George was clenching and unclenching his fists, looking from Cory to Stella.

"George. Cory is from the tattoo parlor. I agreed when I got my tattoo that I'd let them they display it at the shop. Cory was just taking those pictures." She was climbing off the bed, still covering herself.

"You can leave," George told Cory, not looking anywhere but at Stella.

Cory looked at Stella; she shrugged. He held up his hands. "I think I got a couple of good ones. I'll email you. Thanks, Stella."

"Tell Richard no problem." she smiled weakly and then glared at George.

Cory had just turned the corner of the stairs when George pounced on her. He pushed her on the bed and claimed her as his own.

"I don't want anyone else seeing you like this." George caressed her breasts and then kissed each one.

"George, I didn't know he was coming or you either, for that matter." She gasped as he continued to kiss her roughly, making her body feel like it was on fire. She moaned loudly. "We can't."

"We are," George pulled her jeans down and was kissing her hip bones moving farther south.

"There are a ton of people upstairs." Stella was having difficulty collecting her thoughts. "I don't have a door..."

George picked her up and moved quickly into the bathroom, kicking the door closed. "El, tell me it's only me."

Stella gasped as he shoved her against the wall and struggled with his pants. "You," she couldn't get out anything else as he was touching her everywhere.

"You what?" he demanded.

Stella legs were wrapped tightly around him as he had his way with her. "Only you," she barely whispered.

"Say it again, Love, say it again." His mouth moved against her ear.

"Only you, George," Her brain was hurting from him making her so vulnerable. She didn't want to lay it out there, but it was so hard to think with him inside her.

"Good."

CHAPTER THIRTY-ONE

Everything Else

She was lying in bed with the silliest smile on her face. "George, you're tickling me." She squirmed under his touch. "What are you doing?"

He had a red sharpie marker and was drawing on her back. "I'm having fun."

"With what?" She tried to look over her shoulder to see what he was drawing. He was holding her down so she couldn't move around; she felt the cold tip of the marker on her shoulder blade. "I hope you aren't drawing circles on my fat like they do in sororities."

"I want to tell you that you are beautiful, you know that? Inside and out." He kissed her left shoulder blade. "But you are broken. I plan on fixing you."

"Oh really, how do you plan on doing that?" she asked without moving.

He leaned down and kissed her lovingly on the back of her neck, then up slowly to behind her ear. A shudder went through her entire body. "Very slowly, and one piece at a time, Love."

She closed her eyes. *It's too much.* She was letting him in and it wouldn't end well, she knew that. He was getting really close, too close. He held her still and drew a little while longer on her back and then kissed her tattoo. Bending to her left ear, he whispered, "I promise."

Stella got up to clear her head and went into the bathroom. She was trying to see what he had drawn on her back. He came to the doorway of her bathroom, watching her with a smile on his face. He grabbed the top of the door ledge and hung onto it, amused. Stella stopped what she was doing and looked at him, clearly turned on. He used his fingertips to skim down her back all the way to her tailbone. Her nipples responded immediately. He grabbed her and pushed her up against the small portion of the wall in her bathroom that was available. Stella wrapped both legs around him and gasped as he entered her.

After they were done, they got into the shower together. Stella was trying to squeeze past George on the outside of the shower when she saw the outline of the red heart he had drawn on her back now staining her bathroom wall. She turned to address it, but was caught off guard by his mouth and roaming hands.

"El?" Patrick yelled from the side of her bedroom. "You decent?"

"Fuck," she said, exasperated. "Patrick, I'm in the shower."

"Nothing I haven't seen," his said, his voice coming closer. George's eyebrows shot up in a question.

"I'm not alone. GET OUT!" Stella pulled the shower curtain making sure Patrick couldn't see in.

"Who you in there with?" Patrick called, mocking her.

"I swear..." Stella looked at George, who was laughing silently. She hit him playfully, "It's not funny."

George kissed her again and then turned her around, taking care to wash every inch of her. "You're beautiful when you're frustrated."

Although sex with George started off a few times a week, it changed to every night. Stella hadn't relented on her policy that he couldn't spend the night. George was wearing her down though, staying later and later. One night, five months into their thing, her cell phone started ringing. It was 2:00 a.m. She ripped her lips off George and blew a deep breath out, getting her bangs out of her eyes.

"Hold on," she pushed herself off the bed and grabbed her phone. "Dad?" Her voice broke with concern.

"It's your Mom, she's been in any accident. She's in the ICU at Grady. She was in a wreck; a fucking tractor trailer, Stella."

George moved behind her, wrapping his arms around her.

"Is she okay?" Stella's voice was small.

"She...God... Stella, I have no fucking idea."

"I'll be there tomorrow."

"Call me on your way." Her dad's voice was unrecognizable. "Stella, I love you."

"I love you, too." She hung up the phone and shrugged out of George's grasp. "This is just like fucking Jamie," she said to herself.

"Who's Jamie?"

Her eyes snapped to George's like she had just remembered he was there. "You should go, George."

"No, what's going on?" Closing the space between them, he stood as close as he could get without touching her. "Is it your mom?"

A tear fell from one eye. "Yes."

"What can I do?" George tentatively ran his fingertips down her cheek, wiping away her tear.

"You should go," she answered.

"Anything but that, El."

Backing away from his touch, she pulled her suitcase out and threw it on the bed. Stella began throwing clothes in the suitcase, not looking at him. "What am I going to say, George? Sure, drive me down to see my mom, who might be dead. Dad, this is George, we're fucking." She looked at him, his face showing hurt. After a few minutes of them staring at one another, she pulled the closest shirt over her head and walked up stairs.

Stella knocked on Patrick's door. It cracked open.

"What's up?" He asked, his eyes widening.

"My mom's been in an accident; I'm leaving as soon as possible in the morning."

"I'll go with you. Get some sleep, I'll wake you at five." He shut the door.

He's always so robotic in a crisis. She turned around and saw George standing at the bottom of the stairs. "You headed out?"

"No." He pulled Stella to him and breathed her in. "No." George walked her back to her bed, peeled off her shirt, and lifted her off her feet.

"Not really in the mood, George," she said lifelessly.

Laying her on the bed, he laid next to her and held her until she fell asleep. At 4:50, he kissed her awake. For a minute, she kissed him back. Until she woke up. "What..."

"El..." he pushed himself off the bed and slipped his pants on, "Let me help. Please."

"Fuck, George." She rolled over, showing him her bare ass. She left her head down for a whole minute, hoping he would just leave.

"Please," George pleaded.

"Fine. Can you come let Coop out?" Stella reached as far as she could without getting out of bed and pulled her bag toward her.

"Okay. How many times a day?"

"At least three. Run with him if you can. I'll leave instructions on feeding him." She didn't turn around when he kissed her cheek and left.

The nine-hour drive to Atlanta was long and mostly silent, just like when Patrick drove her to Jamie's funeral. George texted her almost every hour. It was exhausting. She wasn't cut out for a "relationship" and this just solidified it.

"El," Patrick put his arm across her shoulders, "your mom'll be okay."

"You don't know that, Patrick, don't make statements that you don't know about," Stella lashed out at him, but he understood and took it.

"I took a couple of days off work, so there's no hurry back," Patrick said ignoring her last comment.

Stella looked at him. "Thanks. You know...you're always coming to my rescue."

"Pretty much." He glanced at her.

"Why?"

"You're in desperate need of rescue on a consistent basis."

Stella looked at her hands clasped in her lap. "I'm sorry."

"For what?" he asked.

"For always needing to be rescued...by you."

"Don't be sorry for that, El, you're the sister I never had. I'd do anything for you, you know that."

"I wish you didn't have to do anything for me, Patrick." She sighed and blew her bangs out of her face. "I can't seem to get right...you know. I'm starting to feel a little more normal. I guess getting laid helps." Stella looked out the window as they passed from Virginia to North Carolina.

"Getting laid always helps." Patrick smiled.

Stella's phone beeped. "Oh My GOD, if George texts me again I will be getting laid by someone else..."

Mom's up she's okay.

"It's my dad, my mom woke up." She felt like a weight lifted off her back. "She's going to be okay." She let one tear fall down her face before she shook it off and smiled.

"See, I'm always right. You should know that by now." Patrick pulled her into a sideways hug.

She and Patrick stayed in Atlanta for two days before heading back to DC They hung out at the hospital pretty much the entire time. Stella's mother had a broken femur and a concussion, but was set to be released the next week.

Texting George that she and Patrick were headed home, she slung her bag over her shoulder and shuffled through the humid, depressing Georgia heat to her car. She sighed; only three steps out of the house and sweat was rolling down her back. Patrick walked out of the front door with her dad, shaking his hand. Patrick smiled at Stella and then saluted her father.

"Ready?" Stella asked as he pulled the door shut.

"Roger."

She laughed. "You know, for the past three years, you've been the most important person in my life." She reversed the car and made her way toward the highway, looking straight ahead. "I know I don't say it enough, but thanks."

"What was that again?" He smirked at her.

"You heard me, jackass."

"Oh, that's what I thought you said."

Patrick was letting Stella drive the first leg of the trip while he was getting work done. Stella let her mind wander. She would have to do something about George when she got back. He was treating her like a girlfriend; she was *not* his girlfriend.

"Whatcha thinking about over there?" Patrick looked up from his iPad.

"Just trying to figure out what to do with George."

"What do you mean?" Patrick put down his IPad and stared at the road.

"I really don't think I can do whatever it is we're doing anymore. It's getting hard." Stella stared straight ahead.

"Wait, are you serious?" Patrick rubbed his shaved head. "It's getting hard? What's hard about it? He does whatever you want him to."

Her head snapped over to Patrick. "Um he most certainly does not. He keeps pushing me Patrick. He's pushing me..."

"Pushing you?"

"I don't know. I'm not sure I can explain, I'm just not ready for what he wants and he doesn't seem to care about that."

"Isn't that a good thing?"

"No. It's not. I'm fine with just sex and nothing else. I can't do anything else."

"El, you've been doing everything else since you hooked up with George."

CHAPTER THIRTY-TWO

Naked Football

After she got back from Atlanta, George began routinely sleeping with his hand on her tattoo, like he was trying to put her back together or pretend there wasn't a hole in her heart. Stella stretched and shifted so that his hand fell from her back. George pulled Stella into his chest and inhaled her hair.

"What time is it?" Stella whispered.

"It's five." George smoothed her hair out of her face. He leaned into her and kissed her mouth gently. "You want me to leave?"

"No..." Stella ran her hand over George's chest. "But, I need you to leave. I'm sorry," Stella whispered.

George gathered her into his arms and whispered in her ear, "What's two hours, El? Let me stay."

"It's what I need."

He sighed and turned over on his back. "You're worth it," he said. He had only been asleep for a couple of hours and he had dark circles under his eyes.

With both hands on his chest, she could barely make out his eyes in the dark. "That's doubtful."

George sighed and kissed her one more time. "Please know I want to sleep with you and wake up with you, okay?"

"Okay." Stella blew her bangs out of her eyes. "I'm sorry."

George sat up and walked in the bathroom and shut the door. Stella got up and let Cooper out the back door. She felt his arms wrap around her and it soothed some of her unease.

"Do you always walk around naked in your house? You live with two guys. You're the best roommate ever." She could hear his smile.

"I've actually heard that before," she said.

"Can I see you later?"

"Sure, I can always use free drinks."

"I mean maybe lunch before I go in?" George tucked a piece of hair behind her ear.

"No, I've got a paper. I have to decide on my topic and I haven't even started yet." She pulled him closer and whispered, "I'll definitely see you tomorrow night, though."

He brushed his thumb over her nipple, which she immediately responded to. "Not fair, George," Stella almost growled.

"Not trying to be fair, love."

Stella was coming out of the bathroom when she heard steps down into her room. She peered around the corner, calling out, "Patrick? I thought you went out?"

"El, it's me!" George called the same time Stella realized it was him coming down the stairs. Cooper got up from her bed, the entire back end of his body shaking happily. George stopped and let Cooper smell him.

"Hey, what are you doing here?" she asked pulling at her tank top self-consciously.

He held up pizza and beer. "I thought we could watch the game."

"What game?" Stella looked at him like he had lost his mind.

"The Steelers and the Redskins. You have no idea what I'm talking about?" George put the pizza and beer on her desk. "I know you watch football."

"I watch college football, George. I don't really watch NFL." Stella walked over to where he was standing and wrapped her arms around him, inhaling his scent of rosemary and mint.

"Really?" he asked, resting his chin on the top of her head.

"Yep, sorry to disappoint you."

George looked defeated. "I guess I can go." He grabbed the pizza and beer.

"No. No...you don't have to go. It's not like I hate NFL, but I don't really have a team that I watch on a regular basis. My roommates watch, but I usually read or study on Sundays." Stella walked to the back door and let Cooper out. "I'll make an exception for you." She smiled.

He put the pizza and beer back on the desk. "Good, I don't want to miss kickoff. You got plates?"

"Sure." Stella went to the kitchen and grabbed two plates and glasses, some napkins and forks. When she walked downstairs, she saw that George had made himself at home and was lying on her bed on his stomach, surfing through the channels trying to find the game. "We have satellite TV."

"I know El, I've been here before," he said, laughing at her.

"Well, we really haven't been watching TV when you've been here," she retorted.

"So you really don't like NFL?"

"That's not what I said, George." Stella walked over to her bed and lay on her stomach next to him. Her stomach did the flip thing it did when George was around. "I like NFL, it's just I'm so busy with school I can only waste one day during the weekend on football and I LOVE college football. "

"Okay, that makes sense." George pulled her to him and kissed her gently. "You want some pizza?"

She shook her head. "But yes for beer."

George got up and got pizza and a beer for himself and got her a beer as well.

"So who do you root for?"

"Steelers." He took a bite of his pizza.

"One of my favorite players from Georgia played for them for awhile. Hines Ward." She took the beer he handed her.

"You know football," George said, looking at her with an expression she couldn't place.

"I guess, why?"

"You just keep getting sexier." George took another bite of pizza. "Could you take off your clothes to watch the game with me?"

"Sure," she said and laughed when his jaw dropped. She took her shirt off and was working on her pants when he tackled her.

George was drinking his third beer while propped on her bed watching the game and Stella was reading with her head in his lap, highlighting what she thought were important pieces of the case she was reading, but she ended up highlighting the entire case. "Kind of defeats the purpose," she muttered.

George had his arm casually on her stomach, which was causing all sorts of concentration issues for Stella. She shifted her body and lay on her stomach with her feet at the head of the bed and her face at the bottom.

"Best game ever," George said.

Stella looked up. "Are the Steelers winning?"

"No, but you're laying there naked..."

"It's not like you haven't seen me before." She winked at him and went back to reading.

"You're so gorgeous, El, it wouldn't matter how many times I've seen you naked. You take my breath away every time."

"Okay," she said, rolling over to look at him. "That was a really good line. You should use it on someone better than me." Stella rolled back over and continued reading. After a significant amount of time of George being silent, she looked back at him; he had an unreadable expression on his face. "What?"

"You're clueless and so hard to deal with sometimes." George rubbed his hand over his shaved head.

"Clueless, I'm not sure. Hard to deal, with yes, all the time." Stella crawled over to where George was sitting and straddled him. "What's so hard right now?" Stella leaned in and kissed his neck.

George groaned and gave in to her without responding to her question.

CHAPTER THIRTY-THREE

Presumptions

Stella swore she would never be one of those people who wore running shoes on the Metro then changed into her heels at the office, but her feet were killing her today. She was wearing a black dress and tights with her running shoes while she made her way through Metro Center. She took the escalator up and navigated through the G Street rush hour pedestrian traffic. Making her way into a nondescript building, she took the elevator to the seventh floor.

Working with Marshals this semester, she'd been dealing with some requests under the Freedom of Information Act. She had a meeting with an attorney from the Department of Justice, Office of Information and Privacy, which was the department that dealt with these sorts of requests. Everyone in DC simply called the office FOIA. Currently, she was working on a FOIA request regarding a prisoner transfer that ended in the prisoner escaping and leading the Marshals on a two-day search. Stella was sent over to their office to collect documents that were redacted in order to produce them to a reporter.

While on the elevator, she had just enough time to step out of her running shoes and slip into black stilettos. As the doors opened, she was stuffing her shoes in her bag.

She hit the call button. "Keith, it's Stella."

"Hey, Stella," a slight African American male greeted and pushed the button to let her in the reception area.

"Hey, Keith." She pushed her hair behind her ear. "You got anything for me yet?"

He frowned. "No, was I supposed to?"

"Hmm, could you call Annie and ask if those documents are ready for me?" She hovered as Keith made a call.

"Okay, I'll send her up." Keith hung up the phone and looked at up at her. "Annie said that Mr. Erickson wanted to talk to you before you left with the documents."

That was odd. "Oh, okay."

"Do you know where his office is?"

"No." She hoped it was close, her feet felt broken.

"Okay, get back in the elevator and go up to seventeen. I'll let them know you're coming."

Fuck... Fuck... Fuck... Her feet hurt just standing, let alone walking to Sam Erickson's office. He was one of the Assistant Directors of the FOIA office. The office had about twenty-five attorneys in all. She was buzzed into the office immediately. Pam, Mr. Erickson's secretary, was waiting on her.

"Hi, Stella. Mr. Erickson wanted to see you real quick before you head back, okay?" She was already walking, so Stella hurried to follow her. She pointed toward an office door that was closed. "In there," she said without slowing her pace.

Stella slowed and stood at the closed door. She'd not prepared herself for this meeting. Taking a deep breath, she reminded herself it wouldn't be a big deal, she was simply a law clerk. There couldn't be anything important he'd want to talk to her about.

She put a smile on her face, knocked on the open door, and entered his office. Looking around his office, she took in the sports memorabilia on the wall and his law degree, which was framed and sitting on the floor propped against the wall.

"Hey..." he paused and looked out the window for a second.

"Stella," she prompted. There was no reason for him to know her name, it didn't hurt her feelings.

"I know," he replied with a glare. "I asked you in here because I wanted to know if you thought of any other exemptions or exceptions for the documents we're producing this week."

She shrank into herself. "No sir, I've been working with your team and the Marshal's office and I think we have them all covered."

"Good." He smiled, his blue eyes twinkling. He wasn't wearing a ring and was very attractive. His copper hair was cut pretty close to his head and was on the verge of turning gray. He had taken off his jacket already and had his tie casually thrown around his neck. Not even taking the time to tie it prior to getting started on his day. "Have you enjoyed your time working with us?" He didn't look at her, but at something out the window.

"Sure," she said. "Everyone has been really helpful."

"Are you planning on staying with the Marshals' office after your internship?"

She sighed; she really didn't know what she was going to do. "I would like to, but they don't have any openings," she said vaguely.

"Staying in the area?' he asked.

"I hope so." She examined him. *Where was he going with this?*

"You applying for this office?" He finally looked at her.

"No sir." She smiled feebly.

"Good." He exhaled a breath it look liked he had been holding. "Let me buy you a drink sometime."

"Excuse me?" *This was very unexpected.* "A drink?"

"You drink alcohol, right? I've seen you at Finnegan's"

OH SHIT. "If you have seen me at Finnegan's, then you know I drink."

"You seem to have a good time wherever you go, Stella."

She really needed to sit down now. "I try."

"We can meet at Finnegan's if you want. I know the owner. Pretty good guy. He's doing what he can with the place since his father died."

"Well, I'd rather meet somewhere closer to the office, if you don't mind."

"I live near Finnegan's so let's do something in Old Town. I assume you live down there as much as I see you at Finnegan's." He smirked at her.

"You're right, I live down there." She gleaned from his smirk he had seen her in her many stages of intoxication. She cringed. "Why don't we meet at the Fish Market?" she said, trying to think of anywhere other than Finnegan's. She didn't want to rub George's face in her grabbing a drink with another person.

"How presumptuous of you." He glanced at his watch, his lips turning up at the corners, and started tying his tie. "I didn't ask you to dinner."

"We don't have to eat," she answered. Turning on her heel, she left.

CHAPTER THIRTY-FOUR

Boyfriends

George slipped into Stella's bed and wrapped himself around her. When she woke up in the middle of the night, she reached around him and made him face her. "What's up?"

"What do you mean?" George smiled at her and kissed her gently, tugging on her bottom lip.

"Stop, you're distracting me." She pushed back from his chest and felt his hands moving up her thighs. "Seriously," she protested, then faded and leaned her head back.

"I missed you." He kissed her neck and behind her ear.

"Bullshit," she whispered as she decided to give in.

He was gone in the morning before they could talk. *Damn it.* That was two nights in a row. She should not engage in a relationship with a bartender. Not even a sexy bartender who knew how to make her scream his name. She sighed and pulled on her spandex, sports bra, and running shoes. When she looked up, Patrick was standing in her room. "FUCK!" she exclaimed, nearly jumping as high as the ceiling.

"Oh, sorry. I thought you heard me come in." He walked in a few more steps.

"Not cool. You didn't even knock, ass. I could have been naked." Stella headed up the stairs and grabbed a bottle of water.

"Let's run outside today," Patrick said casually.

"I need to do legs and triceps today," Stella answered.

"Do them tomorrow. Let's run, I need to talk."

"Okay, something I should be worried about?" Stella pulled out her phone and put it in her armband. She searched her workout bag for her earbuds. "Coop, come," she called as she and Patrick moved toward the door.

"Long or short?" Patrick asked.

"Long, I've been drinking too much." Stella turned to the right and started jogging, holding on to Coop. "You get Coop on the way back."

"Sure."

Patrick ran toward the dog park as usual, Stella didn't put her earbuds in so they could talk. They were silent for the first couple of blocks. "So, what's up?" Stella asked as they turned left onto King Street.

"Well, I broke up with Lisa," Patrick said, staring straight ahead.

"Really..." Stella wasn't surprised.

"You were right."

"Really?" He never admitted when she was right or maybe she hadn't been right in a very long time.

"Yes, okay. I didn't need to subject myself to her for sex. I can get that from someone more amiable." Patrick finally turned and looked at her, smirking.

"That's not what I said," she replied. Stella knew Lisa was not the woman for Patrick, but she didn't want to be blamed for their breakup.

"Sure it is."

"No, I just wondered why you were with her when you don't even like her. You didn't have problem sleeping with her before." Stella shook her head. "What changed?"

"Nothing changed. You just made sense for once."

They ran in silence for a few blocks. "So you want to tell me to do the same thing with George, right?" Stella smiled, figuring out Patrick's game. "You're something else, you know?"

"I'm not telling you anything, except that you made sense when you told me to break up with Lisa when all I was doing was fucking her." Patrick looked straight ahead, his expression stoic.

"That's not what I said, asshole. I said why fuck someone you don't even like to be around them. Everyone likes George." Stella was starting to get angry.

Patrick stepped up his pace, leaving Stella trailing him. She thought about George, his dimple making her mouth curl up automatically. She stepped up her stride and got even with Patrick.

"I like George and I like fucking him, okay!" Stella blurted out.

"I haven't said one word to you about it. You've been inferring shit." Patrick turned around and headed back up King Street. "Seems like you need to reassess what you're doing."

"George and I have nothing to do with you and your ex-girlfriend."

"That's right, my girlfriend. Is George your boyfriend now?"

Stella stopped running and put her hands on her hips.

Patrick stopped running, turned to look at her, winked, and started running again.

CHAPTER THIRTY-FIVE

Every Piece

The Woods Brothers crooned through Stella's speakers as she waited for George to get out of the shower. He had come over after his shift at the bar. She was looking through her closet when she felt his strong arms around her hugging her into his chest. George's hips swayed with the beat of the song; Stella laid her head back on his chest and exhaled.

"How was your day, dear?" Stella could hear the smirk in his voice.

"Okay. I'm working a big FOIA request for the Marshals and we're having really long, boring meetings with other DOJ departments all week." Stella moved her hands to his hips.

George pulled her around so that she was facing him, still swaying with the music. "Who's requesting documents?"

"You *would* know about FOIA requests, I forgot you used to be a reporter." She put her head on his pecs, still damp from his shower. "Do you miss it?"

"Every fucking day." George ran his right hand over her hair, smoothing it back.

"Why did you leave it?" Stella looked up into his eyes.

"Too complicated a story for now..." He kissed her.

"Okay." Stella put her arms around his waist and leaned into him, she wasn't one to push anyone into talking about things they didn't want to.

"What're you doing Sunday?"

"Just reading for school, why?"

"I just thought maybe we could do something not in this bedroom..."

Stella ran her hands down his stomach into his towel, the only thing he was wearing. "Why?" she asked as she pulled the towel off and smiled at him.

When Sunday rolled around, Stella was reading on the back porch after her run with Cooper. Her phone beeped, showing a message from George.

Get in the shower and be ready in an hour

She replied.

ready for what

George texted back immediately.

For me

Stella smiled. She finished reading the case she was in the middle of then went to "get ready" for George. She was pulling a long-sleeved shirt over her jeans when he walked down the stairs. "Hi."

"Hi." He put both hands in her hair and kissed her roughly.

"Well," Stella said, flustered, smoothing her hair back.

"Come on." George grabbed her hand and started pulling her upstairs. He stopped abruptly. "Put on your grey tall boots."

"Why?" Stella asked, looking down at her wedges.

"Please? I'm asking nicely." George's thumb stroked her palm.

"Oh, you like those, huh?"

"Yes, I do." Leaning his head down, George brought her hand to his lips.

While Stella changed her shoes, George let Cooper outside and looked out the window.

"El, are you headed home for Thanksgiving?" he called, watching Cooper run around the backyard.

"No...I don't know. I pretty much never go home unless there's an emergency." She stood up and smoothed her jeans down. "Better?" she asked.

"Why not?"

"I just don't feel like it's home anymore." Stella walked up behind him and circled her hands around his waist from the back.

"Will you spend Thanksgiving with me and my family?" George was still looking outside, waiting for Cooper to make his way back to the door, holding her hands.

"George..." Stella backed up from him, pulling her hands from his. He grabbed her hand and looked at her; she shook her head. "I can't."

"Why, El? Why can't you just do this one thing for me?" His eyes were pleading with her.

"One thing?" Stella fired back at him. "It's been a string of 'one things'...I feel like I'm falling."

"Some people think that's a good thing, El. The falling..." He kissed her hand. "I think that's a good thing. Let's fall together." Seeing her shut down, he pulled her up the stairs to the front door. "Let's go."

She saw his motorcycle parked in the driveway. "Where we going?" A knot was forming in Stella's stomach.

"You'll see," George responded. Pulling her down the stairs, he lifted her up over the bike and used care in securing her helmet. Gently, he kissed her lips, then her forehead.

They headed to 95 North, Stella's legs squeezing George and her arms wrapped around his waist. The wind whipping around her helped her forget the knot in her stomach, spreading through her chest. They pulled into the National Harbor and parked easily. Stella had never been here.

George grabbed her around the waist and helped her off his bike. "Let's grab something to eat." He pulled a blanket out of one of the hard bags on the side of his bike and draped it over his shoulder. He grabbed her hand and led her over to a restaurant called Freshii where they ordered lunch to go. George never dropped her hand. Stella was headed in the direction of pure panic.

George led her to the grass that surrounded a statue called *The Awakening*. There were five pieces of metal buried in the ground that looked like a giant was attempting to escape out of the dirt. The giant's bearded face, in mid-scream, was struggling to get out of the ground.

"Wow." Stella sat on the blanket that was spread out. She set her salad down and stared at the giant. "That's what I feel like sometimes."

"Me too." George bit into his sandwich. "I think it's normal to feel like that. I mean, for me it is."

Before Stella could stop herself, she asked, "Why do you feel like this?" She pointed to the giant's face.

"Several reasons, El." He watched her open her salad and take a bite. "I used to love what I did. Now I'm stuck in a job I never wanted."

"Oh my God, this is so good." Her eyes rolled back.

George smiled, but it didn't reach his eyes. "I'm glad you like it."

She took the rubberband off her wrist and put her windblown hair into a bun. "Maybe it's normal to feel stuck and trying to get free, but can't." She looked back at the giant. "I've never really asked anyone."

"Maybe you should." George tucked an errant hair behind her ear.

"No. That leads to discussions about feelings, of which I have none." She stared at the giant, wondering how long she could continue to convince herself she was still numb. George, with his dimples and expert hands, had awakened her. She was fighting it with every ounce of her being. Numbness was all she could handle right now; anything else scared the shit out of her. "So don't ask, George."

"One day, El, one day you will trust me." George turned back to his sandwich.

Stella looked up at the sky while she lounged on the blanket. "For every piece of me that wants to let go with you, George, there is a piece that's telling me to run far from you. George, I trust you. Believe me, I trust you more than I have anyone..."

"Except Patrick and Millie?"

"Actually, I trust you about as much as Millie. I don't tell her things, either. She's okay with that, just like you are."

"And Patrick?"

"I don't have to talk to Patrick. He already knows everything."

"What does he know?" George pressed, looking out at the water.

"Don't." Stella leaned in and kissed his neck gently. "I'm having such a good day, let's just enjoy it. Why do you feel stuck in your job?"

"Because someone has to pay the bills, right? It always comes down to money, right?"

"That's true," she said slowly. "What bills?"

"My family's," he sighed. George ran a hand over his shaved head. "Someone has to buy the picnic baskets and blankets, right?"

"Your family?" she asked, perplexed.

"My mom and three sisters," he answered.

"You have three sisters, good God." *How did I not know this.*

"Right?" He smiled. "I'm the oldest and, as you know, my dad died, so someone has to take care of them."

She took another bite of food, wondering why his sisters couldn't take care of themselves. Keeping her mouth shut, she leaned back against him. Who was she to have an opinion as to what was normal?

Chapter Thirty-Six

Underwear

Stella was hunched over a handwritten claim by a prisoner, trying to decipher the meaning of the words in the complaint. According to the complaint, the prisoner was requesting five million dollars in damages due to the U.S. Marshals damaging his comb and taking his knife when the prisoner was being transported to Rikers Island. Laughing to herself, she picked up the phone on her desk and dialed Rikers Island.

Twenty minutes, later she was listening to the explanation from a prisoner of why he believed his comb and unauthorized knife was worth five million dollars. She was surprised she was able to quell the laughter until after she finally hung up.

Following up with the marshals involved in the transport, they all laughed at the absolute absurdity of the claim. She drafted an official response to the prisoner and clipped it to the file. She walked into Gary's office and knocked, leaning against the doorframe.

"Hey, Gary, I got my favorite claim so far."

"Oh yeah, will it make for interesting reading?" Gary looked up from his computer and turned his chair to face her.

"Prisoner property is worth much more than I thought. Did you know that damage to a comb and an illegal knife is worth five million dollars?"

"No shit," he replied.

"No shit."

"Come sit down, chat." He nodded toward the chair across from his desk. "How's school?"

"Pretty good; I've got a couple of cool classes and no finals this semester. Although that part is exciting, I have four thirty-page papers to research and write, so I need to get started with that." Gary and Stella had bonded over the past couple of months since she was the only intern that stayed past the summer and they'd worked closely together three days a week.

"I bet."

"The job search is stressful; I really need to get a job lined up."

"I'm sorry we don't have any openings here for you, Stella, I'd love for you to work with us." Gary smoothed his mustache and looked at her pensively. "If you need any references, just let me know and I can get all the attorneys you worked with to volunteer. Wherever you end up will be lucky to have you."

"I really appreciate it, Gary." Stella stood up. "Enjoy reading that disposition, it's awesome."

"See you Thursday." Gary turned back to his computer.

Stella turned and walked back to her office to grab her bag when her phone rang. It was Millie. "What up?"

Millie began talking a mile a minute about being on Capitol Hill for hearings and seeing some famous comedian testifying before Congress on immigration reform. They talked and laughed as Stella walked to the Metro and rode the few stops home.

She pulled on her knee-high brown leather boots and stood up, inspecting herself. Her deep emerald green sweater dress only reached her mid-thighs, but shit, her boots went all the way up to her knees, she thought as she looked in the mirror. She marched upstairs and grabbed a beer. "Damn Billy, aren't you ready to go?" she asked in between sips.

Billy was at his typical place, the couch with a controller in his hand. "Of course, just waiting on your slow ass." He looked up. "Now go put some pants on and we'll go." He laughed.

"Shut up. It's a dress," she said, tugging at the hem of her dress.

"It looks like a shirt to me, but I'm not complaining." He paused his game, "Hey, can you grab me a Corona? They're in the bottom drawer of the fridge."

She stalked over to the fridge and leaned down to open the drawer; only veggies were in there. When she looked up, he was staring.

"Are you wearing underwear?" he asked.

"You fucker! Yes." She turned to go downstairs. "Point taken."

When she came back up, she had a grey dress on that wasn't much longer than the green one, but Billy didn't give her a hard time about it. They walked to the bar together where they were meeting Millie and Patrick.

Once they entered the bar Stella headed to their usual seats. She leaned over the bar and gave George a big hug.

"It's good to see you too, love." He winked at Millie and nodded at Patrick and Billy.

Millie pulled at the bottom of Stella's dress and chastised, "I knew I wanted to see your ass tonight, thank you."

"You know you like it," Stella retorted, pulling the hem down on her dress. Hanging her bag on one of the hooks under the bar, she sat on the barstool and crossed her legs demurely.

"I did, so did the entire bar."

Stella turned and saw many people staring at her. She hopped down from the stool and bowed, she got a few claps. When she straightened up, she saw Mr. Erickson. *Shit.* She needed to not act crazy tonight or maybe take the party somewhere else.

Millie saw the change in Stella's face. "What's up?" She followed Stella's eyes and then asked, "Wait, is that the guy from the FOIA office you were telling me about?"

"That's the one," she said, sitting down and yelling, "Yo, barkeep." George was filling orders on the other side of the bar so Hazel came over. "The regular for the crew?" She smiled.

"Sure." Stella looked back at Patrick; he nodded, looking back to where Mr. Erickson sat with a few friends.

They stayed and drank for hours. When 2:00 a.m. rolled around George came from around the bar and fingered her collarbone, pushing her cowlneck down a little and placing a gentle kiss on it. Feeling the kiss all over her body, she gazed back to where Mr. Erikson had been sitting. She pushed out the breath she was holding. The table was empty.

"Can I come over tonight?" George whispered in her ear; just feeling the heat on her ear and neck was about to send her over the edge. "I have to close so just stay up for me please, it will be a little while. Can I shower at your place?"

No. That sounds too much like a boyfriend. "Sure," she whispered. "You know I'm going to confiscate my key from you at some point, right?"

He frowned. "I know." He threw the towel on the bar in front of Mille and stalked off.

"Oops." Stella hopped off the barstool and followed George to the back of the bar. "George?"

"El, you shouldn't be back here." He frowned and then put his arms around her. "I think you should let me keep your key. You never know when you're going to need something." He smiled mischievously. He smelled of beer and sweat, yet she was oddly turned on. He leaned into her hair, inhaling.

Ignoring his last comment, Stella commented, "There's hardly anyone here. You won't tell, will you, Hazel?" Hazel didn't respond, but walked to the other end of the bar.

"What's her problem?" Stella put her hands on her hips. She'd been very careful about the amount of alcohol she consumed tonight. She was pleasantly buzzed, but not drunk, just right for a good time with George later.

"Don't worry about her." He moved Stella against the corner of the bar where he was blocking anyone's view into what they were doing. His wide shoulders towered over her and he leaned down as he pushed her against the wall.

She gasped, "George?" It came out as a question. She felt his hand go up her thighs until he reached her underwear and he quickly pulled it off her, ripping it on both sides. "Oh, fuck." Her entire body felt like it was on fire.

"I'll buy you new ones," he growled. "Don't fall asleep."

"How long will you be?" she whispered, trying to get her wits about her.

"I'm not sure, but I want you in that dress so that I can take it off you." He shoved her underwear into his pocket.

As she started to leave, he pushed her back and dragged a finger across her collarbone. "Oh shit, George, so not fair." Her head fell back and he kissed her exposed neck.

"Not trying to be fair, El." He moved towards the bar and starting cleaning up, not giving her another glance. She leaned her head back against the wall.

Millie came out from the bathroom and saw her standing there. "You ready, El?"

"I'm not sure I can walk."

"You aren't even drunk yet." Millie then saw El's gaze at George. "Ah, George strikes again, huh?" Millie pulled Stella's arm and walked her back to the bar where Billy and Patrick were talking to a couple of regulars about the Redskins. "I like George."

"Me too," Stella said.

Chapter Thirty-Seven

Someone

It was 4:30 a.m. when she finally gave up on George. She nudged Cooper off the couch and they both made their way downstairs to her room. She fell into the bed and tossed and turned for the rest of the night.

Footsteps upstairs woke her up at 9:00 a.m.; she cringed at the lack of sleep and then looked at Cooper, who didn't even pretend to lift his head. "Me too." She pulled her earbuds out from her bag and put them in her ears. Drifting back to sleep with the Avett Brothers singing in her ears, she attempted to clear her mind of any thoughts of George.

Patrick shook her awake around 11:00, pulling out a bud. "You getting up today?" He sat down and raised his eyebrows. "Why did you sleep in your dress?"

"Too many questions for right now," she said and looked at the clock. "Shit, is it really 11:00?"

"Yep. You going with me to work out?"

She reached out and saw she had a couple of texts from George on her phone. "Hold on..." She looked through them. No apology, just wanting her to meet him at Cosi for lunch. "I think I'll run outside later with Coop."

"Okay, what you got going on for later?" He pushed himself off her bed and rubbed Cooper between the ears.

"Nothing, why?" She stretched her legs and arms in opposite directions as she yawned. "I got tons of shit to read tomorrow, but not doing any work tonight."

"Let's grab dinner." He turned to walk out of her room.

"Okay, Billy coming, too?"

"Ask him. He's still sleeping, the lazy bum."

"Okay." She got up and started moving towards the shower. "Hey, Patrick!" she called.

"Yo," he answered on his way up the stairs.

"George didn't show last night." Walking into her bathroom, she took off her dress; she was still missing her panties.

"I know."

She heard him turn the corner of the stairs and walk through the kitchen, leaving her with her thoughts. George had weaseled his way into her life when she wasn't paying attention. *Damn it, I know better.* The water was hot, very hot, and she let it get hotter to scald all thoughts of being pissed off at George. *He isn't my boyfriend, I don't get to be mad at him. Right?* One of her pet peeves was people saying they were going to do something and then not doing it.

She needed to clear her head. George was her friend; she liked George. George was awesome in the sack and welcome in her bed. They had agreed eight months ago they were only sleeping with each other. She didn't want to share him. *Wait, what? Oh. Fuck.* Thinking back on the last eight months, they did everything couples did except during the day. She really didn't know that much about him. She knew what he liked her to do to him in bed. He was pretty funny, he was a journalist for a while before he got a job at the bar to "pay the bills." She knew he missed his old job. He liked Guy Ritchie movies and comedies. He loved the Steelers and Guinness. She was pretty sure that was all she knew about him.

Postponing the inevitable, she took care in straightening her hair and applying makeup. Before she pulled on her T-shirt, she examined her tattoo, trying to get back to where she was comfortable emotionally. When she finished getting ready, she began the walk to lunch with George. Maybe he would have something enlightening to say; they hardly ever saw each other during the day.

George was sitting in a back corner booth. When she walked in, his breath hitched. She was gorgeous. He loved everything about her. She was hard, though. He'd never dealt with someone so fucked up. She smiled when she saw him and then she gestured she was going to order. He trotted over to her.

"Hey." He leaned down to kiss her cheek and she surprised him by turning and giving him a full-on kiss, parting his lips with hers.

"Hi." Her skin was flushed from the walk and she'd cleared her head.

"Wow, a guy could get used to that," he said as he stared at the menu without seeing it.

"What did you expect, taking a girl's panties like you did last night and then neglecting to follow up?" She hit him with her hip, taking a humorous tone. "Whatcha ordering?"

"My usual," he said and nodded at the guy behind the counter.

"Hey man, usual?" The guy behind the counter was already making it; George smiled.

"Thanks, man."

"What can I get for your friend here?" The guy asked, not looking at Stella. She didn't recognize him from her time working at Cosi, so he must be new.

"El, let me guess. Please?" He took a step forward and explained to the guy behind the counter, "She thinks she should order a salad because she drank last night, but she's debating between the fire-roasted veggie sandwich and the turkey and brie because she's IN LOVE with the bread here. I think she'll go with the turkey and brie." He looked at her.

"Well, don't you just know everything?" She smiled and said, "Turkey and brie sounds perfect."

As they walked down to the counter, George pulled money out and so did Stella.

"El, let me pay."

"You don't have to." She was smiling, but her stomach showed her true emotions. She was queasy.

He swatted at her wallet. "I know. I want to at least take to you lunch. Okay?"

"Okay," she whispered.

"Do you want a cookie?" he asked.

She smiled at the memory. "No, thank you."

After comfortable small talk during lunch, Stella had learned more about George. His favorite color was red. He was an independent, politically speaking. He actively hated both parties, which Stella loved about him. He read constantly, especially when he wasn't working. He worked all the time and right now was exhausted.

"How long have you been up?"

"Never made it to sleep last night," he sighed.

OH. "Oh," she said and leaned back in her chair consciously aware of how close their bodies had been, walls starting to come up. "So why did you want me to meet you here, George? This really isn't like you."

"You know a couple of months ago we said that if we met anyone that we would let the other know so that we wouldn't hurt the other person?" he asked, staring intently at his coffee mug.

"I seem to recall that conversation." Stella felt a shift in her brain, putting things in place that George had been able to puncture. *Walls in place, that was quick.* She had just taken them down a few hours ago. "As I recall, though, it was about eight months ago."

He looked up at her. "I know. The thing is, I met someone and I want to see where it goes."

She scraped her chair back, making a loud screeching noise, and rose quickly. "Okay. Good luck, George." She turned and ran out of the restaurant. *She was so stupid, so STUPID.* She turned and walked as fast as she could toward her house. As she walked, she thought about last night; that was a quick departure from him ripping her panties off.

"El!" George jogged to catch up with her. "El, wait."

She stopped without turning around and waited for him. She felt his hand on her neck first, heat blazing through her body. Then he held her there with one arm and put his left palm on her left shoulder blade and she froze.

"Why are you running?"

"Shouldn't matter to you," she whispered leaning into his hand, cherishing this last bit of contact.

Leaning down, he kissed her neck, "you don't want me?"

She whispered back, "Yes, I do." Then she began walking again. She wasn't crying. She stopped and said, "You know, George, I read somewhere that everything that comes together falls apart. That's pretty fucking accurate." *I fall apart, you walk away.*

She didn't turn around, but walked slowly away from him, daring him to come after her. He didn't.

CHAPTER THIRTY-EIGHT

Thanks

She walked halfway home before she sat down on a bench, dazed. Stella was shocked by the quick turn of events from last night at Finnegan's to now, but not surprised that George had ended things. It surprised her they had lasted this long. He wanted things she just couldn't give him. She pulled out her cell phone and called Millie.

"Hey, sister, what's up?" Millie answered.

"Pretty shitty night/day, sister, pretty shitty."

"I thought George was coming over."

"Me too. He stood me up and then invited me to lunch just now to tell me he was seeing someone."

"Oh, sweetie. I'm coming over now."

"No, don't do that."

"Your protests don't work on me. I'll see you in thirty." With that, Millie hung up.

Stella looked down at the phone and saw the picture that was her wallpaper. *Her and Jamie. Always her and Jamie. This was nothing, George wasn't important. He'd gotten a foot in the door, but nothing a little chocolate and a lot of alcohol wouldn't cure.*

"Okay," she said out loud and that was that. In her mind, she made a little box for George as if he were just some name on a list of people that didn't matter, put him in the box, and started walking the rest of the way home.

Millie, Billy, Patrick, and Stella stayed up half the night drinking, cussing the opposite sex and talking. By Sunday morning, Stella was feeling a little better. She was stunned Patrick had slept later than her. She opened the door to his room to harass him and her eyes grew as big as saucers as she took in the still-sleeping, tangled, naked bodies of Millie and Patrick. *HOLY SHIT! WHEN DID THIS HAPPEN?* She tried to be quiet as she shut the door and walked through the house in a daze.

Billy was outside, tinkering with his bike, and saw her expression when she came outside. "Oh, you saw that, huh?" He looked down with a smile, "At least one of us is still getting laid."

"Um… What the fuck? I don't even know what to say."

"I think I would pretend I didn't see that." Billy kneeled to see something on the chain of his bike.

"Oh, like I can control myself that much," Stella laughed. "This weekend has sucked all emotion out of my body. I'm going to lift weights and kick the shit out of things."

After her shower, Stella heard footfalls making their way to her room. Grabbing a robe, she peered around the corner. A very exhausted, but happy Millie appeared in her room. Stella's smile gave away her knowledge and Millie glanced toward Patrick's room. "You always get what you want?"

"Pretty much," Millie laughed and sat on Stella's bed.

Stella pulled on jeans and a sweater, and then sat next to Millie on the bed. Falling back on the bed she sighed. "Well, I guess that's that."

"Which that?" Millie asked.

"George and I," Stella said, crossing her legs at the ankles.

Millie laid her head on Stella's stomach. "El, all you have to do is tell George you want him back. So, what is the problem?"

"There are many problems: (1) I don't do love; (2) I'm in law school and can't be bothered with a relationship; and (3) he's met someone else." She ticked off the reasons on her hand.

Millie brushed her reasons aside with her hand. "He's totally into you, but you kept pushing him away. No one wants to be rejected on a continuous basis."

She let what Millie said sink in; she didn't feel like she rejected George. On the contrary, she had let him in. He knew things about her and made her feel things she hadn't allowed in years.

"You love him." Millie stared straight at the ceiling.

"I guess I've never thought about it like that, Millie. I never thought what I've been doing is rejecting him. We really have been together, but

I just wanted to keep that last barrier up for some reason. It wasn't even a real barrier. He broke through that months ago." She sighed. She'd made a mess of everything.

"You love him," Millie repeated and turned her head to look into Stella's eyes. "I know you do. Go tell him."

"Uh, no. He just met someone, he wants to give it a go. I'm definitely not going to stop that."

"You should tell him." Millie smiled. "You do love him."

"Shut up and leave me alone." Stella closed her eyes. "Nothing like realizing too late."

"Well, what are you going to do?"

"Nothing."

"Seriously?" Millie's eyes went wide. "You're the most stubborn person I've ever met."

"I'm going to hunker down and finish the last bit of school. I have to get a job, then the bar." Stella got overwhelmed just thinking about it all. "I'm actually quite busy and don't have time for George."

"Only every night," Millie said playfully.

"That, I *will* miss." Stella sighed again. "You know, I think I need a new tattoo and to drink more." Stella rolled over and looked at Millie. "Thanks."

"For what?"

"For being my friend. I know I'm difficult and surly. I'm probably very hard to be friends with…thanks for everything."

"El, you're not that bad," Millie chuckled.

Stella was yelling loudly to Miranda Lambert singing about her heartbreak, quite fitting for how she was feeling. She set the pork tenderloin on the table, along with the oven-baked macaroni and cheese and roasted brussel sprouts. Opening bottles of red and white wine, she put them on the table. She turned up her own bottle of pinot noir she'd been drinking from while cooking, it was almost finished. The table was set for three. She knocked on Patrick's door. "It's ready, lovebirds."

She drank a couple of gulps of wine from the bottle and poured some into her glass before Millie emerged from Patrick's room. She smiled and smoothed her hair back.

"Looks awesome, El." Millie sat down at her seat and waited for Patrick and Stella to join her.

Patrick came out a minute later. "Happy Thanksgiving."

"Whatever, sit down and let's eat before it gets cold."

Millie held her hands out, Patrick took her hand and extended a hand to Stella. "In my house, we say what we're grateful for before we eat."

Stella took Millie's and Patrick's hands.

Patrick nodded. "I'll start. I feel so grateful for being here with two beautiful women. I'm grateful to have a great job and great friends."

Millie squeezed his hand. "I'm grateful to be spending Thanksgiving with my chosen family. I'm also grateful that I'm getting laid."

"Come on..." Stella dropped their hands and took a gulp of wine.

"How about you, El?" Patrick asked.

"I'm grateful for you both. You've made my life livable. I'm also grateful that I didn't have a heart left for George to stomp on."

"El, George stomped on something. You should really talk to him. I feel like you'll get back together." Millie took a gulp of wine.

"Maybe he stomped on my vagina and I'm pissed about it."

"Millie, leave her be." Patrick cut into his tenderloin. "This is great, El, thanks for cooking."

"No problem." Stella ate a forkful of mac and cheese.

Chapter Thirty-Nine

Gifts

tella's back arched at his touch, his fingers gently running in between her breasts, down the length of her stomach. She exhaled loudly as he touched her everywhere. Then his lips were on her, devouring her. "George," she whispered. He looked up at her and climbed up her body, kissing her neck and then jaw line. Stella closed her eyes at the pleasure. All of a sudden, she felt empty. He was missing, his body not pressing into hers. She opened her eyes and it was dark, she was alone.

Fuck, that felt real. Looking over at the clock, she realized it was only 6:00 a.m., but decided to get up anyway. She was still turned on without any relief in sight, so she pulled on her workout clothes and got Cooper's leash. "Let's go, Coop," she whispered and Cooper began his jump dance that he reserved for going for a run.

She pulled her wool cap over her earbuds and grabbed her gloves on the way out the front door. It was still dark when she left her house. She started her run, hoping to get rid of her thoughts of George. She had a final today and would study a little when she got back. Cooper ran back and forth in front of her, taking full advantage of the empty sidewalk.

When she passed Finnegan's, she glanced over to see George's motorcycle parked in front of the bar. *Weird,* but kept running. She chastised herself because she needed to be focused on her final, but her mind kept returning to George and all she had done wrong. *Could she just appreciate the experience of having him in her life and let him go?* She'd been trying, but it was harder than she initially thought. Stella picked up her pace so that it would be harder to think and she would simply have to concentrate on running and breathing. She ran down to the Torpedo Factory and turned around, running back up King Street.

She was panting when she looked up and saw him standing in the middle of the sidewalk. She would know him anywhere. George was wearing a sweater, navy pea coat, and black wool cap pulled down tightly over his head. He was smiling. Stella stopped a block back and stared, wondering if she was dreaming this. She saw his lips moving, but she couldn't hear him. Cooper started pulling her toward him.

"El..." George's cold hand brushed her cheek.

"George?" she asked, wondering why he was outside of the bar at this time in the morning.

George rubbed his thumb over her bottom lip and leaned into kiss her, she jumped back.

"George, what're you doing?" Her earbuds fell out of her ears.

"I miss you..." George put his hands in his pockets and smiled. "I've been texting you and you won't respond."

"What are you doing here...now?" Stella was still mildly confused.

"Oh, I had some stuff to do at the bar." He pointed over to the bar and then said, "I haven't been sleeping well."

"Me either," she admitted before she could stop herself.

"You want to come in for a minute or two, I could make us coffee and we could talk."

"About what? About you and your new girlfriend?" Stella shook her head. "No thanks."

"You're jealous?" George's eyes widened.

"Fuck you, George."

"We could do that too, El. Whatever you want." He smiled his 100-watt smile at her, his dimples making an unwanted entrance.

"I want to stop thinking of you," she said quietly.

"What?" George leaned in, he smelled like sandalwood.

"New perfume for your new girl?" Stella asked sarcastically.

"You like it?"

"Not really." Stella started to put her earbuds back in and George grabbed her hands.

"Come talk to me."

"You haven't really given me a good reason to." She started to move away from him. "I have a final. I don't have time to do this."

"Do what? Have coffee with a friend?"

"We're not friends, George."

"Why?" George's eyes clouded over. "We used to be."

"Well, we're not anymore." Stella pulled her hat off, realized what she must look like, and slammed it back on her head.

"What can I do to change your mind, El?"

"I don't know," she whispered. "I really don't understand why..."

"Why what? Why I want to be friends? Why I can't let you go?" His hands moved wildly expressing his frustration.

"Oh, George...you *did* let me go." Stella looked down at her shoes. Cooper was sitting in between them, wagging his tail and looking back and forth between them.

"I want you back; I didn't mean to let you go. I didn't know you would want me like I needed you to," George stammered.

"Well, you should've asked," Stella said stoically.

"I did ask, Stella."

"Not that day, you didn't." Stella pulled her cap off again. "George, I know it was my fault. I know, okay? I couldn't help it. I can't help what happened between us. What I can help is how I feel now, which is horrible, by the way. I don't blame you for leaving me. I don't blame you ... I just can't let you in again. I can't..."

"Don't be this way El, I'm sorry," George started. He took her hand and put it on his face.

Stella put her other hand on his other cheek and stood on her tiptoes and kissed him. What started out as a gentle goodbye kiss turned into a heated, open mouthed, leave-you-panting kiss. Stella pushed George back by his chest and looked at the desire in his eyes. It mirrored hers. She couldn't help but want him, but he was with someone else.

"I just want you to be happy," Stella said and rushed down the street back toward her house. *Damn, that clear-my-head run didn't turn out as expected.* He still wanted her, but she didn't know if she had it in her to fight for him or that she could bear the hurt that would be involved. Best to rip off the Band-Aid, all the pain, at one time. Then it would fade, eventually.

Stella hadn't told anyone she ran into George or that she had kissed him. Millie would make her go see him and Patrick would drive her somewhere and lock her up before he would let her see him again. She finished all her papers for the semester two weeks ago and she had been sleeping and drinking since.

Stella opened the book she'd bought for George and wrote, "When I saw this I knew you would love it. I hope you enjoy your holiday." She shut the latest book by Bob Woodward and smiled. He'd attended a function at American and she had gotten the book signed then. George was going to love it. Stella hadn't heard from him since that kiss. She put the book in her bag and slung it over her shoulder.

She was wearing a tight sweater and leggings with her gray knee-high boots under her coat and scarf. She walked down King Street headed to Finnegan's for the first time since George had ended things. Stella was driving down to Atlanta tomorrow and wouldn't be back until after Christmas. Taking a deep breath, she pushed open the big oak door to the bar. It wasn't even happy hour yet, but she knew George usually got here about 4:00. There wasn't anyone behind the bar and just one person drinking. He turned and looked at her and pointed toward the bathrooms and the office.

Walking cautiously toward the office, she knocked. George was seated at the desk and was going through documents. He looked up when she knocked and looked at her, shocked.

"Hi," Stella said.

"Hi." George rubbed his hand over his face and head, sighing.

"I didn't mean to interrupt. I...I got you something a while back and planned on giving it to you at Christmas before..." Stella pulled her bag off her shoulder and pulled out the book. "Here, Merry Christmas." She almost threw the book at him before she turned to run out.

"What?" George looked at the book and then at Stella. "You didn't have to do that, El. Thanks."

She turned halfway from the doorway. "Open it. He signed it for you."

"Wow, that's simply awesome." George stood up and walked quickly to her and wrapped her in his arms. "Thank you so much."

Stella took a few seconds to feel him and smell him, then pushed him away. "You're welcome." She started backing away.

"Can you stay for a few minutes?" George smiled. "I miss your face."

"I miss yours, too," she whispered and then shook her head and ran out. She was already two blocks away when she realized she left her bag. "Fucking hell," she said and shook her fists up at the sky, then turned and headed back.

George was standing at the bar when she re-entered. "You looking for this?" He held up her bag.

Stella nodded.

"Have a great Christmas, El." He didn't meet her eyes.

"You, too." Stella didn't even look George in the face when she grabbed her bag and headed back outside.

Well that was a disaster. Shit. When am I going to be normal around him? Stella finally acknowledged to herself that George stomped more than her vagina. *Damn it.*

Later that night, she was sitting at the Fish Market with Millie, Patrick, and Billy for their annual pre-Christmas celebration. She had many big beers and was laughing at something that Billy said when she pulled out her bag to get her money to pay for dinner. She found a small wrapped box. A piece of paper was taped to it.

El, it was great to see your face. I wish you would come around more often. I miss you. It looks like we were thinking of each other.

Love,
G

When she looked up, Millie, Patrick, and Billy had stopped talking and were staring at the box in her hands.

"Wait, didn't we agree no presents?" Billy said.

"Yes," Millie answered. "What's that, El?"

"I guess it's from George." She shrugged.

"What do you mean, you guess?" Millie probed.

"Well, earlier I left my bag in his office and when I ..."

"What?" Patrick interrupted.

"You know that book I bought him? I dropped it off today since I'm leaving tomorrow."

"Didn't we agree to a complete cut-off?"

"Patrick..." Millie chided and put her hand on his arm.

"I just wanted to give him the fucking book, Patrick. I dropped it off and left so quickly I forgot my bag. When I went to get it later, this must have been in there. I didn't notice until now."

Millie grabbed the paper from Stella. "Aw, he still loves you and he misses your face. Open it."

"Open it, El. Let's see what it is." Billy nodded at the box.

"I really just want to return it," Stella said.

"You can't return it, jackass." Millie grabbed it and opened it. "Holy fuck." She showed Patrick, whose face did a weird thing that Stella hadn't seen before.

"What? What is it?" Millie handed Stella the box and covered her mouth with her hands.

"He loves you." Millie couldn't contain her smile.

Stella looked in the box to see two big diamond earrings. "I don't understand." She looked to Billy, then Patrick and then Millie. "Why would he give me these?"

"You're a complete idiot," Millie said and crossed her arms. "Dudes don't buy presents like that for ex-hookups. They buy them for girls they LOVE. HE LOVES YOU!"

Billy took the box. "Maybe they're fake."

Stella nodded.

"Negative, this store doesn't carry fake diamonds." Millie pointed to the store's name on the box. "Oh and look at this, this is the appraisal." She opened it and smiled. "He loves you."

"Shit," Patrick said and took the appraisal, his eyebrows raised significantly.

"I don't understand." She shoved the box and appraisal into her bag. "This is why I shouldn't date. I can't deal with shit like this. Whatever, let's just pay and go."

"Put them in now," Millie demanded. "You have to...they're gorgeous and don't deserve to be in a box any longer."

"No."

"Then I refuse to move from this table." Millie crossed her arms over her chest.

"No."

"You're so fucking stubborn." Millie threw down money and stomped out of the restaurant.

CHAPTER FORTY

No Sex with the Help

She was riding the Metro to her stop when she got a call from a number she didn't recognize; she knew it wasn't George though. It was a 202, not a 703 area code.

"Hello?"

"Stella?"

"This is she." She couldn't quite place the voice. "Who is this?"

"It's Sam."

"Umm…" She didn't know any Sam. "Okay."

"Sam Erickson. Do you have a minute?"

"Sure," she said her voice a little unsure. Sam was from the FOIA office, she was surprised he followed up. She was on the part of the train that didn't have any tunnels for awhile. "I'm on the Metro, though, so if I lose you, I'll call you back later."

"Oh, I'll be quick then. How about the Fish Market Friday?"

She assessed his request. It was Thursday and she didn't want him to know she didn't really have any plans. "I can't tomorrow, Sam. What about Sunday?"

"Okay, I'll meet you there at 7:00."

"Okay. Should I eat beforehand?" she smiled.

"No," he laughed. "I plan on feeding you."

"See you then." She hung up and leaned her head back against the seat. Just one dinner, that was it.

She was having a hard time deciding what to wear on her date with Sam. He was older, an established attorney in the Department of Justice; she didn't need to appear slutty. She was wearing a black strapless top, jeans and a gray cardigan with black, high-heeled boots.

"What do you think?" she asked, twirling around for her two male roommates.

"I'd do you!" Billy called.

"Me too," Patrick agreed.

"I mean, is it too tight, too juvenile? What?"

Patrick paused the video game. "You look fine, El. You don't even like this guy do, you?"

"You're right, why do I even care?" She grabbed her purse and keys and headed out the door.

"I expect to see you in less than two hours, missy," Billy laughed as she shut the door.

When she finally found a parking spot, it was a couple of blocks away from the restaurant. She turned the corner and saw Sam was waiting for her outside. "Hey," she waved, walking toward him.

He was wearing a cornflower-blue sweater that showed off his blue eyes in contrast to his fair skin and hair. He turned and smiled in her direction, said something into his phone, and put it back in his pocket.

"Hi, yourself. You look great."

"Thanks," she said, "you don't look half bad out of a suit." She blushed. "I mean in casual clothes."

He put his arm out, letting her go first into the restaurant, then followed her in to the portion of the restaurant with the bar. It was a friendly, loud restaurant with great seafood.

They ordered and started talking casually about work. She listened to his journey that ended with his current position at DOJ. He'd moved up the ranks quickly.

"Can I ask a question?" She leaned toward him over their dinner, she'd already had two big beers. "How old are you?"

"I'm thirty-six. How about you?" He leaned in closer, too.

"Twenty-six," she answered. "Do you like yours?" She pointed at his plate of fried seafood.

"It's what I always get. I'm weird like that, I get hooked on one thing and that's it for me."

She laughed, "Me too. I've been eating the seafood bake for four years."

"Four years?" He cocked his head to the side, "I thought this was your third year of law school."

She almost choked. "It is."

"You were here a year before you started school. What did you do before?"

"I worked at a restaurant up the street," she answered vaguely.

"Why did you decide to take a year off between undergrad and law school?" he asked innocently, popping a fry in his mouth.

She had answered all these questions before and usually just made up an answer. She sighed. "My fiancé died a few weeks before I was supposed to start law school and I deferred for a year." Stella was proud she had said it without tears.

"Fuck, sorry." Sam looked down at his food.

"Thanks. Shit happens, right?" She took another bite of her fish and smiled weakly.

As they were leaving the restaurant, Sam put his hand on her lower back to lead her out. She'd decided she was just going to leave her car and walk home; she'd one too many big beers too drive.

"Okay, well, I'm going head home. Thank you so much for dinner. I enjoyed it." She actually meant it, it was a pleasant dinner.

"Why don't we stop in Finnegan's and have one more before we head home?" he suggested.

"Why not? It's on my way home." She knew Sundays were the only day that George took off from the bar, so she felt safe going there.

Sam opened the door for her and guided her in by the small of her back. Stella shrank into herself as she glanced over to the bar and saw George. *Why was he there?* He always had Sundays off. She followed Sam over to the table he usually occupied with his friends. *SHIT. What I am going to do?*

Once they made it to the table, she excused herself and made it to the bathroom. Rushing into the stall, she pulled out her phone. "Patrick, can you come pick me up in about ten minutes right in front of Fish Market?"

He responded and she could tell she was interrupting something; he sounded really annoyed.

"Okay, just listen. I drank too much at dinner then we walked over to Finnegan's... oh never mind, I'll walk home." She heard someone come in the bathroom; she whispered in the phone, "He's never here on Sundays. I didn't know he would be here." She hung up the phone and pushed open to the stall door to see Hazel leaning against the wall. "Shit," she murmured under her breath. Putting a smile on her face, she said, "Hey, Hazel."

"You're really something, you know." Hazel frowned at her. "You come into his bar and you're hurt to see him." She almost hissed at her.

"Hazel, I didn't think he would be here. This is none of your business. It's between us or actually, there's nothing between us." She lowered her head and shook it as she tried to push past Hazel.

Hazel wouldn't let her by. "Stella. Do not come back here again."

"You got it." Stella finally made her way around Hazel and pushed the door open. Looking toward where Sam was sitting, she froze as she saw George leaving the table.

Pasting a fake smile on her face, she made way to Sam. She sat down and took a long pull of her Snakebite. She felt better. This had been a mistake; she was leaving.

"Hey, you okay?" Sam reached over and pushed her bangs out of her eyes.

"Oh, sure. What was George doing over here?" Stella recoiled from his casual touch.

Sam looked around and said, "George?" Then a smile broke out on his face. "Shit, Stella, George... that's the name he gives all the girls he wants to get in their panties." The last word died on his lips. "You've known him for awhile, though, you still call him George?"

"Yep, that's not his real name?" She stared at her drink, rage filling her up inside.

"Well, he must've given you that name years ago. He's been in love with this chick for awhile; broke his heart recently, though." Sam took a drink of his beer.

"I had no idea," she whispered and took a look to the bar to see George staring at her with murder in his eyes. She was confused. Stella twisted the diamond earring in her right ear.

"You know he owns this place, right?"

"No, I don't really know him at all." She saw movement out of the corner of her eye and all the stress released. "Listen, my roommates threatened to come find me if I wasn't home in two hours and I guess they made good on that threat. They're by the bar."

"Where?"

She pointed. "The two dudes by the bar. Patrick and Billy, my best friends." She stood up draining the last of her drink. "Thanks so much dinner and drinks. I've enjoyed your company."

He stood up and met her gaze. "I hope we can do it again, Stella."

"Call me," she said and turned to leave. "Thanks again."

"No problem." Sam followed her toward the door, but then took a seat at the bar for another drink.

When she reached Patrick, she realized he was staring at George, or whatever the fuck his name was, in a way that scared her. He put his arm around her shoulders and led her out. Billy walked out backwards, giving Sam the evil eye.

Once she settled into the backseat of Patrick's car, she let loose. "Am I a huge dumbass or what? First, I fuck someone for nine months and didn't even know his real name or that he owned the bar that I drank at for over three years. Then come to find out that he was in love with someone else the entire time anyway. HOLY SHIT. What a mess."

"Well you've totally fucked up our watering hole," Billy said. "Next time we find a bar, no fucking the help."

Chapter Forty-One

A Difference

Stella was sitting on a blanket where she and George had sat over six months ago. She felt comfortable with the sculpture of the giant trying to get out of the ground. She spread her books out and was reading for International Law and Policy class. They had to write a paper as their entire grade and she was trying to determine what she was to write about. Closing her book, she laid back and stared up at the cloudless sky. She attempted to talk herself into feeling numb, she was tired of this newfound pain in her chest that George's absence created. She kept her head down and was thankful for work and school keeping her so busy. After Jamie died, she had welcomed the numbness into her world, it had kept her moving forward even though she really didn't enjoy anything. It cut her off from all her old friends and even her parents. The numbness was stubbornly staying away this time. George had punched a huge, gaping hole in her wall and all the numbness was gone. Now she was all feelings. It was really annoying and puzzling. He continued to text, call her, and leave messages, which just messed with her head. Sometimes she responded, but mostly she didn't. She was still so puzzled by the earrings he gave her, she had sent him an actual letter thanking him. She wore the earrings every day. When she thought of him, she twisted the earrings in her ear.

She dreamed of him every night and thought of him at least thirty times a day. Patrick and Millie were disgustingly cute together and she wanted to vomit on a regular basis. She started reading fiction books again to occupy her mind when she wasn't at work or school. She and Billy hung out more, watching late-night TV since Millie and Patrick were otherwise occupied. She was trying to figure out which bar exam to sit for, since she didn't have a job yet. Every state had its own bar that governed whether an attorney can practice in the state. Because attorneys could waive into DC from any other state, she signed up for the Virginia bar. It would be hellish and she hoped she could pass it.

Davis just got a job in one of the biggest firms in the country. It was so unfair, he didn't even want the job. He went to law school because he didn't know what else to do. Millie had already gotten a job with the Department of Education. It would be a pretty interesting job, policies and legal compliance for school districts in the entire country. She would also be covering legislative affairs in Congress.

Stella was starting to have a pit in her stomach because everyone was getting these kick-ass jobs and she had nothing. She wished she could blink her eyes and have already passed the bar, but she had a couple of months until graduation. The stress of not having a job was starting to outweigh her emotions of losing George, so she guessed that was something.

She parallel parked and walked to the other side of her car, opening the passenger side to let Cooper out. It was the middle of the week so the festival wouldn't be as busy, but she walked with Cooper over to the Tidal Basin and sat on the bench staring out into the water. The cherry blossom trees framed the entire area with their pink and white petals. She closed her eyes and Cooper put his head on her knee, nudging her hand to pet him. This time last year she and George were having a picnic. He'd read to her while she ate and drank; it was perfect. She'd fucked everything up, like she'd done continuously over the last couple of years.

A petal floated across her gaze and landed on Cooper; she brushed it off and held it between her fingers. Stella let herself simmer in self-pity for a few more minutes, then she stood, shook it all off, and started her run to the Capitol. She was going to run the stairs a couple of times, too.

Timing her steps up and down the stairs of the Capitol to the Foo Fighters, she finished her third set in record time. Sweat dripped off every part of her body. She sat on the bottom stair and opened her water. When Cooper sat next to her, his head was even with hers. Taking a sip of water, she poured some for Cooper, too. Cooper was the longest constant in her life; he was her best friend. He knew everything about her and loved her anyway. His love never wavered, it didn't matter if they didn't run or he didn't get treats, every day when she came home it was like she was the best thing on Earth. It was glaring that she wasn't the best thing on Earth, but all Cooper cared about was that she was there and he could sleep with her. George hadn't cared if Cooper had slept on the bed between them. Jamie would've never allowed that.

"Come, Coop," she said, walking toward her car.

She cringed inwardly as she realized it was becoming the season she hated in DC, tourist season. Once spring rolled around, tourists were everywhere, they didn't know how to ride the Metro, to stay to the right on escalators and clogged up the Mall area. She usually stayed out of this area after April.

She cursed when she saw the traffic leading out to the GW Parkway. It was going to take her forever to get home.

An hour and a half later, she opened the door to their house. Billy and Patrick were sitting in the den eating dinner. "Yo," she said, throwing Cooper's leash on the floor.

"Where've you been?" Billy asked, scooping a spoonful of pasta into his mouth. "Patrick's been worried."

Stella looked from Billy to Patrick, "I fucking hate tourists. It took me and hour to go like five miles because of the Cherry Blossom Festival."

"Why would you subject yourself to that?" Patrick asked.

"Just wanted to look at the blossoms." Stella slumped on the couch. Cooper was splayed on the floor, panting.

"Well..." Billy asked.

"What?"

"Were they worth the hour and a half drive?"

"No," she answered.

CHAPTER FORTY-TWO

Where There's a Will

S he looked over to right field, where the fielder was talking on her cell phone and drinking a beer. Smiling, she hit the ball directly at the fielder and ran all the way to third base, while the woman ran after the ball with her beer in one hand and her phone in the other. Everyone on her team cheered; she knocked in two runs. The U.S. Marshals were now ahead of the DOJ, FOIA office. She smiled as she bent over, putting her hands on her knees for a minute before turning to give their thirdbase coach a high-five. He was one of the attorneys in her office at the Marshals service.

"Nice work Stella," Gary, the head of the interns, called from the bench. He was also the coach of the softball team for the Marshals. All the departments of the government had softball teams and they played each other on the fields located at the Mall. Their game today was in the shadow of the Washington Monument.

"Thanks," she smiled. She loved softball and was excited that she could continue to play after college. Even if it was a slow pitch, beer-drinking league. Sam was the third-baseman for FOIA. Playing softball with adults was fun and frustrating at the same time. Stella had been playing some sort of softball since she was six, when her dad starting playing catch with her in their front yard. The people that played didn't take the game seriously enough for her.

"Good hit, Killer," Sam laughed. He walked over to the base where she stood. "How you been?"

"I've had worse days." She smiled back at him. She ran at the crack of the bat, scoring the winning run for the Marshals. After the game, both teams headed over to a bar south of the Capitol. She ended up sitting in a booth with a couple of the interns. They were chatting about what they had lined up after graduation and she, again, got the feeling of dread. Stella had been sending out resumes and applying to jobs, but nothing had panned out so far.

Sam leaned in from the booth behind theirs. "What about you, Stella? What are you going to be doing after graduation?"

"Taking the bar," she said and took a long pull of her margarita.

"You haven't lined up a job yet?" Sam was looking at her intently.

"Not for lack of trying, Sam." She smiled feebly.

"Well, let's do lunch this week; I may be able to help with that." Sam winked at her and then turned back to his table.

"Thanks," Stella said to his back. As they were all leaving the bar, Sam caught up with her. His cleats were making a clicking-grinding sound as he hurried to catch up with her.

"You want a ride?" Sam jiggled his keys at her and pointed toward his car.

Feeling like it would be rude to say no, Stella smiled. "I don't want you to go out of your way."

"I live down that way, too. It's really no problem."

"Okay, sure. Thanks so much."

They walked over to his car in comfortable silence. Self-conscious about being so sweaty in his car, she pulled her shorts down as low as they could go on her hips. He didn't seem to mind getting in his car with his cleats still on. She followed his lead.

"So, you must've played softball before to be such a good place-hitter." Sam pulled onto the road and headed toward GW Parkway.

"Yep, I've played since I was six." Taking in the memorials on the way toward Virginia, she took a deep breath. She loved DC at night; all the monuments lit up were almost breathtaking.

"Let's grab one more drink before I drive you home." He looked at her quickly as they drove through Crystal City.

"Oh, I wish I could, Sam, but I have so much reading to do for school." Stella counted the lights they passed and looked longingly at the shortcut to her house as they passed it. She was beginning to feel uncomfortable.

"Come on, Stella, one drink. You forget I went to law school, too. I know your third year all you do is write papers at the end of the semester. We can talk about possible jobs."

"Okay...one drink." Her heart sank as he parallel parked in front of Finnegan's right behind George's motorcycle. She drew in a huge breath and steeled herself to play this right.

"So, I haven't seen you around here lately." Sam popped open his car door and quickly crossed the street.

"My friend's boyfriend just opened a bar and we've been over there a bunch," she lied easily, "Nothing like free beer."

"Oh." Sam opened the door for her and she walked through, scanning the room, her eyes locking on those grey-green eyes she loved so much. Her stomach flipped a dozen times. "Let's sit at the bar," Sam said as he put his hand on her back to guide her.

"I'd rather sit at a table if you're going to tell me how I can get a job..." Stella objected.

"Stella, we're only staying for a drink. I don't want to mess a table up." Sam nodded at George and then smiled. "Hey, Will. Can I get a Guinness? Stella, what do you want?"

Her eyes never left George's; it was the first time she'd heard anyone call him Will. "A Snakebite please."

George's eyes were full of many things, anger, concern, and one she couldn't quite figure out. "Hi, Stella," George said stiffly.

"Hi." She didn't know what to call him and broke off eye contact with him. He looked good; his hair was a bit longer than usual and he was wearing a red, short-sleeve, v-neck t-shirt that showed off his biceps.

"Coming right up, Sam." George moved down the bar and began making their drinks, his eyes pinning her to her seat.

Stella felt like she couldn't breathe. "I'm going to run to the restroom." Sliding off the barstool, she willed herself to walk the distance to the restroom without running. She pushed the door open and stood against the cool wall instead the stall. Taking several big gulps of air, she convinced herself she was fine. "Okay, not a big deal. He's not even an ex-boyfriend." Returning to her seat just as George was putting their glasses down, she avoided his stare and looked at Sam.

"So, I have a friend at the GC's office of the FBI. I know someone's leaving in a couple of months and I think if you can get me your resume I may be able to get you the job over there." Sam lifted his glass and seemingly inspected it.

Stella was baffled. "Really? That'd be so great; I can't tell you how stressed I am about not having a job."

Carefully sitting his glass down, he looked into her eyes. "Look, I like you. You seem like a pretty bright person. Plus, I know you must be a good person if Will is so taken with you." He looked over at George and nodded.

"What do you mean?" Stella was baffled again.

"I don't know what happened with you two, but I know he's broken up because of you."

Stella began shaking her head. "No. It's not me. Believe me, he made it clear what he wanted."

"Stella. Trust me, the man is in deep. I'm willing to help you out as a favor to him."

Tracing the cracks in the bar, she spoke slowly. "Sam. I really appreciate your help, but I'm afraid you have me mixed up with someone else."

Sam laughed and shook his head. "Okay then, I'll forward your resume anyway." He waved George over. "Will, how's it going?"

George smiled and looked at Stella as he answered, "Can't complain."

"I was just asking Stella here why she hasn't been around lately. Do you know that her friend's boyfriend just opened a bar? She dumped you for free drinks." Sam looked from George to Stella. "I gotta hit the head. I'll be back."

Stella concentrated on her drink.

"Stella, it's good to see you." George leaned on his forearms on the bar making his face just inches from hers. "I've missed your face."

"You too," she answered, flustered; that didn't even make sense. He grabbed her hand and kissed it.

"I need to see you more often, Stella." He kept using "Stella" like it was stab against her.

"I don't think that's a good idea for me."

The next night, she declined going out and was lounging on the couch watching a really bad reality show. Her dad had told her about the show about some redneck men in Louisiana who had made millions from making duck calls. She had to admit it was pretty funny.

Earlier in the night, she had poured her entire bottle of red wine into a tumbler and had been sipping the wine for the last hour from a straw stuck into the glass so she wouldn't have to sit up to drink. Stella finished her large glass of wine and she closed her eyes. Seeing George the night before had bothered her more than she was going to let anyone know. She couldn't understand why she still acted like an idiot around the fucker. He was a liar.

There was no reason for him to have lied to her. He was getting laid with no strings. Isn't that what all men wanted, to be fucked without having to do all the relationship-type things? Apparently, that wasn't enough for George, he still lied about everything. She was more confused than ever. Sam had acted like George cared about her, but she knew that he was seeing someone else. It was all so bewildering.

CHAPTER FORTY-THREE

Your Story

Stella put her Metro card through the turnstile and walked to the platform to wait on her train. She was busy with school and work and had been on about fifteen different interviews, but still hadn't landed a job. Getting rejected for jobs was becoming her least favorite hobby. Her phone rang as she was stepped on the train. It was a DC number that she didn't recognize.

"May I speak to Stella Murphy, please?" a gruff male voice demanded on the other end.

"This is she." She moved through the train until she found a seat.

"This is Stan, from the GC's office for FBI. I wanted to let you know you got the job. Congratulations."

A weight the size of a Mack truck lifted off Stella and she smiled a genuine smile. "Thank you so much."

"We'll be sending you all the paperwork via email. You start the week after the bar exam. See you then." Stan hung up.

She smiled as she remembered Stan from her first interview with the FBI. He was older and during her interview he had offered her cashews, joked about his office without a window, and made her feel less stupid than most attorneys. Stan's sense of humor was evident at their first interview. He didn't take himself too seriously, even though he was serious. Stan wouldn't sugarcoat anything and she knew she would gain invaluable experience from him. He would be her immediate supervisor and until she got her results, everything she did would be under his name. Initially, she would be doing research projects and responding to claims for damage to personal property under the Federal Torts Claims Act, which was the same thing she did for the Marshals.

Stella fist-pumped for getting a job and closed her eyes the rest of the ride, listened to Ben Harper, and enjoyed the weightless feeling of having a job.

I haven't seen you in awhile, y'all coming by the bar tonight

No

Why are you avoiding me

busy

Come on

Stella threw her phone across the room and blew her bangs out of her eyes. George had left her alone for awhile, but had been texting and calling her daily since her visit to the bar with Sam. At first she was just ignoring him, but decided that was really rude. Closing her eyes, she pictured him naked and asleep in her bed.

Instead of going to Finnegan's like they had every Friday for years, she'd been making everyone go to a different bar down the street. It was fine, but it wasn't Finnegan's. It lacked character; it lacked George. She rolled onto the floor from her low platform bed and did ten pushups for thinking about naked George.

She looked up when she heard a creak on the stairs leading to her room.

"George, huh?" Millie was smiling at her doing pushups.

"Of course." She put herself in child's pose before sitting on her knees and looking at Millie.

"Have you seen him recently?"

"Just when Sam took me to Finnegan's a few weeks ago. I was so annoyed."

"You know I like George. I think you should talk."

"No way," Stella sat with her legs crossed, looking up at Millie. "Being rejected from a relationship that I didn't even know I allowed myself to be in was tough enough. He got tired of me shutting him out. I understand that. I don't even want to open that door in any way again. It's only one-nighters from now on... I've decided."

"That's a great idea," Millie said sarcastically. "Why can't y'all be friends?"

"Because I don't want to be friends with George. That never works for anyone; one person always ends up falling in love and being devastated in that situation. Haven't you seen any romantic comedies?" Stella turned down her music. "Look, I just know that I opened up a little and totally fucked up. So I'll go back to not dating *or* fucking the same person on a routine basis."

"You're so stupid, Stella." Millie came and sat down next to her. "You and George had something real, you know; something to fight for, instead of fighting, you bowed out. The first mention of someone else and you said go ahead. SO STUPID."

"I never said I wasn't stupid." She picked at her sweater. "He's a great guy. He deserves to be happy. I can't make him happy."

"You could..." Millie looked at Stella, "You just have to try, El. Why won't you try?"

"I simply don't have it in me, Millie. I'm not the girl who gets the guy. The guy dies in my story. The girl is alone."

"Fuck that, El; change your story. Only you can do that." She got up. "I'm going to change my story now in Patrick's room."

"Ewwwwwwwwwwwwww, gross! You keep that story to yourself." Stella laughed and threw a pillow at Millie. Her phone beeped again as she received a text message.

"You're more than capable of rewriting your story, El. You just have to do it."

CHAPTER FORTY-FOUR

Messing With My Heart

She lay on the chair in the tattoo parlor with her sports bra on so that Richard could ink her back. Stella had been sitting there for about an hour already and needed to get up and stretch. She turned her head to the side. "Richard, I need a break."

"Alright, I'll get a smoke quick. Be back here in three minutes."

Stella lifted her torso off the chair and stretched her back and arms. She was sweating from having been pressed into the plastic chair for an hour with the pain of needles in her skin.

"Oh, that is going to be sweet, Stella." Cory examined her almost-done tattoo. "I love the script you picked."

"Thanks." She tried to turn and get a glance of it in the mirror. Cory grabbed her and held her still.

"You know Richard will kill you if you look before it's done."

She smiled and then nodded. "How's Patrick? He hasn't been in a while."

"He's good. Been busy with work and other shit." She bent over at the waist and hung the torso portion of her body upside down, her hands dangling right above the floor, stretching her back. Patrick didn't even know that she was getting this tattoo. This tattoo she wanted to get herself.

"Well, I'm surprised he didn't come with you." He touched both her sides and looked closer at the script.

"Some things you have to do by yourself, right?" She got goose-bumps from Cory's touch.

He walked over and sat down in the chair opposite her. "You almost done with school?"

"Yep. I got three months left." She had been working her ass off trying to get everything ready for graduation and the bar.

"Then the bar, right?"

"Don't fucking remind me, Cory."

Just then, Richard walked in, "Remind you of what? What an asshole he is?"

Cory's face looked offended and Stella laughed. Richard was a gruff guy, but he was an artist when it came to tattoos. Her first one had been done over a couple of different sessions and he'd met with her to plan it and draw it a couple of different ways before it was perfect.

"Something like that..." Stella said, laughing.

"No," Cory said at the same time.

"Stella, you know that Cory's the reason we have a 'no fucking the clients' policy." Richard sat in his chair and motioned her to come back to hers as well.

"I don't understand a policy like that. Isn't that part of the reason you work here." Stella glanced at Cory, who turned a bright shade of red. "I mean really, y'all can't have sex with customers? Ever?" Her lips turned up at the corner as she stole a glance at Cory.

"The policy is to not fuck at the store." Richard looked at Cory. "I mean this guy can't keep it in his pants. It's ridiculous."

"Oh, I get that then. Kind of a health hazard, Cory." She looked down as the needle started drilling into her back again.

"I can too keep it in my pants," Cory whined like a toddler.

"Whatever, man, I found the used condom that one time. That was enough for me."

Stella laughed. "Gross, Cory. You didn't bother putting it in the trash?"

"Stella, this is going to be tight. I like the location you picked, too. I think the off-centered script is going to look amazing." Richard worked for another thirty minutes and then said, "Okay, this is perfect. Really good. You ready to see it?"

"Sure." Stella blew her bangs out of her eyes and pushed herself up. Walking to the mirrors, she closed her eyes and let Richard position her; when she opened them, it was there and exactly what she wanted.

Positioned midway up her back, just to the right of her spine, in script, it read, "I'm the hero of this story."

"It looks great, exactly what I wanted." She turned and hugged Richard. "Thanks."

"Just doing my job." Richard rubbed salve over the tattoo and then covered it. "You know the drill."

"Yep."

A couple of weeks later, Patrick pushed the door open and yelled, "Hey fellas? Where are you?"

Stella and Patrick had gotten the first morning appointment for her to get a new tattoo, her third. Richard headed out of the back of the parlor and made his way to Patrick. They embraced with backslapping and then he looked at Stella.

"I can't believe you're getting another one already." Richard moved to his area of the shop and started pulling out all his tools.

"What can I say; I guess I'm addicted." Stella pulled off her shirt to reveal a very small sports bra.

"I told her she was getting too many, but as you can see, she doesn't give a shit what I say," Patrick was walking around the shop and looking at the recent additions to the pictures. Both of Stella's tattoos were on display on the wall in black and white. Cory had taken both pictures from behind, showcasing Stella's muscular physique and her profile with her hair cascading down her back. They were gorgeous.

"This isn't really a new one, just kinda modifying the hole of heart one..."

Richard's eyes snapped to her when she said she was modifying that tattoo. "You didn't tell me that," Richard looked at her and then at Patrick.

"Um... I realized you may have a strong reaction to what I want and wanted to talk to you about in person."

"This is going to be good," Patrick muttered, rubbing his palms together.

"Which tat do you want to modify?"

Stella turned her back to Richard and explained, "Okay, I want a half of a heart added, like it was drawn with a sharpie."

"Fuck no." Richard pushed his chair back, glaring at her. "Do you know how long it took me to design and complete that shit? I'm not fucking with it."

"I kinda thought you would say that," She pulled her shirt back over her head. "I guess I'll just run down the street and get it done." Smiling, she turned her back to Richard, waiting for him to give in.

"No. Fucking. Way. Are you getting my tattoo fucked up with at that place," Richard growled. Then he slumped on his stool.

"I was hoping you would see reason… I want it to look like a red sharpie." Stella smiled at Patrick; he'd told her he thought Richard would refuse to do it.

"This is so fucked, man." Richard looked to Patrick. "She can't be serious."

"Oh, she's serious. Seriously stupid," Patrick laughed.

"Whatever, it's my tattoo. I want what I want. Now get it done." Stella pointed at Richard's sketch pad.

"Don't really need to sketch what you're talking about, Stella." Richard started pulling out all the materials he would need. "The least you can do is tell me why you're doing this."

"Because she loves a dude," Patrick replied.

"Then get his name somewhere." Richard looked at her hopefully.

"Not going to happen."

She only had one real month left of law school and it would be taken up with writing papers. She'd be so busy she wouldn't even know her name. She'd finally landed a job. Things were falling into place. Running down Cameron Street with Coop, she saw a familiar figure out of the corner of her eye. George was walking with a tall gorgeous brunette. *Shit.* She almost turned around. Stella took the next right and then a left to be parallel with them, but running toward the Potomac. Witnessing George with his new girlfriend was not on her priority list of things to do, but maybe this was good. Closure was necessary to help her move on.

Taking a left on North Union, she ran until she hit the dog park. She let Cooper off his leash but she unconsciously kept looking toward where they would be coming from.

Stella was looking out at the river when she heard her name; her back was to him exposing her new tattoo. *Fuck, please don't make me do this.* Turning, she faced him. He was trotting towards her, leaving his new girlfriend walking toward the dog park.

"El!" George was wearing a green and white striped v-neck T-shirt that showed the lean muscles in his torso. She wondered if one of his sisters got him v-neck t-shirts in every variation.

She looked away and tried not to picture him naked.

"Hey," George said, but it sounded like a question.

"Hi, George." Stella blew the bangs out of her face and leaned on the fence, praying that he would leave soon. She turned one of her diamond earrings he had given her, which she did now when she was nervous or worried or thinking about George.

"You look, great," he said, giving her his 100-watt smile, his eyes going to her earrings.

"You do too." She looked down self-consciously at her racerback tank and spandex then over to the gorgeous brunette that was almost to them now. "I can't do this," she whispered, looking at the woman. "Coop, come." She opened the gate and ran back toward the opposite end of the park, Cooper at her heels.

"El, wait," George yelled at her back.

Stella took one quick glance back, George looked heartbroken and the woman was irritated and talking with her hands, pointing toward Stella. Lunges when she got home, only the most punishing exercise for the thoughts that would enter her mind on her run back. She was turned on just by seeing him, even though he had moved on.

Her phone beeped and she slowed. It was George, she could tell by the area code.

WTF. You can't even talk to me now?

She turned up LMFAO and ran back to the house with Cooper in tow.

CHAPTER FORTY-FIVE

Nothing Helps Like
Getting Laid

Stella emailed her last law school paper EVER to her law professor and fell back on her bed. She closed her eyes, exhausted, but her mind was buzzing. Cooper nudged her hand, demanding her attention, and she rubbed his head mindlessly. She'd stayed up all night editing and finalizing her paper for her International Law class. If she never drank another cup of coffee again, it'd be too soon. All the coffee she drank in the last three years had probably caused some sort of permanent damage. Cooper jumped on the bed and put his head on her stomach.

She, Millie, and Patrick had plans to go out tonight and celebrate. Her graduation was two days from now and her plan was to stay drunk until her parents got there. She was giving herself a week off of everything and heading to the beach with Millie after graduation.

"Coop, I think life is easier when it's just me and you." She rubbed his head and only saw love in his eyes. Cooper moved his head from her stomach to her chest so that his tongue could reach her face. Her mind drifted back to the brunette with George and her heart ached. Cooper's wet nose nudging her hand reminded her to continue to pet him.

"Hey... What about me?" Patrick walked down the stairs. "Done?"

"Finally." Stella sat up and looked Patrick's way. "The bar is going to be a bitch, too. I just want to get through all the hoops."

"You've got a job all lined up." He walked over and sat next to her on the bed, dropping his arm around her. "I'm proud of you," he said.

"Wouldn't have done it without you," Stella said sincerely, leaning her head on his shoulder.

"Sure you would've." Patrick sighed. "Where we going tonight?"

"Have you talked to Millie?"

"She said it's your party."

"I'm going to run, then hopefully take a nap. I'll think of something."

"You doing okay after seeing George?" Patrick rubbed his hand over his shaved head.

"I'm going to kill Millie." Stella stood up and huffed. "I'm fine. As a matter of fact, I feel like dancing tonight. Celebrate the new chapter, which means getting the fuck over George or whatever the fuck his name is."

Patrick looked into her eyes. "Nothing helps like getting laid."

"That's a good idea." She smiled, but it didn't reach her eyes.

The dance music pulsed and she moved to it, instinctively letting the man in front of her pull her into his arms, press a leg in between hers and move with her. She threw her arms up and her head back; dancing never felt so good. She needed it. She and Millie had just graduated from law school and she was about to start studying for the bar. She needed the release.

Stella, Millie, and Patrick had gone to a bar for awhile to celebrate her new job and their graduation, but ended up at this dance club in Clarendon. She opened her eyes and saw a very attractive African American man keeping up with her pace. The edge of a tattoo peeked out the neck of his black t-shirt, his biceps were covered in tattoos as well. *Nothing like a bad boy.* She felt an arm on her waist other than the hot dancer and looked behind her to see Patrick glaring at her. Stella peeled herself off the very handsome man, struggling to look away from him. Holding her finger up, she requested her dance partner to give her a minute.

Patrick motioned they were leaving; she pulled her phone out. It was 3:50. *Good call, so they could get a cab before the road was flooded.* Moving back toward her dance partner, she leaned into his ear and yelled, "My friends are leaving."

His arm snaking around her waist, he pulled her closer to him and his lips skating across her ear. "Let them." He bit her earlobe and smiled.

Giggling, she looked at him; it was nice to feel wanted. His eyes were deep chocolate and brimming with sex. She shook her head. "Can't."

"I'll make it worth your while. Come home with me." Something told her he wasn't used to having to ask a woman for anything twice.

"Sorry, gotta go." Stella turned and followed Patrick out of the bar.

When they got on the sidewalk, Millie pulled her in for a hug. "That was so fun. Why don't we do this more often?" They waited on the sidewalk as Patrick attempted to grab a cab.

"No idea." Stella was sweating; her white tank top was soaked through, the details of her black bra clearly visible. It was impossible for Patrick to get a cab, so Stella walked to the street and saw a limo idling a couple of blocks down. Walking that way, she signaled for Patrick and Millie to wait. She leaned into the driver's side of the limo. "Hi."

The guy looked up from his smartphone and didn't make it to her eyes, but stayed on her chest. "Hi."

"You waiting for someone." Stella leaned giving him the best view of her very sweaty cleavage.

"Yep." He looked around.

"You got time to take me and my friends home?" She attempted her best flirty look.

"No." He eyed her one more time then went back to Facebook on his cell.

"How can I change your mind?" She stood up straight and looked around, about to head back toward the bar. As she stepped back, he grabbed her wrist.

"Take your shirt off." He smirked at her, knowing she wouldn't do it.

Stella pulled her white tank top off. "What else?"

His mouth dropped open and said, "Give me your number." He took a picture of her with his phone.

Stella motioned for Patrick and Millie to come and leaned down, giving him her phone number. Just as he was entering her number in his phone, it went off. "That's my client. Jump in the back."

She walked around the front of the car, putting her tank back on and meeting up with Patrick and Millie.

"What's going on?" Patrick's brow furrowed.

"Just get in the fucking limo." Stella opened the door, quite proud of herself, as she looked back toward the club and saw her dance partner making a beeline to the limo. She jumped in the limo and waited for it to take off. Instead, her dance partner got in the back and smiled at her.

"So I hear I'm taking you home and my driver has your phone number. It must be my lucky night." His eyes roamed her body and then went to Patrick and Millie. "Where are we taking you two?"

Patrick's face was hard. "We're going to Old Town."

Millie looked at Stella and mouthed, "Oh my God." Stella composed herself. "I'm Millie, this is Patrick, and that's Stella."

"My driver just sent me a picture of your boobs, Stella." His smile was genuine and he had the whitest teeth she had ever seen. He turned his phone to show her the photo. She scooted next to where he was sitting on the backseat. He draped his arm around her shoulders. "So Stella, I'm going to take your friends home and then get Jimmy to take us to my hotel. You on board with that?"

"Sure." "No." Stella and Patrick said at the same time. Her dance partner laughed as she glared at Patrick. She hadn't had sex since George and maybe this was what she needed. She definitely need a release, sex with this guy would be a good one.

CHAPTER FORTY-SIX

Don't Ask Questions

Stella walked in her house and was met by a grinning Millie and a scowling Patrick. She didn't even get to the kitchen before Millie started asking a million questions. "Where's Coop?" Stella asked, interrupting Millie's questions.

"Billy took him to the dog park to pick up chicks," Patrick answered. "He needs all the help he can get."

"So you are really going to make me wait to hear about Jesse?" Millie literally squirmed in her chair where she was sitting, eating cereal. "I'm going to strangle you. OUT WITH IT."

Stella smiled. "I like him. Sex was good. The end."

"No way. You know who that is, right?" Millie asked, incredulous.

"It came up last night...after awhile. He's testifying on the Hill about football and concussions. He's a pretty cool guy." Stella opened the fridge and got a bottle of water.

"And..." Millie pressed.

"He definitely knew his way around the bedroom. That's all I'm saying, other than he tried to get me to be his ho in this area code."

Patrick spit his coffee out and Millie busted out laughing.

"I politely declined," she said with a smile. "Then he reminded me he already had my number and he would call me when he was in town."

"Oh my shit, El." Millie looked at her, inspecting her.

"Yep. It was good, but I hope he doesn't become a hassle." She sat at the kitchen table and rolled the bottle between her hands. Jesse had the hotel bring up breakfast this morning before he would let Stella leave.

"Oh my shit. You had sex with Jesse McIntyre from the Atlanta Falcons?"

"Fuck, Millie, are you upset you came home with me?" Patrick asked, annoyed.

"Don't ask questions you don't want to know the answer to." Millie smiled sweetly.

Her parents were coming up for a week before her graduation; she was going to take them to all the Washington tourist traps, the memorials, and her haunts. She couldn't wait; she'd given them hell in the past couple of years and she was going to show them how she had been living. They'd been so supportive, even when she wouldn't let them. Letting her push them away until she was able to have a normal conversation was a blessing. It was something for which she would be forever grateful. She knew this wouldn't make up for her behavior, but it was something.

Her parents were staying at the Westin in Old Town and she was meeting them there once they were settled. The doorbell rang and, puzzled, she walked to the door. "Stay," she said to Cooper. Opening the door, Stella saw an enormous bouquet of dark pink peonies. They were gorgeous. "Hi," she said to the deliveryman.

"El Murphy?" The man didn't look up from his clipboard.

"Yes." She grabbed the vase of peonies out of his hands and put them on the floor. She looked for her purse. "Hold on," she said and shut the door on him. Running into the kitchen she grabbed a few bucks from her bag and hurried back to the door. She ripped it open and gave the money to the deliveryman. "Thanks." Shutting the door, she looked over at Cooper. "Coop, you shouldn't have."

Bending down, she picked up the vase and carried the peonies to the kitchen. She pulled the card from the bouquet.

I'm so happy for you. Congrats on graduating to a different sort of hell. I miss your face.

G

Stella smiled in spite of herself. George remembered she was graduating. Then she frowned. She missed him, damn it. She did ten lunges on each leg.

Her phone dinged, her parents were at the Westin. "Coop, outside," she said as she walked toward the back door. Opening the door, her phone dinged again. It was Millie.

I need drinks. Where and when?

She replied.

Parents here. I'll be occupied until after dinner. Drinks in Old Town somewhere?

sure

After meeting up with her parents that night, she met Millie for drinks at a bar in Old Town. Stella told her about George sending her flowers and the card. Millie told her she needed to text him. While Stella initially refused to even discuss text-messaging George, after seven drinks she agreed.

I got my flowers today. It was so thoughtful, thank you.

She and Millie had gone through over a hundred iterations of the text she sent, but Stella eventually just sent whatever. George was probably working tonight, so she wasn't expecting the quick reply.

I'm proud of you. You did it.

Stella was baffled by George; she couldn't figure him out. Millie squealed at the text.

"What?" Stella asked.

"El, do you think a guy who you just used to fuck would care about your graduation and get the date right?" Mille turned up her drink.

"I don't know. Maybe…"

"NO. El, the answer is no." Millie looked at Stella intently. "I'm not sure how many guys you've 'just fucked,' but they don't care what your name is, let only what school you're in or when you graduate. HE LOVES YOU."

"I'm pretty sure he doesn't, Millie." Stella's walls wouldn't even let her believe that George caring about her was possibility.

"You don't know shit about most things, believe me, El. He cares about you. You guys just have to figure it out."

"I'll take that into consideration," Stella said, hoping to change the subject. "So you ready for a week at the beach, with no papers or tests?"

"Are you fucking kidding me? I'm not going to know what to do with myself. I'm bringing my Kindle with four new books on it. I don't do free time anymore."

"I know. What's free time and what do you do when you have it?" Stella laughed and tipped her glass back.

She and her parents had fun the entire week before the graduation ceremony. They met everyone who was important to her, except George. They planned a big dinner for her, Patrick, Millie, and Billy at her favorite sushi restaurant, Café Asia in Roslyn, even though her father didn't eat sushi. She took her parents to one of the most famous restaurants in the city, Old Ebbitt Grill, where they had steaks, really expensive wine, and oysters.

The ceremony was boring. Nothing would be as exciting as turning in her last final and getting passing grades. People talking to hear themselves talk seemed to be the theme. Politicians and lawyers talked more than most, because they believed they were smarter than everyone else in the room.

Happy that the ceremony was over, Stella glanced at her parents as she made her way out of the auditorium. Their grinning faces made every painful minute of the ceremony worth it. When they left her at National Airport, they were smiling ear to ear. She told them not to expect to hear from her until after the bar exam. They understood.

Her mother kissed her cheek. "I'm so proud of you." She smiled, a tear fell down her cheek.

"Don't cry," Stella sighed.

"It's a good cry. I can't believe you're through." Her mother smiled.

"Not quite done yet," Stella said. "The bar is no joke."

"You'll be fine," her mother said, grabbing her pearls and rubbing them. "I know you and you'll be fine. You got that from me." She kissed Stella's cheek and walked into the airport.

"Well, you did get your stubbornness from her. So I guess she's right." Stella's dad hugged her. "Just text me every once in a while, let me know you're alive."

"It's a deal."

"I love you." Her dad smiled. "You're my smart baby girl. I can't wait to see what happens next."

CHAPTER FORTY-SEVEN

A Break

Driving through heavily wooded streets, moss draping from the trees, Millie and Stella pulled up to the house Stella's parents had secured for them. Stella opened the car door and unfolded herself from the seat, stretching her arms and back. She let Cooper out of the backseat; he ran immediately to the beach.

The house was yellow with a black door and a wraparound porch. The house itself was on stilts and the stairs leading up to the black door were white. Stella couldn't wait to try out one of the white rocking chairs she saw on the front porch.

"Well, someone's excited to be here," Millie said, trotting to catch up with Stella.

"I'm excited. I haven't had a vacation in four years. This will be great." She looked over at her friend. "Thanks for coming with me."

"A free week at the beach?" Millie put her hand over eyes, shielding them from the sun. "Um, it was a really hard decision."

"My parents wanted to do something fun for me. This is a friend of my dad's house." She ran back to her car and grabbed the house key. "Let's go check it out." They walked up the front stairs. "Cooper! Come!"

"So, what's the new ink about?" Millie asked after they both changed into their bikinis; Millie in a white string bikini and Stella in a lime green bandeau.

"Which one?" Stella asked as she dragged two chairs down the stairs to the beach.

Millie was carrying the cooler. "Let's do the gross one first." Millie stopped and pointed at Stella's old tattoo that now looked someone had taken a sharpie to it.

"After Jamie died, I thought I'd never be able to feel again, I was so decimated by what happened. George made me realize maybe I could feel again... Maybe I would want to."

"Okay, but that doesn't clear up the fact your old tattoo looks like someone took a marker to it."

Stella actually blushed. "So, one night George took a marker and drew a heart on my back and told me he would put me back together piece by piece. I got this for me to remember who helped me when I didn't think it was possible." She shrugged. "I have half a heart instead of no heart."

"Wow. Has George seen it?"

"Of course not."

"And the other one?"

In white ink, she had "I'm the hero of this story" in script on her back. "I think it's pretty self-explanatory, don't you?"

"Humor me." Millie smirked at Stella.

"Okay." Stella blew out a long breath. "So I've just been existing, but I'm going to start living again and only I can do that for myself."

"I love them both." Millie smiled, laid on her lounge chair, put her earbuds in her ears, and closed her eyes.

The next day, Stella was stretched out in a very skimpy red and white striped bikini on her lounge chair. She had her earbuds in her ears and was listening to The Black Keys while she read her latest obsession. Millie was running around with Cooper in the water and laughing like a little kid. Making her way up to her own chair, Millie looked toward the house and then looked down at Stella.

She tapped Stella's foot to get her attention. "We have company." Millie wrapped the towel around her barely-there black bikini and slumped in the chair.

Stella turned so that she could see where Millie was looking. Patrick was making his way down the stairs with Lisa in tow. "What the fuck are they doing here," she muttered. Then she looked at Millie. "I did *not* invite them."

She pushed herself up off the chair and walked quickly to meet Lisa and Patrick. "Patrick, what are you doing here?" She took a quick glance at Millie. *What the fuck is he thinking?*

"Your parents told me that I could come for a few days." He smiled at Millie and waved. "I hope that's okay."

"Umm…negative, ghost rider." She took in Lisa, debating coming down the stairs in her heels. "You might," she emphasized might, "be okay, but her. NO!"

"Oh, Lisa here is just dropping me off." He pushed his sunglasses back up his nose. "She's headed to some convention in South Carolina for the weekend. She dropped me off, so I can just ride back with you and Millie." By the time he stopped talking, Lisa and taken off her heels and made her way to where they were both standing.

"Yep, just passing through. I wish I could stay. The beach is gorgeous and so private." She giggled and looked at Patrick in a way to convey what she was thinking.

"Oh, okay." Stella muttered, not sure if it *was* okay. "Well, there's plenty of room." She figured there was nothing she could do about it now. "I really wish you had some fucking manners, dude. All you had to do was send me a text or something." She turned, muttering under her breath, "Jackass."

"Love you too, El," he laughed. "Which room is mine?" he called to her retreating figure.

Stella didn't bother answering him.

Later that evening, Patrick and Stella were lounging on the couch with the television on. Millie was making dinner in the kitchen.

"So, you excited about starting your job?" Patrick asked Stella.

"Sure. I think for the first couple of years you basically do the same thing you do as an intern though." Stella patted the couch and Cooper jumped up and lay on her legs.

"Really, you won't be in the field?" Millie asked from the kitchen.

"I could be, but it would be doing document review or helping with research and witness testimony. Not really in the streets with a gun or anything."

"I like the General Counsel attorneys for the ATF. They're pretty cool. They help the agents know the laws and do trainings, fix fuckups, things like that."

"Well, we'll see." Stella smoothed Cooper's hair; although she kept it shaved, the hair on his head was always longer. Cooper had been enjoying the surf more than the three of them and immediately started snoring.

"Well, Sam helped get you that job, right?" Millie smiled at Stella from the kitchen.

"What?" Patrick said, pushing himself off the couch moving to get another beer.

"Umm, thanks Millie. Sam helped me get in contact with the General Counsel for the FBI and set up the interview."

"I don't like him."

"I don't care." Stella sighed loudly, blowing her bangs out of her eyes. "We aren't fucking, if that's what you're implying."

"I would probably know if you were," Patrick said stiffly.

"You don't know everything about me," Stella said defensively.

"Yea, he kinda does," Millie spoke up from the kitchen. "Dinner's ready."

"Whatever," Stella said as she moved to the table and sat down.

"We're roommates, you know most things about me, too." Patrick shrugged.

"I didn't know you were seeing Lisa again."

Patrick scowled at Stella. "Well, that's because I'm not seeing her again."

"Okay, I'm just confused how she ended up driving you down here. You know that's weird, right?" Stella glanced at Millie to gauge her reaction to this conversation. About that time, Millie pushed her seat back and excused herself.

"Why did you have to bring that up, El?"

"Oh, you thought if I didn't bring it up, Millie would forget about Lisa dropping you off?" Stella got up to follow Millie, but Patrick put his hand on her shoulder.

"I got this," Patrick said as he followed Millie toward her room.

Millie and Stella walked down the beach with drinks in their hand, Cooper running in the water next to them. Stella pushed her sunglasses up her nose. "I really needed this break. The next two months will be insane."

"Agreed." Millie bent to pick up a shell.

"All I plan on doing is studying and working out." Stella went on, shielding her eyes from the sun. "We need to set up a schedule. One of my friends said treat studying like a job, 9–5 everyday."

"That sounds like a plan. We can map out group study in the morning and then alone in the afternoon, subject by subject. We can do it, we're smart." Millie said, always organizing their studying.

"Sometimes it doesn't matter how smart you are," Stella answered, starting to worry about her future again.

"Well, that's fucking depressing." Millie stared out at the ocean. "Don't worry, we'll get a schedule together. We're going to kick the bar in its teeth."

"Whatever you say." Stella bent down and picked up a light pink shell.

"Tell me about Jamie." Millie looked at Stella.

Stella was taken aback by the abrupt change in topic. One of her favorite things about Millie was that she never pried or pushed Stella. "What?"

"Tell me about Jamie, El. Tell me about your relationship with him. You've never talked about him before."

"Right..." Stella looked out at the ocean. "Not going to start now, Millie."

"Come on, El. It was years ago; you've moved on to George."

Stella stopped walking and looked up at the sky and let a huge sigh. "Millie, you'll never understand how much I've been through. He was the love of my life and was taken from me. We should've had more time together. We would've been happy together. I guess to the outside it may appear that I moved on to George, but I didn't. I really just can't. I was open to George because he agreed it was just sex, but then he changed his mind. I didn't."

"You keep telling yourself you didn't or don't love George, but you did and you do. You've admitted it and now you're just trying to convince yourself of the opposite. I'm sure having your fiancé die is hard, the hardest thing you'll ever go through, but you can't stay stuck." Millie took Stella's hand.

Stella pulled it back, not keen on anyone touching her. "What's going on? Millie, why are you asking me this now?"

"What's your favorite memory of Jamie?" Millie asked.

Stella looked up at the sky to keep from crying. "It's stupid."

"I'm sure it's not, El."

"Jamie played baseball in college, so he could never go to any of my softball games. The one game he was able to attend my senior year was so perfect. I played second base and had a really good game, but my favorite memory is of him cheering for me and the look in his eyes when I was playing. After the game, we sat on the bleachers and talked for hours. It was so perfect, just a day in the life...you know?"

Stella sat on the beach and looked out toward the water; Millie sat down next to her. "If I would've known I wouldn't have him for long, I would've cherished everything. The way he took over my apartment with all his things. The way he smelled. His skin and clothes were always permeated with the smell of clementines from some soap his mother always sent him. The way he looked at me. The way we fought."

Millie put her arm around Stella. "But isn't the saying right, that it's better to have loved and lost than never loved at all?"

"No. That saying is bullshit." Stella had all of her Jamie feelings in a little box in her brain. She never opened it anymore.

"Oh, El. I thought George was pulling you through all this. You were acting like a real live person."

"George helped me, but I'm not there yet, Millie. May never be." Stella pulled her bathing suit up to cover more of herself. "I always act like a real live person," she said sarcastically.

"Oh sweetie, no. The first year I knew you, it was clear you were fucked up. You acted like a Zombie."

"Shit, you should have seen me the year before. I thought I was better." The first year after Jamie died was a blur of pain and alcohol. Her first year of law school was a blur of reading and alcohol. The second year a blur of sex and alcohol. *At least there is a theme.*

♥ ♥ ♥

Sitting on the back porch facing the ocean, Patrick, Millie, and Stella watched the sun set while sipping their drinks.

Millie turned to Stella. "Did you hear back from Jesse?"

Patrick looked at Stella, a question in his eyes.

"Yes, I told him we would get together later." Stella looked at the waves.

"I thought that was a one-time thing?" Patrick asked.

"It's just sex, Patrick. We both know it." Stella took a sip of her wine.

"You're cool with being one of many?"

"We used a condom, of course." Stella scoffed at Patrick's tone; she was always careful.

Stella had been on birth control since she was sixteen and used condoms, always. She and Jamie had given up condoms after being tested, but they were still piled high in the drawer next to her bed from her relationship with George. "It's actually better that way. There's no pressure on either of us. We know what it is."

Patrick looked down at his hands. "Isn't that the same agreement you had with George?"

Stella looked at him, stunned and a little speechless. He was right. "I don't plan on doing anything with Jesse on a regular basis."

"Patrick, leave her alone," Millie scolded. "If she wants to fuck someone else to get over George, so be it."

"I just don't want you hurt." Patrick pushed himself off the chair and walked over to where Stella sat. He leaned over the railing.

"I'm pretty sure that's what I feel on a consistent basis, Patrick. I don't know what happened with George. He wore me down; he made me feel again. I needed it. I was totally broken and didn't feel anything until he elbowed his way into my life. Did it hurt like hell when he left? Yes. Do I regret it? No. He made me stronger. My hurt isn't going to change if I fuck some football player in his big, swanky hotel room."

"Okay, you're a big girl. You do what you want anyway."

"Correct," Stella answered, her gaze never leaving the water.

The next morning, Patrick was in the ocean with what looked like a surfboard, but he was standing and paddling his way out to sea. He'd been paddling out there for over an hour.

"So, I'm a pretty patient person, Millie, but are you going to tell me what's going on with you and Patrick?"

Millie signed and shielded her eyes when she looked out at where Patrick was in the ocean. "I'm pretty sure he's going to propose to me," she said with seriousness. Then she looked at Stella's mouth hanging open and burst out laughing. "I'm just kidding. We're just hanging out, having sex, taking it as it comes."

"That sounds familiar," Stella said, looking back at her book.

"Hmm. I have no idea what you mean," Millie commented, her voice dripping with fake innocence.

"Y'all are exclusive?"

"Yes."

Before she could ask her next question, her phone beeped. She started looking through her bag for her phone.

I'm in DC for the weekend. let's get together.

Stella looked at the message again, not knowing the number, and then she began laughing. "This is priceless." She showed it to Millie.

"Are you kidding me?" Millie said incredulously. "Is that Jesse McIntyre?"

"I believe so... I don't know anyone else from Atlanta that would want to get together with me."

"El, you are so lucky."

Stella's face fell a little before she replaced it with another big smile. "Whatever."

"What are you going to do?" Millie asked, giggling like a twelve-year-old.

"Nothing, I'm not in DC right now so we cannot get together." She responded quickly to his text that she was out of town for the next few days. His reply was quick.

Next time

"Okay, should I come up with something charming to say back or just leave it?" She looked at Millie, who was watching Patrick with a look of desire on her face.

"Ewwwwwwwww, keep that face to yourself. Did you hear me? What should I say back?"

Millie slowly turned her head to face Stella. "Nothing. It'll drive him crazy."

"Not really trying to drive him crazy, but I don't have a problem with nothing." She threw her phone back in her bag and picked up her book. Not looking at Millie, Stella commented. "You know it won't end well, right." Patrick was her best friend, her brother, and she would like nothing more than her two closest friends to fall in love and live happily ever after. She just didn't see it happening. Being the alpha male that he was, Stella couldn't see Patrick being okay with Millie making more money than him.

Millie breathed out, "Yep. I'm aware."

"You ever heard the expression 'don't shit where you eat'?"

"Yes." Millie answered shortly.

"Don't be pissed at me when my house becomes a battle zone when it goes down."

"You'll just have to come to my house then."

"Well, you just have an answer for everything, don't you?"

"Pretty much." Millie smiled and went back to admiring Patrick.

CHAPTER FORTY-EIGHT

These Two Girls Go Into a Bar

Throughout the months of June and July, Stella maintained a routine of studying, throwing up, studying, and running. Her brain was so fried when she left school every night, she couldn't complete full sentences. Turning her brain off after 7:00 pm every day and running with Cooper was mandatory for her not to lose the delicate grip she held on sanity.

Before July 4th, Stella and Millie took a mock bar exam. The mock exam took four hours and at the conclusion of the test, Stella sat on the Metro, grading her test and crying. She'd failed miserably. Taking the weekend off from studying, she drank heavily and felt sorry for herself. Then she headed right back into the library on Monday to her study group with Millie and Davis.

Time for the actual exam finally came. It seemed like no time had passed since her graduation, but each day had also seemed endless. Stella's mother surprised her with a massage the day before the bar in order for her to relax. Stella ate lunch at Cosi and then went to the spa across the street. She took off her clothes and lay on her stomach, waiting for the masseuse to come in and work magic.

"Okay Stella, you've come in for some relaxation today. Anything in particular?" the man asked in a low relaxing voice and he rubbed oil on his hands.

"I'm taking the bar exam tomorrow and just trying to relax," Stella replied with her eyes closed.

"Really?" The rubbing on her back stopped and her eyes popped open. "I got arrested the other day because someone hit me in a bar fight at Finnegan's. I think it's bullshit; I was defending myself. What should I do?"

Are you fucking kidding me? My masseuse wants legal advice? This is classic.

"Needless to say, my massage was not relaxing." Stella was telling Millie about her bizarre massage over dinner. They were sitting in the restaurant of their hotel in Norfolk, Virginia, where the Virginia Bar was being conducted. The entire bar process was the most ridiculous thing Stella had ever voluntarily done to herself. The application process took months to complete and after today she wouldn't know if she actually passed until the November.

"That would only happen to you." Millie's eye was twitching and had been for several hours. They had gotten adjoining rooms so they could relax tonight before they attempted to sleep and make sure they got up on time. "Two days and it will be over."

"Can you believe it?"

"Not really, I'm so stressed I don't know how to deal with it."

"You should just throw up like I do. I feel much better after that." Stella smiled weakly, taking a big bite of her hamburger.

Two days later, Stella exited the huge ballroom where over 400 graduates were taking the Virginia Bar exam and fell on the floor in exhaustion where Millie was stretched out waiting for her.

"Holy shit, I guess I need to go ahead and sign up for the February exam. That kicked my dumb ass." Stella scratched her head and looked at Millie. "Let's get the fuck out of here."

"Agreed," Millie replied as she pushed herself off the floor. "What did you think about the question on Riparian rights?"

Stella put her hands over her ears. "No. We never talked about exams in school and I'm not about to start now. We can't change our answers, so it doesn't matter. "

The ride home was mostly silent, as Millie and Stella were drained. Millie dropped her off at the curb in front of her house.

"You not coming in?"

Millie shook her head. "I just want to sleep."

Stella leaned back in the window of the passenger side of Millie's Volkswagen. "You okay?"

"As okay as I can be, I guess. We'll talk tomorrow... And drink. Let's drink tomorrow," Millie said.

"Sounds like a plan. See you tomorrow." Stella walked toward her house and saw Cooper jumping at the door. Stella stuck her head in and Cooper jumped up on her, putting his huge paws on her chest. Cooper never failed to show her how much he loved her; she needed that.

CHAPTER FORTY-NINE

Fact or Fable

Stella had been sitting in her office at the General Counsel's office on her second cup of coffee when Stan stuck his head to tell her to come with him to a meeting. This, she'd determined, was not uncommon. Younger attorneys were pulled into all sorts of meetings with the other, more seasoned attorneys, for all kinds of reasons, ranging from being eye candy to taking notes. No matter the reason, young attorneys were not prepared for these important meetings, but had to catch up during the meeting itself. It seemed to be a form of hazing. The meeting was at the ATF's General Counsel's office.

She pressed her palms down her grey trousers and looked around at the conference room where they waited. The windows spanned the entire length of the room. She was nervous and trying not to show it by talking to Stan too much.

He was pleasantly sipping his coffee. He scowled at her. "Stop fidgeting," he ordered.

"I'm not," Stella answered. She took a sip of coffee as the door opened and an older African American woman walked in wearing a black pantsuit, followed by a grey-haired man in a cheap-looking brown suit. She sat back in her chair, then in came a disheveled guy with long matted hair and a ratty beard. He walked in with his head down and didn't really look at her or Stan until he sat down directly across from her. She thought she was having some sort of mental breakdown until his eyes went wide at the sight of her. She closed her eyes and it was like fireworks went off behind her lids, she took a deep breath and then opened them again, hoping she was just hallucinating. She wasn't. She pushed back her chair abruptly and mumbled something about the bathroom. She ran from the room and down the hall and made it to the first stall before she vomited. She kept throwing up, over and over.

Not sure how long she had been in there, she sat on the floor and leaned her face against the cool tile wall. She didn't believe it. It was Jamie. He'd lost a significant amount of weight and his hair and beard were disgusting, but it was him. She would know those eyes anywhere. *What the fuck? He's ALIVE.* Stella could honestly not wrap her brain around what she'd just seen with her own two eyes. A knock came at the door. Stan pushed it open a bit.

"Stella, you okay?" he poked his head in.

"Shit, Stan, I must have food poisoning. I'm so sorry." Her voice shook a little, but she assumed that would be normal, given how much she had just thrown up.

He sighed and shut the door.

"Holy mother of fuck." She leaned her head back and closed her eyes. She pushed herself up and went to the sink to look at her face, she kind of looked crazy. Maybe she was crazy. She splashed water on her face and swished it around in her mouth. She pushed the door open and Stan was waiting for her. "You got any gum?" she asked.

"You better not be pregnant." He turned and they walked down the hall. "I've been briefed. I'll share everything with you in the car." He'd driven the ATF offices and they were expected back to brief the General Counsel for the FBI.

She sat in Stan's car, numb and shocked, as he filled her in. The ATF wanted the FBI's cooperation with a four-year undercover operation that had gone bad. The operation was out of Montana and involved the undercover agent that was sitting across the table, a Jack or Jimmy or something; Stan couldn't remember.

"So what is it exactly they want us to do?"

"When we get back to the office, I'll check to make sure with Jeff, but I'm pretty sure you'll be able to handle this one yourself. The ATF has already done our work for us, with the exception of fucking it up, so you'll just go and be the DC presence with the FBI team out of Montana that's already there. We need you gather intel for us and work under the FBI attorney from the Montana office."

Shocked didn't begin to describe what she was feeling. "Okay."

"Like I said, I got to check it at the top, but I'm pretty sure you leave tomorrow. It'll probably be for a few weeks, or months, depending."

Weeks or months? What the fuck did it matter? Her entire world just imploded. She wasn't going to mess up the only good thing in her life; her job.

"Listen, I know you're sick, so I'll drop you off at the Metro before going to headquarters. Keep your phone on and start packing. I'll get you all the deets later."

"Okay."

"This is going to be easy; a cake operation." He smiled at her, mistaking her quietness for nervousness. "You don't need to have passed the bar. Pretty cool first assignment, though, right?"

She nodded. "Very cool. I'm just trying not to throw up in your car right now."

"Appreciate it." He pulled over at the McPherson Metro station. "Stella, if I don't see you before you leave. Good luck. Be in touch."

"Of course." She started to close the door, then leaned back in. "Thanks, Stan."

She turned and walked in a daze into the Metro station.

CHAPTER FIFTY

Suit Up

"Suit up, Cooper," she said as she walked into the house. He jumped off his chair and followed her into her room. She pulled on shorts and a tank top, put her earbuds in and fastened her phone to her arm. "Nothing like a mind-numbing run to make it better," she said and rubbed Cooper's ears. Cooper started doing the dance he did when she got his leash out. She grabbed a bottle of water and made her way to the street and to start a punishing run.

Kid Cudi blaring in her ears, she ran down King Street and turned left when she hit the water. Running until she hit the dog park, she let Cooper off his leash and watched him bound around. Then she let herself go, falling to the grass and sobbing. Laying on her back, she opened her eyes as Cooper finally made his way back to her and licked her tear-soaked face. Cooper lay next to her, making sure he was touching her, and closed his eyes with his nose nuzzled into her side. Running out of tears after awhile, she simply closed her eyes. Her body felt hollow. She opened them when felt someone standing over her.

"George," she said flatly, no feeling or emotion left.

"Hey, El, whatcha doing?" He sat down next to her in his running shorts, his shirt off and tucked into the waistband at the small of his back.

"Nothing much," she said, looking around and pushing herself up on her elbows. Her phone buzzed and she checked the messages, ten from Patrick. She ignored them.

"Looks like that; middle of the day, laying in the dog park." He brushed the hair that had fallen out of her ponytail out of her eyes.

"Don't touch me!" she exclaimed and jumped up. "I've had enough of everything, shit."

He raised his hands in surrender. "Whoa, sorry, Stella."

"I've had a shitty four years and today's been right up there, so sorry. I don't want to chat." She bent to put Cooper's leash back on and doubled over.

"El," George stayed where he was, "let me take you home."

"I don't want shit from you."

"I know." He shook his head. "How did I fuck this up so much?" he asked himself, rubbing his hand though his black hair. Then he got up and lifted Stella over his shoulder. "Come on. I'm taking you home."

She had no fight left. She had fought life for too long. She curled into to him.

"Come on, Coop." He slapped his thigh signaling Cooper to come with him. Cooper happily followed them both to a townhouse right across the street.

"I thought you were taking me home?"

"This is my house."

She looked up and took in the townhouse that overlooked the park and the Potomac. The location alone made the townhome worth over a million dollars. "You live here?" She thought nothing could surprise her anymore. "Fuck, I didn't know you at all, did I?"

"You know the important stuff."

"Oh, like how you like your dick sucked?" Her insides were turning; she was going to be sick.

George sucked in a breath and let it pass. "That's pretty important," he laughed.

Stella was currently incapable of seeing humor. "You're liar, just like everyone else. George or whatever the fuck your name is..."

Putting her down on the stoop, he looked into her eyes. "I'm not sure what's happened, but let's talk. Let me get you and Coop some water. Talk to me, El. Please." He ran his thumb across her jaw line. You could call me a motherfucker for the rest of my life and that'd be fine if you would just talk to me."

"Well, that might be embarrassing for you," she said without smiling, but followed him in the house. Taking in the den area, the corners of her mouth turned up infinitesimally. It was just like she would have thought, cluttered and homey.

"I see you got some new ink," George commented letting his fingers sweep over her left shoulder tracing the half of a heart. He smiled.

"I don't want to talk about that." She instinctively moved away from him and sat on his worn brown leather couch. Three of the walls in his den were bookshelves full of books. "I love this room. The smell of books makes me happy." She closed her eyes and Cooper walked over and plopped down on her feet.

"What do you want to talk about, El? What was so bad today or four years ago?"

Her phone buzzed again, it was a message from Stan.

Stel, all a go for tomorrow. Your flight is a 2:55 out of National. Pack for a couple of weeks, you may be able to fly back if you're there longer. Good luck.

She sighed and texted back.

great I will come by the office and pick up the deets.

He responded immediately.

no need, ATF agent will be accompanying you on flight and will fill you in

"Just when you thought things couldn't get any worse," she muttered. *NO. FUCKING. WAY would she sit next to Jamie the entire flight to Montana.*

George crossed the room in a few strides and grabbed her phone; scanning through her messages from Stan and then Patrick; he cocked his head to the side in a question. She struggled to get her phone back, but he moved quickly from her and held her away with one hand.

"Nosy much?" she said, finally getting away from his grip and snatching her phone back.

"Come on, Coop, let's go." Cooper lazily stretched his legs and arms, then sat back down.

"You going somewhere, El?" George moved in front of the foyer, effectively blocking her way to the front door.

"Got an assignment for a few weeks out of town." She looked down. "Come on, Coop, let's go."

"Why won't you talk to me? I mean, you even told Sam." Hurt emanated from his eyes.

"Well, then you already know." She sighed; she had no energy for this conversation. "If you ask me questions I'll answer them."

They stood toe to toe staring into each other's eyes.

"You were engaged?"

"Yes."

"Jamie?"

"Yes."

"He died?"

"I thought so, yes. I saw him today, so I guess not really."

George's eyes got wide. "What do you mean?"

"I guess instead of breaking up with me, he and the ATF decided to fake his death to start a four-year-long undercover operation for him." Her knees almost gave out at the admission. Not being able to look at George, she closed her eyes.

George absentmindedly ran his hand through his hair. "Wow, they do that? Are you okay? Holy shit."

"What do you think?" she answered without opening her eyes.

"Okay, that was a stupid question." He leaned his head, back looking at the ceiling as if an answer to the situation would fall out of the sky. Taking a deep breath, he closed his eyes, trying to figure out how to play this.

Gently, he reached out and took both of her hands and pulled her into him, wrapping his arms around her. She let him hold her, move her to his leather couch and ease her into the cushy pillows. He put his hand on her leg and she leaned her head on his shoulder. They sat like that for several quiet minutes. Without moving, Stella asked, "So did it work out?"

"What?" He turned to look at her.

"The girl you met last fall, did it work out?" Looking down, she examined her hands.

"Not at all," he answered honestly.

"What happened?" Stella needed to know, but still couldn't look at him.

"She wasn't you." He didn't look at her, but resigned himself to the fact that this might be the last time they spoke.

"What?" she whispered, a small glimmer of heat shooting through her.

"It's just that I love you and can't seem to get past it." He smiled down at her. "You're really hard to love, but even harder to get over." He pulled at a stray hair that was stuck to her face.

"You love me?" She closed her eyes, unsure she could deal with anything else today. Opening her eyes, she looked into those green flecks. "George, we can have this conversation or we can wait. It's up to you, but I want you to know that I'm in shock. I threw up, like thirty times when I saw Jamie this morning. I just found out I'm headed out of town for a couple of weeks and my world is kind of imploding right now."

"El, your life always seems to be in some sort of state of implosion. We can wait, but know that I love you. I'm not going anywhere. I can listen to you, hold you, love you. Whatever you need." He took a deep breath. "But, I need something from you. You have to give a little bit. I need you to tell me how you feel about me before you go." George was cradling her now, Stella's face pressed against his bare chest. He pushed her far enough from him so that she looked at him. "I need this one thing from you."

She grabbed his face and slammed her lips against his, launching an all-out assault on him.

He pushed her back gently. "Not that I don't really appreciate that and hope to receive more. I need to hear you say how you feel about me, please."

"Why?" she hedged. All the months she'd tried to convince herself he was nothing other than a good lay weren't enough to convince her of that, but she wasn't ready to profess her love. *Was she ready to tell him or was this it? If she didn't, would she lose him?*

"I'm starting to put you back together." He kissed her jaw line up to her ear.

She groaned. "It's impossible."

"Let me be the judge of that." George worried that this fiancé coming back into her life would be the end of them, if there was a them. "By the way, I've had the best view of your runs the last few months. You're very ritualistic. I could tell time by your visit to the dog park with Cooper on Tuesdays, Thursdays, and Saturdays."

"Oh you liked the view, huh?" Her phone went off again, like it had been every five minutes since she went on her run.

They were all from Patrick.

Where are you?

We need to talk

Have you talked to Jamie?

El come on

where are you?

Are you okay?

FUCK reply to my texts please.

She scrolled through her texts and things clicked into place. Who had told her about Jamie? Who had driven her to the closed casket funeral? Who had been in her life every day making sure she was okay since he "died"?

"Are you fucking kidding me?" All the things that had happened in the last few hours hit her like a ton of bricks and that crack that she worried about all those years started. Stella took in a deep breath, dropping her phone. The one person that she'd trusted more than anyone had been lying to her for four years. This threatened to end the sanity she was struggling to maintain.

"What is it?" George leaned in to see the plethora of texts from Patrick.

"Patrick knew all along that Jamie was alive. That MOTHER-FUCKER." Rage filled her mind, made her see red, actually see red. She flew up and grabbed Cooper's leash. "I gotta run."

George grabbed her arm. "I'll run with you."

"No." She pushed past him and he pushed her against the wall.

"Yes." He looked into her heartbroken eyes. "I'm going with you."

They ran the three miles back to her house in silence, Cooper leading the way. When they walked through the door, Patrick was pacing through the kitchen, livid. He ran to her, throwing his arms around her. "Are you okay?"

She shoved him back. "Am I okay?" she asked incredulously. "Really, Patrick? That's what you're going with?"

George took Cooper and released him from his leash. Cooper stood in between Stella and Patrick, looking confused.

"You've been lying to me for years and have the fucking gall to ask me if I'm okay? I can't even start to tell you how un-okay I am."

"El, I'm sorry. I..." Patrick looked down at his hands. "I umm..."

"You at a loss for words, huh?" She pushed past him. "Listen, I'm leaving for awhile, okay? Don't worry about me, I don't need your ass. I'm going to pack my shit and Cooper and I'll be outta here. I'll get the rest of my shit later."

"Don't do that, El." Patrick reached for her again. "Don't leave like this."

Sidestepping his arm, she yelled, "Guess what, Patrick?! Fuck you! You don't get to tell me what to do." She stomped down the stairs and a stunned Cooper looked to Patrick and then George and followed her down the stairs. "George!" she called. "Grab Coop's food and put it in my car, please."

Patrick looked like he was about to cry.

George moved toward the cabinet where they kept the dog food. "Give her some time, man."

"It had to be you she ran to, right?" Patrick seethed. "She's my best friend and she ran to you."

"I love her, man. Get used to it. Also, a best friend wouldn't have done what you did." Patrick looked at his phone as it buzzed and then threw it against the wall, smashing it to pieces. "This is fucking ridiculous. All of this because of that asshole? He has ruined her."

Stella stomped up the stairs carrying her suitcase, laptop, and workout bag. She brushed past Patrick, who was just standing there looking defeated. George and Cooper followed her out the door and down to her car.

"El, please…let me explain." Patrick called to her back.

"Get a new roommate!" she yelled.

Patrick ran and grabbed her arm. "El, please." His eyes were pleading with her.

"I HATE YOU." She jerked her arm away from him.

Stella didn't even hesitate as she walked out the door without looking back. She did stop for a second when she realized Patrick's car was blocking hers in the driveway. "FUCK." She took a breath and turned to George. "Do you mind asking Patrick to move his car so that we can leave?" She opened the trunk and threw everything in. Digging in her purse, she pulled out her cell phone and dialed Millie. "Hey, listen, today has been the biggest pile of shit that has happened to me in a while. Can I stay with you tonight?" She was talking as she opened her passenger side door and folded the seat up so Cooper could get in the back seat.

George came up behind Stella and took the phone gently from between her ear and shoulder. She jumped and then glared at him when he started talking to Millie. "Hey, Millie. Long time…it's George. Listen, El is going to stay with me tonight and then she has to go out of town for work. Cooper is staying with me while she's gone." Stella was just staring at him. "I think it would be best to have Patrick fill you in right now."

Stella moved to the driver's side of the car and started it, waiting on George to get in. Kid Cudi filled the car before she reached to turn the music down. George leaned over to her, phone still on his ear, and gently kissed her cheek.

CHAPTER FIFTY-ONE

Enough

W hen they pulled into the driveway of George's townhouse, he showed her how to park in his two-car garage under the unit. A Toyota 4Runner was already parked in the garage. She didn't even know he owned a SUV. It reminded her that he'd lied to her. He got out of the car, let Cooper out of the backseat, and moved to her side of the car. Stella was still sitting in the car in somewhat of a fog. It was almost like she had to concentrate to remember to breathe.

He opened the door and pulled her to him, wrapping his arms around her. "You're going to be fine," he whispered in her ear. Then he picked her up and carried her up two flights of stairs into his bedroom, where he lay her gently on the bed. He knelt down and untied both of her shoes, pulled off her sweaty socks, and then leaned over her body. "I'm going to go start a bath for you. I'll be right back." He disappeared and she could hear the water starting. She turned her head to look at the wall of his bedroom and was surprised, it was in order. His bed was huge, with a leather headboard that went all the way to the ceiling. A walk-in closet was on the same wall as the entry to the bathroom. George appeared above her again; he leaned down and kissed her tenderly.

"George..." She was fighting so many emotions. "This..." Her voice cracked and a tear fell down her face.

George's face pinched together and he kissed her tear away. "You don't have to talk about anything right now. Let me take care of you." He pulled her pants and underwear down in one swift move, examining what was underneath. Then he peeled off her workout top and gazed hungrily at her naked form on his bed. George carried her into the bathroom and put her in the bath. His bathroom was just as impressive as the rest of his house, but a little more messy. There were towels and clothes everywhere. "Please relax for a little while. I'm going to get you a glass of wine, red or white?"

"Your choice," she said softly. Stella plunged under the water and stayed under as long as she could. Under the water her mind started racing; she was still so pissed. All the things that didn't make sense about George ran through her head, but then were surpassed by the realization that she just didn't fucking care anymore, about anything. The numbness that she had after Jamie's "death" came back in full force, that familiar hardness spreading through her chest and brain again.

After a while, Stella raised herself out of the water; she was all wrinkles after staying in the bath for so long. She walked into his closet and pulled a long-sleeve henley shirt down over her naked body. It smelled like him. She padded down the stairs. Going downstairs in only his shirt would short-circuit any conversation he wanted to have with her; she hoped, anyway.

Stella stepped off the last step onto the main floor, turned to the kitchen, and saw him. Shirtless, his muscles flexed as he prepared dinner. She pushed her wet bangs off her forehead. Licking her lips at the sight, she said, "A girl could get used to this."

George turned and faced her with his smile and his abs; she wanted to jump him immediately. "Wow. Can you wear my shirt, always?"

"You'd rather me wear a shirt than be naked?" Stella asked, feigning innocence.

"Well maybe... No, I'd rather you'd be naked." George attempted to pull his shirt off her.

"Not yet," she said firmly. "I'm famished." Stella sat on the stool provocatively, giving him a peak at what was under her shirt.

George stared at her and then went back to cutting vegetables and cooking dinner for them both. "El, I don't think I can concentrate on cooking with you sitting like that."

"Oh, do you want me to come over there and help?" She smiled; this was a great distraction from thinking about her day, but she was still pissed at him. There was still so much they needed to talk about. She stood in front of him, her thighs pressing against the cabinet. Stella pulled his arms around her, her skin tingling with his touch. She felt him lean into her hair and inhale. "So let's talk," she said. "What's your name?"

He grimaced. "My name is Willston George Finnegan."

Stella turned around to look at him, her eyebrows arched in disbelief. "I feel like an idiot, George. I felt like I knew you, but I didn't even know your real name."

"I'm sorry." George held her arms so that she stayed facing him, putting his left leg in between her legs pressing her against the counter. "Okay, so I told you my name was George initially because that's what I do with all women I want to get in my bed, but shit, a year later I liked how it sounded on your lips."

"Give me a fucking break, George." Stella took a long pull from her wine.

"I fell in love with you before we even had sex. You agreeing to fuck me was so surreal..." George put both of his hands on her, one on her face, the other on her neck. "I played along with your arrangement because I thought it was better than nothing, but you would let me in and then push me away. I couldn't continue to play it cool with you. I wanted more. I wanted you to meet my family..." George trailed off, his lips barely touching hers as he spoke.

"George..." she breathed out anticipating his kiss that never came. "Us being apart has been really hard for me. I need you to touch me."

"Where do you want me to touch you?"

Stella pushed herself onto the counter and spread her legs. "Where do you want to touch me?"

George couldn't hide the shudder that went through his entire body. "I love you." He attacked her, not able to control himself.

Stella's walls were still up until he started kissing her, but her body reacted to him immediately. She missed him and she finally let herself go, feeling everything.

"I'm sorry, Stella. I should've told you my real name and that I owned the bar, but I didn't think it mattered." He cradled her face in his hands.

"What else am I missing?" she asked, looking intently into his eyes.

Stella and George were intertwined on his king-size bed. She sat facing him, her legs around his waist, their faces inches from each other. His arms were loosely around her and she was tracing an outline of something on George's chest. "I've missed you," she whispered.

"Somehow I don't believe you." George rubbed his thumb over her lower lip.

Stella sighed. "Should I tell you I'm sorry again?"

"For what? We were upfront with each other. I knew you believed you needed certain things, but I was hoping I would be enough. I wanted to be enough for you." George brushed her bangs to the side.

"I don't know what to say, George. I fell in love with you, but I couldn't even admit that to myself until after you said it was over."

"You fell in love with me?" George's eyebrows went up in surprise.

"Yes," she whispered. Admitting it felt like jumping off a cliff with no parachute, no cushion, and no idea what was next. "This is against everything I've…I really don't know if I can do this or if this can work."

"Oh, it'll work." George said, smoothing her hair back. "You don't know it yet, but this," he pointed to himself and Stella, "is going to work."

"George, you really are a masochist."

"I guess when it comes to you I am. You're the best kind of pain." George kissed her gently. "Let's go over the rules, shall we?"

"Whatever," she said.

"We love each other."

"That's not a rule," Stella protested rolling to her back and staring at the ceiling.

"Oh, but it is." George leaned over her. "You're now my girlfriend."

"George, come on." Stella pressed her hands against his chest.

"No. These are my rules. You are my girlfriend. You must text and call me on a regular basis. The fact you're going out of town tomorrow really puts a damper on my plans for you. You will stay with me, all night, as often as I will allow it, and let me warn you, that will be an everyday allowance. Also, I need you to answer all questions I ask, whether it's about Jamie or your job. I want to know everything. I need to know everything. I love you with every ounce of my being and I need things from you. Can you handle that?"

"I'll try," Stella whispered.

They stayed up all night talking, apologizing and making plans. Stella really couldn't believe something good was finally happening to her. Her life was taking another turn and this one she liked.

When she woke up, he was gazing intently at her. Stella smiled. "I really like waking up in your bed with you." She gave him a chaste kiss. "Who knew?"

"I knew," George replied.

Chapter Fifty-Two

Your Love

S tella pushed her way down the aisle of the plane with her earbuds in her ears. She had selected a very mellow playlist to keep her as calm as possible during this flight. Changing her seat on the flight and cost her over one hundred dollars and resulted in her sitting in the last row of the plane. She was going to be professional, but had decided she wasn't going to talk to the ATF agent, formerly known as Jamie.

As she turned to slide into her seat, she shoved her bag under the row in front of her and leaned back. This would be a very trying couple of weeks. When she saw the ATF agent enter the plane and begin looking up and down the aisles for his seat, she studied him. His blond hair was longer and darker than she'd ever seen it, a dirty blond-brown mix. At its current length, it was wavy; he'd always kept his hair short and out of his eyes in college. His once long, lean body looked very thin, but his walk was the same, all ego. His beard was a light brown and covered most of his chiseled features, including his mouth. Closing her eyes, she pictured Jamie as he was that last night they had spent together and sighed.

He sat without looking for her; he probably figured she was running late. As they taxied out of the gate, she saw him turn and glance around the half-empty plane. *Not too many people headed to Montana.* His eyes landed on hers and she looked away. Pulling out her iPad she logged into the airline's internet and logged into her email.

She reviewed the email from Stan, which again reassured her that her position was just to gather intel and make sure the DC office knew what was going on in the Montana field office. She was basically being sent to babysit. "A cakewalk," he had told her. *I HATE CAKE.* Once they were in the air, she felt a shadow to her right and took her right earbud out of her ear, refusing to look up from her email.

"Stella?" Jamie began.

"No," she said. He continued to stand there and she turned the volume up, The Civil Wars drowning out whatever he was saying.

He reached down and pulled the cord, making her earbud fall out. She looked up, her expression steely.

"Stella, I'm supposed to brief you..." He looked around.

"Just give me the file. I'll review it on the way." She snatched the file out of his hands and put her earbud back in her ear. *Bastard.*

She didn't look up, but could feel when he left her side a few awkward minutes later. She would review the file in a few minutes; she wanted to send George an email first. The problem was, she didn't have his email and what she wanted to say was too long for a text. She googled Finnegan's in Old Town and pulled up the website. There was a contact email. She clicked on it and started typing.

George or whatever the fuck your name is,

I'm on the plane, leaving you, and I'm miserable. This assignment will be long and I'll be bored. Per our discussion, I will text you often. I plan on giving you what you need, George. You have given me what I thought I needed since I met you. Months ago, when you broke things off with me because you met someone else, I was coming to lunch to tell you that I was falling for you. I mean, hard. I was willing to try this thing, but I shut all that down once I heard you met someone. You know how I told you about one of my favorite authors who said everything that comes together falls apart? I still believe that. However, in that same book, it is said if you know that everything falls apart, stop grieving about it falling apart and enjoy the together time. I am going to enjoy us together. I promise.

I have always wanted you to be happy. I just never thought that would be with me. You, alone, made me realize that maybe I can be put back together. That I could possibly be happy. The realization that you could be happy with me is almost too much for me to fathom.

I love you. I love that you let me figure it out on my own (mostly). I will tell you what I don't love, I don't love that you know so much about me, but I don't know that much about you. How selfish am I? I do know some things... but I want to know everything. I don't love that you give so much to me. I want to give you what you need. What do you need George? I know you're thinking of a sexual comment to answer that question, which is fine, but I want to know what your heart needs. What does your soul need?

Do you need reassurances from me (I would) that I'm in no way interested in the agent I'm currently sitting 20 rows behind? If so, I can quickly give you those. Do you need reassurance that I will be dreaming of you every night in Montana? I can guarantee you, that after last night, that is absolutely the case. Do you need anything else, George? Because I plan on proving to you that I do, in fact, love you.

BTW- Please take care of Cooper. He has had my back longer than you have. Take him on his run; take him to the Dog Barkery. He likes the female collie that hangs there around 1:00-2:00 on Saturdays. Let him sleep with you, he can keep my spot warm for me. Maybe we could Facetime. Okay, just kidding.

I miss you already.
Your love

Chapter Fifty-Three

Contact

Stella grabbed her bag and filed off the plane once they landed in Montana. Stan had arranged for her to pick up a rental car for the one hour drive south to her hotel. She headed to pick up her suitcase and make her way to the rental car pick-up. Jamie was nowhere to be found. *Good.*

She texted Stan and her dad to let them know that she'd made it safely. She had several messages from Patrick and one from Billy. She skipped Patrick's, she wasn't in the mood. She wondered what Patrick told Billy, if anything.

Where's coop? i need my drinking partner.

She replied:

not to worry, he's not drinking without you. had to leave quick, didn't know your schedule for dog sitting.

She hit send. Immediately her phone buzzed again; it was Stan.

Have fun babysitting.

She smiled, grabbed her bag and stood at the rental car counter. When she walked out into the parking lot, she smiled at the Escalade that agency had gotten her. *Sweet.* She plugged her hotel address in the navigation system. Her phone buzzed; George. She quickly opened the message, hoping he had already gotten her email.

It was a picture of Cooper lying on her sweatshirt and looking pitiful. It was captioned:

"He is not the only one who misses you."

She replied.

Good.

She threw her phone on the passenger seat and made her way to her hotel.

Once she checked into the hotel, she set about settling in, as this room would be her home for awhile. She took her time hanging up clothes and putting out her makeup, blow dryer, and hair straightener in the bathroom. A knock sounded at the door. She looked at her phone, it was 9:30 p.m. She walked to the door, peering through the peephole. Jamie was standing in the hall in a black hooded sweatshirt pulled down to his eyebrows. *No. She wouldn't even entertain this.*

She pulled the door open a sliver, with the latch closed, and looked through at Jamie. "No," was all she said.

"Stella, wait." She shut the door on him. "I need to talk to you," he begged.

She opened the door again. "I don't give a fuck what you need," she said, the rage evident in her voice. She looked at him one more time through the door. Any love she felt for him was replaced by pure, unadulterated hate and it was written all over her face.

Good, he thought. "I'm sorry!" he yelled at the closed door.

She never responded or even acknowledged she heard him. She rested her forehead on the door as he turned to leave. His eyes. Those eyes that had been her haven for so long now made her want to vomit. They were the only thing even remotely similar to the Jamie she knew.

She wasn't going to look him in the eye again, she decided, which shouldn't be a problem since they weren't even supposed to be in the vicinity of one another. He'd come to DC only to brief the office on the operation since he'd been on it since the beginning. He was going back undercover and she would be nowhere near any real action. She flung herself on the bed and felt all the tension of the day start to leave her body. She stared at the ceiling for several hours before she finally fell into a restless sleep.

Stella spread a blanket on the ground and opened the bottle of wine she bought from Mountain Mission Winery. She passed it on the way to Polson the first night and swung by after her first day at the field office. Although it was August, there was no humidity here. The lake was surrounded by looming mountains like she had never seen on the

East Coast. The rich greens of the trees were in stark contrast to the crystal-clear blue sky. The sky looked different here.

She reflected on the turn her life had taken in the span of twenty-four hours. Everything was so surreal. *His parents had a funeral for a son that was still alive. Why? Why did Jamie propose in Savannah when he knew it wouldn't be for long?* He was a liar. She wondered if she really knew him at all. He obviously hadn't given a shit about her. Why drag out this long lie? She wondered what had been in the casket they lowered in the ground, the one she had cried next to until Patrick carried her away. She regretted the year of her life she wasted mourning him. She regretted how she had treated everyone in her life because of her grief, especially George.

Stella and Jamie's relationship had been so easy. She fell for his blond hair, blue-eyed, long, lean body immediately and she never looked back. He was fun, loving, and easy to be around. She was blown away by the absurdity of it all, the ridiculousness that was her reality. Now she couldn't share this shit with anyone or his life would be in danger. He was dead to her. The Jamie she knew was dead. She'd mourned him already and decided not to waste anymore of her life on that piece of shit.

Stella drained her second class of Cab and shoved the cork back in the bottle when her phone dinged. She smiled; it was from George.

Two days out. Cooper is now pissed.

She replied:

Me too. First day report... Bored outta my mind.

Stella wondered if George had gotten her email yet; he hadn't mentioned it. She walked over to her rental and put the half-empty bottle in between her laptop and purse so it wouldn't move and made her way back to her hotel. After she got to her room, she finished the rest of the bottle and scrolled through her unopened emails from Patrick. She felt more betrayed by him than Jamie, for some reason. They both lied to her, but Patrick lied every day for four years; worse for a whole a year when she couldn't even put herself together. He let her get a tattoo for some fucker who didn't have the common courtesy to break up with her. Then he continued to lie to her for the three more years. She wondered if she could ever forgive him. She doubted it.

Before she went to sleep, she texted George:

I miss you.

CHAPTER FIFTY-FOUR

Don't Freak Out

George was putting up clean Pilsner glasses when Kara, one of George's younger sisters, came out of his office.

"Um, I think this email is for you, George?" She handed him a printout of an email she'd found going through the inbox for the bar. She blushed and looked away.

"What?" He took it and looked at his sister's blushing face. "Why is your face doing that?"

"First of all, who calls you George? Second, what's going on...is all this true?" she asked, motioning to the paper.

"Fuck if I know, someone sent an email to the bar? And my fucking name *is* George."

"Um...your middle name is George, and read it." She sat down on the closest barstool, watching her brother read with a furrow in his brow until he got to a couple of lines in, then a grin broke out on his face.

"Can you explain this?" Kara asked.

"Not to you." He continued to read as he spoke to his sister. When he was done, he folded the paper and put it in his pocket, turned around, and started straightening the liquor bottles.

"Who was that from?"

"Her. It was from her." he turned and looked at Kara.

"Stella?" Kara was shocked, the last she'd heard, Stella was out of the picture and had run from them at the dog park.

"Yes, a lot has happened in two days."

George looked up as Patrick walked through the front door, he was looking at his phone. Setting down the glasses he was drying, he walked to the end of the bar near the door. "Patrick," he greeted, noting the anxiety on Patrick's usually cool features. A tingle of panic ran down George's back. "What's going on?"

"Okay, don't freak out..."

"Not a good start," George interrupted.

"There was an incident in Montana field office." Patrick examined his hands, not looking at George.

"What do you mean, an incident?" George asked.

"Well, there was an explosion." Patrick started.

"What the fuck are you talking about?" George's voice was almost a yell.

"Is there somewhere we can go and you can sit down?" Patrick looked around at the few people in the bar.

George shook his head a few times, like he was trying to shake the cobwebs out of his brain. "Okay." He walked around the bar and motioned for Patrick to follow him. "Hazel, I'll be right back." George sat down behind the small desk and Patrick sat across from him. "The field office where El was working was bombed. There have been reports of casualties and injuries, but no names yet."

"I honestly can't even understand what you're trying to tell me right now." George rubbed his shaved head. "So you're telling me that El is either hurt or dead?"

"She may be okay, but I haven't heard from her and I've texted her seven times. Have you heard from her today?"

Relief washed over George. "Yes. She texted me this morning at..." he pulled out his phone and looked at the time, "at 9:00 a.m."

Patrick shook his head. "That's 7:00 a.m. in Montana. The attack happened at 8:15. Text her and see if she responds."

George just stared at his phone.

Patrick blew out a breath. "Look George, I wouldn't have come here, but I know if anyone had heard from her it would be you. I'm trying not to jump to conclusions, but..."

George texted Stella:

Tell me ur ok

George and Patrick stared at the phone for what seemed like an hour, but was really only five minutes.

"Shit," Patrick muttered and got up. "George, please let me know if you hear from her and I'll keep you updated from my end."

They exchanged cell numbers and looked at each other, the two men who loved Stella, trying not to think the worst.

CHAPTER FIFTY-FIVE

Return to Me

Three months later...

Stella walked hesitantly down the stairs, holding onto the railing for support. When she got to the sand, she smiled as she felt the warm grains surround each toe. Looking up, she saw Cooper, his expansive back to her as he sat watching the waves crashing on the shore, his tail wagging back and forth making a fan shape on the sand. Cooper's straw-colored fur was longer than usual because George hadn't known to get him shaved.

George sat next to Cooper, his tan, lean back was bare and showcasing a tattoo of a half of a heart covering his shoulder blade, which looked like someone had drawn it with a sharpie. Stella walked cautiously toward the water and eased her body down carefully next to George. They stayed silent, but she leaned into his side, touching him from his shoulder to his ankle until Cooper rose from George's side and nuzzled in between them, forcing Stella to separate herself from George.

She put her hand on Cooper's back, sighed, and pushed her sunglasses up her nose. "I love you, you know."

George turned and looked at her, a tear threatened to fall from his eye. "I swear, El, you're going to be the death of me."

The bullet had clipped her heart and traveled through her shoulder blade and her back, wreaking havoc on internal organs and bones. She had heinous scars on her chest, spreading across her from one side to the other, where surgeons had to repair the internal damage. At one point, staples and stitches were the only things that held her together. All the doctors said she had been lucky, an inch this way or that way and she would have been dead. Lucky that the bullet had gone through her shoulder blade and not her spine or she would've been paralyzed; lucky that the bullet exited her body at all. *Lucky.* Her doctor told her that going out in the sun with the scars was a bad idea, but she could cover them up with bandages, which is what she'd done. She was a walking bandage.

"Maybe..." Stella smiled faintly. "Maybe it wouldn't be a bad way to go, would it?"

He grabbed her hand.

"You know George, I don't know if I'm digging the new tattoo. It's kind of lame."

He looked at her with wide-eyed astonishment; he thought she'd love it. "You don't like it?"

"I love the thought behind it, but it looks like someone started something and it's not finished."

George used his thumb to stroke her hand. "First of all, I could never have a tattoo as badass as yours." They both laughed. "You have an actual bullet hole through where your heart is supposed to be. How can I match that?"

Stella ran her hand down Cooper's back and stared at the waves.

George reached out and took her hand, kissing her knuckles. "It's not finished, Love. You and I aren't finished."

ACKNOWLEDGEMENTS

This part is hard for me. This book happened because a number of things and people came together at the same time. First, I have insomnia. Therefore, I was able to finish a story about characters I grew to know and love. Second, people that I trust said it was good and I should finish it. Third, I threw caution to the wind and gave into the characters that were in my head. My husband bought me an iPad for Christmas a couple of years ago and Good God, the writing I've done on that thing. I have a three-year-old and a full-time job, I write when I can; that device makes it possible. I wrote this book after my son went to sleep, when I should be talking to my husband. I wrote during family functions (I know, inappropriate). I wrote on airplanes and in cars.

Getting back to thanking people...I will start with those that without, in all honesty, this book wouldn't even been written. My husband (whom I've been friends with since I was eighteen) is truly my knight in shining armor and made me believe in love. He always believes in me, whatever I do. I really appreciate that support and without it, this book would still be in my mind. He also gets woken up in the middle of the night when I dream of these characters and have to write it down, lest I forget. He *sometimes* is a good sport about that.

Also, when this story was in its first stage (I call it the bones of the story) my parents sat down and read it in two days over Thanksgiving. They gave it the go-ahead, like I might actually have something. They also helped with me trying to bounce ideas off them for titles and other things. My mom made me and my dad laugh many times with all her questions. This is not her type of book: too much cursing, drinking, and other things. Notice I didn't mention sex...that's an inside joke for you, Dad. I should probably thank my mom for taking me to the library or the bookstore every weekend when I was little and buying me every single Babysitter's Club book. I can still spend an entire afternoon in a bookstore or a library, if I had that sort of time. I guess I should also thank them for raising me to believe that I can do whatever I set my mind to. Appreciate it.

Next, I sent the draft to one of my best friends, my roommate in law school, John. Your thoughts and opinions about this story were invaluable. As usual our conversations regarding this book always spiraled back to our law school days and how ridiculous we were. I'm very sad the Brickskellar is no longer open, because that would have been a pretty funny chapter.

One of my friends who made this book better is my girl Lizzie. She is amazing and I appreciate all the work she did for me, for wine and food. Thanks, I'll pay you back one day. When I was working on Tension I met the fabulous Erin Roth who did the re-edit of By A Thread. I hate that I met her after it was published, but so excited for this shiny version to be put out there.

Last but not least, my sister, Kelei, who bought into Stella and her circle of friends totally. After she read it she asked me all sorts of questions that helped get the perspective from the reader, not my all-knowing self. She put up with numerous emails, texts, and calls from me on a daily basis at one point about different aspects of the book and trying to get it out. I don't know why she helped me so much through the process, but she did. I'm sure I could not possibly pay her back for all of her help, which included her being a nanny, PR representative, website designer, bouncer of ideas off, and all around help-me-make-decisioner (I just made up that last one, but it fits). Maybe I should take her shopping...

Also, I want to make sure everyone knows who designed the cover art. The cover was designed by www.georginagibson.com.

To anyone else whom I talked to about this book, thanks so much for listening.

Check out Stella's next adventure at:
www.rlgriffinauthor.com

Also, you can get more information about the
characters and the author at her website,
but also by following R.L. at:

http://www.goodreads.com/rlgriffin
http://www.twitter/RLGriffinauthor
www.facebook.com/rlgriffinbyathread

You can also contact R.L. Griffin via email at:
rlgriffinauthor@gmail.com.

Stella's adventure continues in Tension,
out August 1, 2013. Here is a little taste:

Prologue

She heaved in the toilet for the third time in a row, but it was only bile now. The noise echoed through the empty bathroom. Hunching over the bowl, she tried not to grasp the sides with her hands. Because she was more aware of her body and its reactions to stress, she hadn't eaten or had any coffee this morning, thinking maybe she wouldn't get sick. Pushing herself off of the cold tile floor and flushing the toilet, she spit the remaining bile from her mouth into the toilet. Fighting the urge to wipe the excess saliva on the sleeve of her expensive suit jacket, she pulled a few squares of toilet paper off the roll and patted her mouth. Pushing the door of the stall open, she examined the image she saw in the mirror.

What she saw gave her pause and she stopped just shy of the sink to take in her appearance. Her new outer shell was almost unrecognizable. She'd recently cut her long black waves into a straight, chin-length bob, currently tousled. Her weight loss over the past several months made her cheeks look sunken; she'd attempted to hide her sallow skin with makeup, but she still looked just a little bit haunted. The new grey suit she was wearing was wrinkled. Irritated, she smoothed down the length of the pencil skirt to where it hit just above her knees. Her soft pink shell underneath was chosen to make her look more fragile. *As if it's possible to look any more fragile.* Some of her scars were visible above the collar of the shell; all perfecting the image Millie said she needed to show the world.

Washing her hands quickly, she dried them and pulled out a comb. *Breathe.* She pulled the comb through her hair. Her stomach rolled again and she dug in her pewter handbag for her medication. She'd finally gotten around to going to the doctor, who diagnosed her with some sort of stress-induced disorder that causes her to throw up. *No shit, I diagnosed myself years ago.* Throwing the pill in her mouth, she swallowed it dry. Reaching into another pocket, she pulled out lip gloss and reapplied the pink color to her lips, trying to feel the least bit "normal."

She popped a peppermint into her mouth and closed her eyes, counting to ten slowly before she pushed open the door and walked to the bench just outside the courtroom. As soon as she sat down, the door opened and the U.S. Marshal assigned to the courtroom called her name. Her heels clicked and echoed against the marble floor. The courtroom was full, but she had tunnel vision. She didn't allow any of her terrified thoughts to enter her brain; she could break down later. In private.

Making her way to the witness stand, she concentrated on not tripping in the six-inch black pumps she always wore. They were her lucky heels for court and she needed them more today than any other day. She took a deep breath, sat down on the stand and took her first glance at the defense table. Her entire body shook with fear at the sight of the man sitting in an ill-fitting suit next to his attorney; she knew the entire case rested on her testimony. *No pressure.* Shoving the fear down inside her, she folded her hands in her lap and stared at them. *Calm.*

"Ma'am, please state your name for the record."

"Stella Murphy."

CHAPTER ONE

Reliving the Rollercoaster

George gazed out at the waves crashing against the shore as Cooper, Stella's 100-pound Labrador-Golden Retriever mix, ran up and down the beach in front of the house. He woke early this morning and made coffee to take on his walk with Cooper. His eyes drifted up and down the shore line as Cooper attempted to catch the sea gulls that were taunting him. He and Cooper became fast friends when Stella left the dog with him and traveled to Montana, and now Cooper treated George as one of his people. They'd been on the beach for a couple of hours, leaving Stella to sleep. Stella was beginning to shows signs of her old self, the one he'd fallen head over heels in love with, but he could tell she was holding something back from him. She slept a lot these days.

His life had become a rollercoaster since the day this wondrous, broken woman walked into his bar. Stella had come into Finnegan's, the bar he owned, and changed his life with her sad green eyes and witty banter. When they first met, she was completely closed off, wounded, and grieving, but eventually he felt her open up to him. They had many glorious months together before he'd bumped into that last wall that he couldn't break. So he bolted, thinking it would be better just to rip the Band-Aid off.

He was wrong.

He knew he made a huge mistake the second he told her he met someone else, which was a lie. The walls he managed to push through came crashing down right before his eyes. The way she looked at him changed, all emotion dissipated, and she walked away like he was nothing; like what they had was nothing.

That was the *first* time George lost Stella.

He tried everything, short of begging, to get her back. He tried all the usual things: jewelry, acting casual, texting, even having friends argue his cause. Nothing worked until he saw her collapsed, Cooper lying next to her, on the ground in the park. He picked her up, threw her over his shoulder, and took her home, where they finally had it out. He finally told her his real story; finally told her the truth. He admitted that his real name was Willston George Finnegan and he owned the bar. He explained, with difficulty, that he'd been burned several times by women who found out he owned the bar and seemed to want to stick around for his money, so he had a strict policy of not giving out his name. He met Stella as George, and he loved her as George, not as Will. Stella breathed life back into George and he loved her for it.

Confessing that he loved her and missed her being in his life had been one of the hardest things he'd ever done. Stella was a loose cannon; he never knew how she was going to react. Since the time he realized he wanted her in his life, she'd been a whirlwind; teasing him, laughing with him, loving him. Stella couldn't admit how she felt about him, but he'd grown to accept it, hoping in time she'd come around. He told her he would spend his entire life trying to put her shattered heart back together and he meant it.

That day, the day George found Stella and Cooper in the park, Stella seemed dazed and utterly devastated. She listened numbly as George bared his soul, and in typical form, she didn't care about the fact he owned the bar, but was pissed he wasn't completely honest with her. Stella told him that she was, once again, in the middle of an emotional upheaval. *Then* she told him that her dead fiancé wasn't really dead, but working undercover, that she'd just seem him. He'd been "dead" for four years, and she just saw him. At work.

Stella had been assigned to the Montana field office to babysit the cleanup of an ATF undercover operation that had gone awry. She told George her role was minimal; she was simply supposed to report back to the DC office. There was no real legal work involved. The problem was that not only was her ex-fiancé part of the operation, but her best friend, Patrick, had known he was alive the entire time.

George did what any scared shitless boyfriend would've done. He ran Stella and Cooper back to her house, where she confronted Patrick. Patrick tried to apologize and explain, but Stella wouldn't give him a chance to. Stella was devastated. All the pain and all the healing over the last four years were for nothing; it was just practice.

Afterward, he drove them back to his house. George carried his broken love into his bedroom, undressed her and ran a bath. It was incredibly difficult not to touch her then, but Stella seemed so fragile. Later that night, when she admitted that she loved him, it was a like his heart grew three sizes. Stella told him she was uncertain that she could even be in a relationship, but she was willing to try. Happiness bloomed and filled every inch of him as they lay entangled in his bed. He'd slept with his hand on her tattoo, right where the half of a heart now appeared because of him.

He took her to the airport the next morning; they were sending her immediately to assist in the cleanup of the mess in Montana. The loss in his gut felt like the size of a cavern, but he put on a brave face. He couldn't believe he was kissing her and seeing her off, watching her get on a plane with her former (and no longer dead) fiancé.

Cooper stayed with George while she was in Montana. She'd sent an email while she was on the flight with *him*; a message that made George want to fly to Montana to be with her while she worked. He printed the email and kept it in his wallet, always.

George or whatever the fuck your name is,

I'm on the plane, leaving you, and I'm miserable. This assignment will be long and I'll be bored. Per our discussion, I will text you often. I plan on giving you what you need, George. You have given me what I thought I needed since I met you. Months ago, when you broke things off with me because you met someone else, I was coming to lunch to tell you that I was falling for you. I mean, hard. I was willing to try this thing, but I shut all that down once I heard you met someone. You know how I told you about one of my favorite authors who said everything that comes together falls apart? I still believe that. However, in that same book, it is said if you know that everything falls apart, stop grieving about it falling apart and enjoy the together time. I am going to enjoy us together. I promise.

I have always wanted you to be happy. I just never thought that would be with me. You, alone, made me realize that maybe I can be put back together. That I could possibly be happy. The realization that you could be happy with me is almost too much for me to fathom.

I love you. I love that you let me figure it out on my own (mostly). I will tell you what I don't love, I don't love that you know so much about me, but I don't know that much about you. How selfish am I? I do know some things ... but I want to know everything. I don't love that you give so much to me. I want to give you what you need. What do you need George? I know you're thinking of a sexual comment to answer that question, which is fine, but I want to know what your heart needs. What does your soul need?

Do you need reassurances from me (I would) that I'm in no way interested in the agent I'm currently sitting 20 rows behind? If so, I can quickly give you those. Do you need reassurance that I will be dreaming of you every night in Montana? I can guarantee you, that after last night, that is absolutely the case. Do you need anything else, George? Because I plan on proving to you that I do, in fact, love you.

BTW- Please take care of Cooper. He has had my back longer than you have. Take him on his run; take him to the Dog Barkery. He likes the female collie that hangs there around 1:00-2:00 on Saturdays. Let him sleep with you, he can keep my spot warm for me. Maybe we could Facetime. Okay, just kidding.

I miss you already.
Your love

When George read that email he knew they'd be together, for real this time. Not just falling in bed every time they saw each other, although he really enjoyed sex with her. He wanted her in every way he could get her. He wanted to see her every day, see the wry smile on her exquisite face when she said something sarcastic. He wanted her to meet and love his family as much as he did. He knew he was asking for too much, but planned on being with her every step of the way until she accepted it. Accepted that they were made for each other—he'd known it as soon as they had real conversations on her lunch break when she was working at Cosi. His lunches with her became his favorite time of his day.

Stella texted George after her first full day in Montana, bored out of her mind. Prior to heading to the field office her second day in Montana, George received another text.

Headed to the office for another titillating day
Wish you were here to titillate me

Later that day, Patrick Greer, Stella's roommate, had come to the bar to see if Stella had contacted him. There was an explosion and Patrick didn't know if she was dead or alive.

That was the *second* time George lost Stella.

The long hours between Patrick's visit to the bar and Patrick's subsequent strained call that evening, notifying him that Stella was in the hospital and not the morgue, were excruciating. Time seemed to stretch forever. George told Hazel to run the bar and took the first flight to Montana. He didn't remember the flight or the drive to the hospital. The only thing he remembered about that day was that he cried. George hadn't cried since his dad died.

The nurse ushered him into the room, and there she was, unconscious, with what seemed like a dozen tubes coming out of her body; a tube and bandage-covered replica of his Stella. Seeing her brought a fresh round of tears to his eyes; he stood staring at her broken body for what seemed like hours. Then he gently crawled into bed with her and touched her. And he did another thing he hadn't done since his dad passed. George prayed.

That's how he met her parents. He was laying there, holding her and mumbling comforting words between sobbed prayers, when he heard people enter. He knew before he looked up that it had to be her parents. They walked with nervous shuffles, not the brisk efficiency of medical staff.

Stella's mother sobbed openly and her father had stood there staring, stoic. George had carefully gotten out of the bed, wiped his eyes with the sleeve of his shirt, and held out his hand to Stella's dad. "I'm Willston Finnegan."

Stella's dad was tall, probably over six feet, with salt and pepper hair. His lined face was worn and covered in stubble. His eyes were dark blue and vacant.

"Who?" Stella's mother asked. George looked to Stella's mother; her shocked faced outlined by her black bob, which shone in the florescent hospital lights. She was wearing tortoise shell glasses, a pink cardigan set, and jeans. She was the total opposite of Stella.

"Oh." George cleared his throat. "George. Stella calls me George."

Stella's father never took his eyes off Stella, but shook George's hand with a nod.

Stella's mother took in George from head to toe, making careful note of his blotchy face and disheveled clothes. "George. Of course.

I'm Miranda. Oh, God. I can't believe this. This is Frank." Miranda pointed at Stella's dad, but his eyes never left his daughter. "Frank, remember when she broke her arm when she was ten? That's what she looks like." Miranda's voice broke.

Stella's father finally spoke. "She looks dead."

George flinched.

"Frank!" Stella's mother cried.

Frank looked to George for some sign of support. "This is nothing like a broken arm."

"The nurse told me she's doing the best as can be expected with all the injuries she sustained. Um…" George took a deep breath and rubbed his hand over his short hair. "Her vitals are good. They don't think she'll be paralyzed, but they won't know until she wakes up. They repaired the damage to her heart. There was a slight rip where the bullet grazed it and then exited out her back."

"They told you all that?" Stella's mother asked, her eyes wide in surprise.

"Heather, her shift nurse, felt sorry for me," George said, rubbing his head with his hands. "Also, they think I'm her brother."

Miranda smiled weakly. "George, would you mind going to get us some coffee? I think we need a minute."

"Sure." George nodded and walked out. This wasn't the way he imagined meeting Stella's parents.

CHAPTER TWO

FBI What?

Stella walked hesitantly down the stairs, holding onto the railing for support. When she got to the sand, she smiled as she felt the warm grains surround each toe. Looking up, she saw Cooper, his expansive back to her as he sat watching the waves crashing on the shore, his tail wagging back and forth making a fan shape on the sand. Cooper's straw-colored fur was longer than usual because George hadn't known to get him shaved.

George sat next to Cooper, his tan, lean back was bare and show-casing a tattoo of a half of a heart covering his shoulder blade, which looked like someone had drawn it with a sharpie. Stella walked cautiously toward the water and eased her body down carefully next to George. They stayed silent, but she leaned into his side, touching him from his shoulder to his ankle until Cooper rose from George's side and nuzzled in between them, forcing Stella to separate herself from George.

She put her hand on Cooper's back, sighed, and pushed her sunglasses up her nose. "I love you, you know."

George turned and looked at her, a tear threatened to fall from his eye. "I swear, El, you're going to be the death of me."

The bullet had clipped her heart and traveled through her shoulder blade and her back, wreaking havoc on internal organs and bones. She had heinous scars on her chest, spreading across her from one side to the other, where surgeons had to repair the internal damage. At one point, staples and stitches were the only things that held her together. All the doctors said she had been lucky, an inch this way or that way and she would have been dead. Lucky that the bullet had gone through her shoulder blade and not her spine or she would've been paralyzed; lucky that the bullet exited her body at all. *Lucky.* Her doctor told her that going out in the sun with the scars was a bad idea, but she could cover them up with bandages, which is what she'd done. She was a walking bandage.

"Maybe..." Stella smiled faintly. "Maybe it wouldn't be a bad way to go, would it?"

He grabbed her hand.

"You know George, I don't know if I'm digging the new tattoo. It's kind of lame."

He looked at her with wide-eyed astonishment; he thought she'd love it. "You don't like it?"

"I love the thought behind it, but it looks like someone started something and it's not finished."

George used his thumb to stroke her hand. "First of all, I could never have a tattoo as badass as yours." They both laughed. "You have an actual bullet hole through where your heart is supposed to be. How can I match that?"

Stella ran her hand down Cooper's back and stared at the waves.

George reached out and took her hand, kissing her knuckles. "It's not finished, Love. You and I aren't finished."

The next morning, Stella's eyes opened hesitantly. It took a few minutes to realize where she was. George must've gotten up early again. Her long raven locks covered her face. Light shimmered through the closed burlap curtain; the bright green of the walls reminded her of the Jell-O they served in the hospital. All the artwork in the room she was sharing with George was happy, palm trees and sunsets on beaches. She knew it was meant to be relaxing. It was a beach house after all, but it was so cheery it made her want to vomit. Hate curled around her, nuzzling her neck. The past weeks had been full of doctors, physical therapists, and people talking in hushed voices. Hushed voices pissed her off. All the doctors and nurses had walked on eggshells around her. She was alive. She'd been poked, prodded, talked about, and basically degraded for weeks. Her bitterness was difficult to hide, but she was trying. *The least they could do was talk honestly.*

As she rolled onto her back, the dull pain in her chest made her rake her hand over the battered skin above her breasts. Her chest ached;

she'd been told it may always ache. *Just another thing to make it impossible to get that motherfucker out of my mind.* The stitches and staples that had once covered her chest had either disintegrated or been removed, but the jagged scars and the feeling of being ripped apart remained. It might never go away. She was reminded on a daily basis, often multiple times a day. *Hate.*

She was getting better at smiling, laughing, and talking about normal things. It was hard work to push away the feelings she felt toward *him.* The betrayal and the hatred threatened to smother her and invaded her thoughts on an hourly basis, sometimes more. Stella was trying; she was working on perfecting her fake smile. It had come a long way since waking up after weeks in a drug-induced coma.

She'd opened her eyes and felt a weight in the palm of her hand; someone was clutching her fingers. Not quite able to see clearly, it took several minutes to take in the room. There was someone on her left and that person was most definitely holding her hand. There were two more dark figures in the room, but her vision was hazy. Someone was pacing at the foot of her bed. She heard the low rumbling of music off to her right. The level of light coming through the window kept the room in shadows, showing it was daybreak or sunset. *Where was she?* Opening her mouth to speak, she was stunned to find that she couldn't. Then she realized there was something down her throat and she started to choke on it. Choking, she involuntarily squeezed her hands and the person on her left yelled.

"El? Oh God, get the nurse. El!"

The person at her feet ran out, the one on the right started crying. She tried speak again, but couldn't. Panic started to set in. *What the fuck?* Her mouth felt as if someone had poured an entire sandbox into it and then banned her from drinking water. The room suddenly came into view, her eyes clearing substantially.

George was leaning over her, clutching her hand. He looked as if he was going to cry or had been crying, his eyes red-rimmed and bloodshot. There was so much exhaustion in his eyes that the familiar green flecks were barely noticeable.

Her mother was standing on the right and blubbering, her hair disheveled, which never happened. She tried to say "Mom." She couldn't.

"Stella, baby!" her father yelled as he bounded back into the room. "Holy shit, I ..."

Nurses and doctors swarmed her bedside, pushing everyone else out of the room. Tubes were pulled, her throat opened and she took a huge gasp of air. She began coughing uncontrollably, which made her entire body fill with a weird sensation. *Pain.* Her gown was pulled down as the doctors and nurses examined her entire body. Stella was mortified.

"Stella, I'm Dr. Houston. I've been watching over you for the past couple of weeks. We're going to check some of your vitals and other parts of you and then I'll allow your loved ones back in. Okay?"

When she didn't respond, the doctor asked again. "Okay?"

Stella nodded. She couldn't talk; her throat felt like sandpaper. A nurse finally offered her a plastic cup with a straw and put it to her lips. Stella took a long drink of the cool liquid. It tasted like a watered down sports drink, but was like heaven and soothed her parched throat.

As the doctors and nurses went through the routine of checking all of her vitals, she looked around the room. She tried to remember how she got here or how long she'd been here; anything. Her brain couldn't think of anything except Jamie's eyes as he pulled the trigger, making her entire life veer in a different direction, again. Her stomach turned at the thought that Jamie, the person she'd once thought was the love of her life, had shot her while looking into her eyes. She felt a tiny growth in her gut, an unfamiliar feeling she couldn't quite place.

All the memories came rushing back and she dry heaved. A nurse held a plastic bowl in front of her in case she threw up. The memory that this person she'd followed to DC and who she had planned to marry, faked his own death to go undercover with the ATF, reverberated throughout her body. She heaved again. And then the fucker came back from the dead and shot her. Angry tears sprang from her eyes. He did this to her. She was ripped to shreds, literally and figuratively.

The sun was blistering her bare shoulders, warming the scars that reached across her chest and making her pull her hat down on her head. The waves crashed off to her right as she walked down the beach. Cooper ran up and down the beach and dove into the white crest of the waves. Stella had been unemotional when she was in the hospital and even more so in rehab. She had the pain medications to thank for that convenience. Taking a sip of the Bloody Mary she'd made that morning to drink with her cocktail of medications, she stepped in the surf. She pulled the pill box her mother bought her out of her pocket and threw it into the crashing waves. The pills dulled her senses, made her forget things, and made her so drowsy that she'd sleep for most of the day. They'd been a godsend in the hospital; it was the only way she'd been able to handle what had happened to her in Montana, but now she needed to get back on her game.

After she'd woken up, it took several weeks for her to feel like herself again and to get a grasp on how colossally different her life would be when she left the protected area of the hospital. She squinted and blinked her eyes at the sun, having forgotten her sunglasses in the house. Stella remembered the first couple of days after she woke up in the hospital as though no time had passed.

Even through the haze of pain medication, she remembered the second she realized her life had turned into a three-ring circus. Cue the music.

Shortly after the doctors and nurses had rushed in, Stella fell back to sleep, the pain medications knocking her out. Her eyes popped open some time later at the sound of her name. Looking around her hospital room, she couldn't see anyone talking to her. Glancing at the television, she saw a picture of her face filling the entire screen. *Holy shit! What the fuck is going on?*

"Why the fuck am I on TV?" she asked no one in particular.

Her mom's head lifted from the couch. "Oh honey, you're awake!" She rushed to Stella's bedside and grabbed her hand, patting it gently. She gestured to the TV. "It's been like this since the incident."

"Like what?" Stella honestly had no idea what her mom was talking about. She turned her attention to the news story on the TV. The reporter was in Athens, Georgia, where Stella had gone to college, "talking to the best friend of the FBI Beauty." She tried to sit up too quickly and knew immediately the sudden movement was a bad idea. "Shit."

Her mother shrank away, ready to hit the call button just as George rounded the corner with four coffees. "Stella, are you feeling okay? Should I call the nurse?"

"I'm fine," Stella muttered. She really didn't feel anything. "What the fuck are they calling me?"

"The FBI Beauty," he answered. When he saw the look on her face, he chuckled. "Seriously, El. The FBI Beauty."

"Are you guys fucking with me?" Stella looked around like there was a camera somewhere and this was all one big joke. She looked to her dad, who sat silently in one of the chairs in the corner, for confirmation.

"Stella, you don't have to cuss in every sentence," her mother chastised.

"Ever since they started getting pictures of you, it went from 'an attorney with the FBI' to 'The FBI Beauty.'" Her father almost snarled. "Next thing you know, some wacko's going to send you a sash."

She ignored her father and addressed her mother. "Oh, excuse the fuck out of me. I just wake up from almost dying to see my face on TV and I'm supposed to be calm and cool about this? And who gave them all my pictures?" she asked, looking right at her mom.

"Oh no, ma'am, this has nothing to do with me! According to Patrick..."

Stella interrupted her mother at the sound of Patrick's name, she actually hissed. "Patrick?! Where the fuck is that bastard?!"

The surprise in her mother's eyes was quite comical and George actually started laughing. "They had a bit of a falling out, Mrs. Murphy."

Her mother scowled. "Well, if I was the one to give them pictures, it wouldn't be the ones they're using. Undoubtedly, there were tons of pictures on Jamie's website of you and him. Several are of you in very tiny, inappropriate bikinis." She shook her head and her face looked as if she had tasted something awful. "I would've chosen more tasteful photographs of my daughter."

"El, you were the only one who lived," George announced, handing her a coffee. "They're calling you a hero. It's been the top story for weeks."

"Fucking 'FBI Beauty,'" her dad muttered. He took the coffee offered by George and stomped out of the room without another word.

Stella watched him go and then she turned her gaze toward George. "Wait...what do you mean, I'm the only one who lived?"

"Love, the other three people in the office at the time of the blast died. You were the only one who lived." George pointed toward the door. "The FBI has had two agents assigned to the room since you've been here. They've been trying to talk to you since you woke up, but your dad has been out there beating them away."

Numb. Stella couldn't understand her detachment from the situation. She didn't feel anything. She looked at her mother and then down at her hands. "This is all so ludicrous. I'm not a hero. I got shot. I didn't save anyone. I didn't apprehend anyone."

"Well, according to the news, you're a hero for surviving. Especially since one of the guys left many identifying marks on you and your clothes," George sneered. "And by the way," he attempted a smirk, "your whole backstory is very tragic."

"No shit," Stella agreed as she looked at her mom. Her mom nodded, tears silently streaming down her cheeks. Stella turned back to George. "What do you mean, marks?"

"Well, he left fibers all over your clothes and skin," George answered, not making eye contact.

"Who—"she started. "Oh," was the only response Stella could muster as the information sank in. *Fibers on your clothes and skin. You're a lawyer, you know what that indicates...* Stella shook her head, clearing away the cobwebs, trying to remember what happened before she was shot.

George cleared his throat and changed the subject. "There was a really funny bit where an entertainment tabloid show went to your house and Patrick answered the door without a shirt on. It was quite funny and has gotten tons of airtime. You should've seen him go off. I'll show you the You Tube video later."

"I don't understand." Stella ran her hands over her face. "Why are me and all my friends all over the media and why are there agents at the door?"

"Because they haven't caught them," her mother answered softly.

"Oh, for fuck's sake. Caught who? You just said everyone else died." Stella blew her bangs out of her face. "I need a fucking haircut."

"Yes, you do." Her mom smoothed her black bob into place. "And language, please. I didn't raise you to speak like a trucker."

George spit his coffee across the room. "I hope you cut your bangs so you don't have to blow them like that."

Stella glared at him. *Men.*

Stella finished her Bloody Mary and contemplated going back into the house to make another, but instead she sat down at the bottom of the stairs that led to the back porch of the house they were renting from her parents' friend, toes still blissful in the sand. She gazed out at the water.

"Coop!" Stella called from the stairs. Cooper came running at full speed, stopped in front of the stairs, and shook all the water and sand from his fur. "Damn it, Coop." Stella laughed. He flopped down on her feet, panting from the exertion of running in the waves. She scooped out an ice cube from her drained glass and chewed on it, thinking about her precarious situation.

Stan, her supervising attorney at the General Counsel's office for the FBI, had walked into her room less than 48 hours after she woke up. He popped his chewing gum and hummed as he walked to the right side of the bed and pulled up a chair. "So, sleeping beauty wakes," he quipped, grinning. He sat across the bed from George and looked directly at him. "Son, I need to speak to Stella alone."

George frowned. Stella's parents were at the hotel, showering and taking a much needed break. He didn't feel comfortable leaving her alone. "Whatever you need to say to her you can say to me."

Stan laughed obnoxiously and shook his head. His white hair was disheveled from the flight and he wore jeans and a plaid button down, instead of his typical suit. "That's not how it works, kid. Get out of here. I'm trying to get her ready for what's coming." He looked intently into Stella eyes. "Soon."

George turned to Stella, fuming. Stella nodded weakly, a pained expression on her face. She'd explain later. Now, she needed to know what was going on with the investigation. "Real piece of cake you sent me on..." she said as George slammed the door.

"Look, Stella, I'm real sorry about how everything went down, but you need to prepare yourself for this investigation. You're the only witness; they have no leads. The only evidence they found was on you. The *entire* case will be on you." He looked at the door and then whispered, "The media is going crazy with all this 'FBI Beauty' shit. I'd be worried about my job if I were you. They're digging into everything and splashing it all around."

Closing her eyes, she asked. "So you know?"

He nodded. "Know what?"

She looked at him, puzzled.

"If you happened to have some relation to an undercover agent for some reason, I certainly don't know that. I'm not the only one who doesn't know. That knowledge is, like, top secret information, though, so I'm hoping it doesn't come out." He stared intently at his hands, which he'd propped on the side of the bed. "But, you know how we are, Stella. The FBI's dick is bigger than the ATF's and no one is agreeing to share any information. I seriously doubt they ever will."

What?! Stella's brain wasn't working as fast as usual to translate what was innuendo and what was truth. "What do I do?" she whispered. The realization that Stan was here to help her, even though he had no business in Montana, was making her panic. He was here to warn her, obviously. But why?

"Keep your head down. Tell the truth about what you saw and no matter what, *keep your mouth shut* about unnecessary shit." He glanced at the door again like he was expecting someone to burst through any minute. "You get me?"

The answer went unspoken. She nodded at the same time a man and a woman entered the room without knocking.

Stan stood up. "I'm so glad you're feeling better, Stella. We'll talk later, okay?"

She nodded, her brain still processing what he'd told her.

The two suits didn't even blink at Stan as he left. "Ms. Murphy, I'm Monica Peterson, the Assistant Attorney General heading the investigation into the terrorist attack in Montana. This is Special Agent Jason Harris. He's the agent in charge of the case."

Stella just stared at the middle-aged woman in her navy skirt suit and navy heels. Her tan hose were sorely outdated.

Just then, George burst through the door. "You okay? I just saw…" He pulled up short as he saw the two suits at her bedside.

"Yes, he was just leaving as Agent Harris and Assistant Attorney General Peterson came in," she stared intently at the door hoping George would follow her lead.

"Ms. Murphy, we need to discuss the investigation," Ms. Peterson declared, looking pointedly at George.

"Look, I want to get these guys as much as you, but I just woke up and I'm still a little cloudy. I'd rather George stay in here just because he'll be able to tell you if I'm going off the rails."

Ms. Peterson glanced at George and nodded. "At this stage, it's fine, but once we get into details, we'll need to proceed differently."

George sat down and handed Stella a cup of coffee. "Fine with me," he agreed.

Agent Harris pulled out his pad. "So, can you tell me everything you remember?"

"Sure, with the understanding that I'm hazy and things will probably change or get clearer. I'll do my best."

"Start at the beginning," Ms. Peterson prodded quietly.

"Well, I got to the office pretty early that day because I was still on DC time. I'm not sure the time..."

George interrupted. "She texted me at 9:00 a.m. Eastern Time and she hadn't gotten to the office yet."

"We're going to need that text, sir," Agent Harris demanded.

"I can forward it to you now," George agreed, pulling out his phone.

"So you headed to the office early. Did you get any coffee? Did you stop anywhere on the way there?"

"No."

"When you got to the office did you notice anything out of place?"

"No."

"Okay. Walk us through it."

"There were only a few cars in front of the office. I got out of the car and walked into the office through the front. I nodded at Special Agents Trey Williams, Jeffery Riggins, and Peter Richardson. I put my bag and laptop at my desk and walked to get a cup of coffee. I sat down at my desk and the entire front of the building blew off. It knocked me out of my chair and onto the floor." Stella closed her eyes, silently counted to three, and tried to remember. "I couldn't hear anything after the explosion." Opening her eyes, she grabbed George's hand. "It was so surreal. I was trying to figure out if I was injured. I...I felt these hands grab my arms from behind and pull me up." She shuddered, remembering the feel of his hands on her.

"So you were knocked to the floor?" Agent Harris confirmed.

Stella nodded. "Yes, didn't I say that already?" She looked at George and he squeezed her hand. "He was big, very round. His fat stomach and gun were pressed against my back. I still couldn't hear. I could see his lips move, but I couldn't hear anything."

"What did he look like?" Agent Harris was scribbling furiously on his pad.

"He was wearing all black and a mask. I couldn't see his face. He ripped my shirt and spoke to me, but I couldn't hear him." George squeezed her hand again and then put his other hand on hers. "He grabbed my face and yelled something at me. Then I saw another guy."

"Anything on him?" Agent Harris asked.

"Same black outfit and mask. They were all wearing the same thing."

"How many did you see?"

"Three," Stella answered.

"There were three?" Ms. Peterson butted in. "All in black with masks?"

"Yes."

"Then what?" Agent Harris motioned Stella to continue.

"The big one pushed me on my back and starting ripping my pants off. I kicked him in the face with my boot. I started crawling away and he pulled me back and flipped me over. Then he ripped the button off my pants. It was then the third one came up behind the big one. They exchanged words and then the third one shot me."

"Did the third guy look any different?"

"No. It's fuzzy. They were all in black with masks." Her mind released a flash of all three around her when Jamie shot her, staring directly in her eyes while he did it.

"Do you remember anything after being shot?" Agent Harris inquired.

Stella shook her head. "That's it."

Made in the USA
Charleston, SC
11 April 2015